The critics on Michael Collins

'Michael Collins is undoubtedly an exciting talent, capable of writing razor-sharp prose and he has produced a gripping, stylish novel that deserves to be read'
Times Literary Supplement

'Reading Collins . . . is like being mugged in a savage land'
The Times

'Colourful, surreal and vividly characterised . . . already prompting comparisons to Joyce and Beckett' *The List*

'Michael Collins is a considerable stylist . . . his prose has a thoughtful, sinewy quality, a kind of subliminal toughness of mind' *Weekend Telegraph*

'[Collins] makes apparently simple materials work powerfully . . . his aim is exact and his effect eerie'
Observer

'Collins is operating at a level that's beyond the reach of most of his practising colleagues' *Toronto Globe & Mail*

'Energetically brilliant' Michele Roberts

'Michael Collins's vision is breathtakingly black and his writing so sharp you could cut yourself on it' *Irish Times*

'A style so arrestingly visual it hijacks the reader's concentration; dazzling with the energy and originality of the language' *Independent*

'Readers . . . . grateful to Collins. He is a stylist, blessed v . . . . . . of having something worth saving well' *The . . . .*

'Collins writes with a kind of furious zest: a passionate colloquial patter half-Irish, half American . . . The writing hums with its own electricity' *Glasgow Herald*

'One of the most exciting talents to have emerged not only in Ireland but anywhere in recent decades'
Susan Hill, *The Times*

Michael Collins was born in Limerick in 1964. His fiction has received international critical acclaim and his work has been translated into numerous languages. His first book was a *New York Times* Notable Book of the Year in 1993, his short story 'The End of the World' was awarded the Pushcart Prize for Best American Short Story and the *Toronto Globe and Mail* selected his most recent collection of stories as 'one of the must-read books of the year'. *The Keepers of Truth* won The Kerry Ingredients Book of the Year Award for Best Irish Novel and was also shortlisted for the Booker Prize.

By Michael Collins

The Keepers of Truth
The Meat Eaters (stories)
The Life and Times of a Teaboy
The Feminists Go Swimming (stories)
Emerald Underground

MICHAEL COLLINS

Emerald Underground

PHŒNIX

A PHOENIX PAPERBACK

First published in Great Britain in 1998
by Phoenix House
This paperback edition published in 1999
by Phoenix,
an imprint of Orion Books,
Orion House, 5 Upper St Martin's Lane,
London WC2H 9EA

Reissued 2001

A CIP catalogue record for this book is available
from the British Library.

ISBN: 0 75380 734 3

Printed and bound in Great Britain by
The Guernsey Press Co. Ltd, Guernsey, C.I.

For my family
And to Maggie McKernan for faith

JIM KEMMY R.I.P.

Purgatory

I spent two months marooned as an illegal immigrant at The Stars and Stripes, a motel in Paramus, New Jersey – all chemical refineries and endless intersecting highways, total shite. I had this Gregor Samsa-type metamorphosis the first week in America: the skin came off me in sheets, flesh blistering like I was about to erupt. The burn of chemicals made my eyes sore, my throat dry. Either bed lice or the chemicals in the air or the blistering sun – Jasus, I was in total isolation, some sort of moulting snake man from one of those movies you'd see on a Saturday afternoon.

Of course, there was no going home. Once you did the shite I'd done, once you never finished your leaving cert, you got your walking papers and got the fuck out of Ireland. Immigration was the name of the game. England, Australia, Canada. Sneak into America. Anywhere but stay at home.

This motel was an isolated kip of total moral meltdown, doors and membranes of cheap curtain hiding things, banjaxed bodies drugged and shrunken, the paranoid hiding from the light of day. Businessmen came for a few hours to fuck whores who specialised in leather or sadomasochism or were not women at all but transvestites or skinny punks who walked with canes and looked like skeletons, benders who shoved rodents up each other's arses.

The walls were thin. You could kick your way into the next room, which happened more than once when I was there, especially with the Mexicans who got pissed drunk every night and flung bottles off the balcony. They called me

'Amigo' and 'Hombre'. They were all dishwashers and bus boys.

I was totally incapacitated with the skin disorder in that first week in America. I look back at it now and think, how the hell didn't I take a razor to my wrists? I was this freak, abandoned to my room. I'd labour down the hallway like the Mummy, a damp web of gauze around my face as I went for the Coke machine. Dealers huddled in blankets like a primitive sect, creatures on the edge of this great metropolis. I watched the deep pulsars of light moving out on the road, the alien paradise of non-illegals. Doors remained open in a night-trade of skin hunger and longing where pilgrims arrived shaking for salvation, slapping dead veins. I stood in the crimson glow of the Coke machine, drank through the small tear in the gauze around my face and listened. In the dark of small rooms they fed veins, giving themselves to their god with a pinprick of sacrificial blood. I felt the dark figures inside, listened to the low whisper of their moans, saw the blue flames of their methane burners throwing shadows. For a while I thought I'd succumbed to some plague from that spunk-infested hole of vapid desire. I was something tragic, part of the fear of disease, part of the architecture of American despair, and the joke was that I wasn't a week in America and already I was a symbol of isolation and abandonment.

Welcome to purgatory. My room smelt of diesel and insecticide. Grease hung on everything. Carpet encrusted with vomit. There'd been a fire, walls scorched brown. It smelt like after a flood, a wet mousy dampness of decay, cockroaches waiting in the brown heat. The place was baking all that summer. The sweat poured off me in buckets. No wonder I had the skin problem. I was a creature of the North Atlantic, a cold-blooded creature of a rainy island. It posed a formidable challenge to my genetic heritage, to adapt or go extinct. A sort of nihilism beset me in those early days of hibernation. I relived my past life, crying softly with the detailed memory of what happened to me back home. I felt the immensity of America open like a wound. Trucks trundled on the edge of consciousness through the inebriating darkness out there on the highways. I was lost in nightmares inside my head, roaming around a past that had suddenly been eclipsed in one transatlantic flight. Images of the leaving flickered in a grey reel of film as I curled up alone.

It wasn't like I picked this shithole for my new existence. The story of my demise is a long, harried saga. You see, a friend-of-a-friend type of deal hooked me up with the room and the emigration in general. It all transpired back at the old house in Limerick, a tea and biscuits affair with a white tablecloth. Eddy McDonald, this immigration broker from Limerick City, had connections in the States with what he called the Emerald Underground. He came over with this itinerary for me – fuckin *itinerary* – but it got to the parents. Eddy got them to spring for the first month down for me. Eddy, a family friend, and I use the term loosely, had me signed up for a meat-packing house in New York. He said the money was great, better than arsing around behind bars in the Bronx. They loved the Irish at this meat plant. We were hard workers, and that's all that matters in America.

All this sanctimonious grandeur and pomp, the tea in its cosy, the fry hissing on the pan, lovely slices of brown and white currant bread.

'It sounds good in theory,' is all my Da had to say. He rubbed his chin like he knew something. I knew he wanted to know how much it was going to cost him to get rid of me. I was the oldest. I had to be made an example of.

Da was in his officious suit, a big frog with this big belly and skinny legs. He worked as a ticket collector down at the railway, a mindless job that could have easily been given to a badly trained ape. I had these names for my Da, 'The Bean Counter,' tight with the cash he was, or 'The Chiseler.' He wouldn't give you the steam off his piss. 'It sounds good in theory,' Da said again, his mouth stuffed with a poultice of currant bread. Such wholesome shite. He brought the tea to his lips and drank, patted down his greasy grey hair and began nodding his head. He said, 'Teddy Boy, you listen to Mr McDonald.'

On the day of the flight, Da was polluted drunk by the time we hit the road. He had a big grievance against me, because I'd got myself into trouble with the law and got blacklisted from running. The running had been my ticket out of Ireland, once upon a time, a full scholarship to America. You see, there was a time when nobody in the land could touch me in the cross-country. But it wasn't to be like that in the end. I ended up with no offer and was just floundering around home, doing no running, doing nothing, just keeping shy of Da most of the time, backing a few dogs at the track, but I was no good at picking winners. I was just hanging around corners whistling at the schoolgirls going back and forth from the convent school.

I was down at the White House before we left for the airport, getting a few quid off the locals. They shook my hand and wished me the best, more out of consideration for Da than any real sympathy for me. 'You heard Tommy Flannigan won the Munsters? He's set for a scholarship,' Paddy Morris said with genuine remorse. 'You had the beatin of him by a mile.' Morris was a local bookie, a man forever out on the roads with a tentacle of greyhounds extending from his long rake arms. Morris was the one who showed me how to rub potcheen into my legs before a race, showed me how it eased the nerves and brought blood to the joints. He was the one who gave me the trick to clear out the intestines by taking half a loaf of brown bread with water forty-eight hours before a big race. He had intestinal flow and excretion down to a science. 'You'd have had him by a mile, you know that, don't you?' He had this tight, plaintive smile on his small face.

'Central Tennessee State isn't it?' this other ol man said. 'Damn shame, really.'

'Full scholarship and all,' Mr Morris said, and took a drink and wiped his lower lip. 'You know they'll take anything over there in America. You could get a turnip a college degree over there.'

Da was red in the face. 'And look at him now, Corner Boy

is all he is,' he muttered. I could see Da wanted to have a go at me.

'This Teddy Boy never had what it takes,' Da said in disgust. Droplets of sweat rolled down his forehead. A vein swelled at his temple. He looked at Setanta, our mental terrier mix who was slobbering away at a bowl of Guinness mixed with a raw egg. The place was electric with tension. I was dressed up like I was on for aggro at an FA Cup Final in this black ill-fitting suit, my head cut to a bristle of black stubble, my Doc Marten's spit-shined and this Munster Scarf around my neck. I stood in the darkest corner, anxious to get out of that shitehole without a fight.

Mr Boyce, the life assurance man, drummed his hands on the counter. He had a half-chewed piece of cabbage in his mouth, a shot of Paddy's and a dinner of spuds and steak steaming before him. Da led me to him, and sure enough Mr Boyce had this policy for me, beneficiary none other than one Mr Bean Counter Samuel Kennedy, a fifty-thousand-quid policy for accidental bodily dismemberment or death. Boyce took a lovely fountain pen from his inside breast pocket. He had this big soft nipple of pudgy fat. Da punched me in the lower back, pushing me toward the policy. The pen was warm, like something incubated.

'The grannies can rest easy tonight,' this ol fella said behind my back. The place erupted.

'Bollocks . . .' Da stumbled. His glass tumbled and smashed, and Setanta did his nut barking at me.

Outside Da roared, 'Teddy Boy! Corner Boy! Boot Boy! Bollocks!' and telegraphed a blow. I let his fist get me on the side of the head. It was raining cats and dogs. I heard this low level hum in the ear that never really left me.

Da brought Setanta along for the ride out to the airport on the pretext that he needed walking. Setanta was vicious when he had drink taken, snappy bastard, borderline alco. He had to ride up front, relegating Ma to the back seat with us. I hated the dog. The indignity of that brute coming to see me off at the airport. He tore into my calf when I was kicking a ball around one day – Da said Setanta was only going in for a clean tackle, took the dog's side. Setanta was Da's exclusive property, part savage, part mental deficient. He was called into municipal service during the Gaelic Football and Hurling matches – when the drunks beat the head off each other on the trains, Da would set the dog into a frenzy and clear them. For this Setanta earned an extra few bob and had the status of the employed, 'something you've never achieved,' Da would shout if any of us said shite to the dog as he guzzled his egg and Guinness.

We were nearly killed on the way out to the airport. 'If it wasn't for Setanta barking, we'd be all dead,' Da said as we backed out of this ditch. Such shite. Setanta, under the influence of booze, saw a rabbit and went at the windshield like a madman, bashed into Da and sent us hurling toward Eternity. Three families nearly snuffed out just like that, all the cars in this slow waltz spinning out of control all over the road. 'Good man yourself,' Da said and patted Setanta on the head. 'Saved our lives, you did. You good ol dog.' Did Da think our heads were filled with fuckin sawdust?

I wanted to run for the plane. My poor ol Ma was dressed up to the gills in her Sunday best, this little hat like a Christmas pudding on her head. She'd not long to live by my estimation. After my trouble with the law she got this stroke, a noticeable palsy of the left side of her body. It was as though she was slowly turning to stone; a cement-grey colour affected the dead side of her body. If I was sorry for any of the things that had happened, it was for causing her pain. She'd always been a big supporter of me and the racing. The running was all from her side of the family. By the time I left, I'd hear her in the bathroom groaning something awful. Her eyes betrayed that her insides were in bits. She was reduced to wearing long coats to hide the betrayal of her own bowels.

It was the kind of thing that makes you an atheist. No matter what happened to me, I was a bollocks. But you'd have to ask yourself what sort of Supreme Bollocks would invent colon cancer to humiliate a poor woman who'd never said a bad word against anyone in all her life. Our Aunt Bridie, my mother's sister, had died of colon cancer. It was in the family. It was like that at her house when we went there years before, the same sour smell of shite that no spray could conquer.

Da checked his pocket watch like he did down at the railway. He was eyeing me as I said my goodbyes to Ma. She moved like a hen on a brood of eggs, shifting in pain and settling herself every few minutes. 'You'll let us know how things are, Liam, won't you?' I said I would.

Da came over and said, 'Teddy Boy, you better get a move on. Mother, do you want tea?' She did.

I kissed my Ma and followed my Da. He grabbed a young fella in a dicky bow and pointed at my Ma. 'Get that woman a sandwich like a good lad there.' I watched Da dealing with people in his officious manner. He wanted ham and cheese sandwiches with salad cream. I just looked at him and was thinking of all the names I'd had for him down through the years. The Turnip. The Automaton. The Dalek. The Bean Counter. The Chiseler.

My brothers Martin and Pat, twins, were playing the video games, all dressed up for my farewell bash in their confirmation suits. They were the next for the immigration, two eejits who couldn't hammer a nail into a block of wood. I used to think that one brain must have been divided up between the two of them, they were that thick.

The Bean Counter was getting edgy, fumbling with loose change in his pocket. The dog wouldn't sit still and attacked the video machine because of the intergalactic space alien noises it was spitting out. The lads kicked at Setanta because he was messing up their game. The dog did his nut and twirled around like a tornado. He ended up raising his leg and pissing on this family's suitcase. A young man shouted, 'Hey! Bollocks!'

Da gave Setanta a boot in the snout, and the dog skidded backwards, but shut his trap. He knew when Da meant business.

A policeman ran over and began to lay into Da about the dog, but Da put his hand to the side of his mouth like he was going to tell a secret, and said real loud, 'I bet you there's drugs in that case. This is no ordinary dog. This dog is a trained drug sniffer.'

The family was flabbergasted. The dog had his usual toothy grin of grim satisfaction that he was fuckin up people's lives.

In the aftermath of the piss, Da needed to vent his rage. He retreated and went over to the video machine and plopped Setanta down on the glass so he could see what was happening in intergalactic space. Martin said, 'Fuck off,' to the dog, and Da dropped Martin like a sack of coal. Total animal. The roars of Martin. Da gave him a boot in the back. People were staring at us. The dog went into convulsions of barks, his long nails scraping the glass as he went after an invading enemy ship.

Meanwhile this Irish dirge music was playing over the speakers, this banshee haunt of souls departing for other lands. Jasus, it gave me the willies. Families were taking leave of their sons, huddled in circles of black like funeral wreaths. You could see the ol dears with their teary eyes and the stiff fathers and the shots and pint glasses piled up. I was jealous for a moment.

Da took me by the elbow to the bar, bought six ceremonial shots of Jameson, and said to me, 'You'll remember there's others here needs lookin after. You're the first of many to fly the nest.' He said he paid six hundred eighty quid to get me to America. He wanted it back with interest. The dog came over, already bored by the video game, to show his support for Da. He looked up, moving his eyes between the volley of words. Da tapped my arm with his fat fingers, impressing his point. 'The disgrace you brought to this family . . . You can forget all that running shite now. Don't be gettin ideas into your head. It's all good enough for Mr Morris and his dogs to be on about sport, but you've to start earning your keep.' He jabbed his fat finger into my chest. 'Listen sunshine, you've done nothin but disgraced us.' There was the look of a madman in his eyes, like he was ready to beat the head off me. My ear had the usual ringing sound, so it was easy to ignore what he was saying, though a tear sprang from somewhere deep inside me. 'To think you could have been goin off a hero, on a scholarship, no mind.'

Behind the bar was this standard Irish farewell poem, 'May the road rise to meet you.' It was done on this quilt with a famine girl in a shawl walking a donkey carrying turf. The girl, staring off at the ocean, was thinking of her love gone over the sea. Jasus, I felt a lump in my throat.

'Listen to me, Bollocks!' Da nudged me. He knew I was off in my own world. 'You'd better get some sense.' He tapped his head, then he tapped my head. 'The noggin is what gets you on in this world. You've a brain in there right enough. But you won't use it. Why?' He tapped my head again with his knuckles. He was going at me in a big way, trying to drink and speak at the same time, and ended up spluttering all over me in a fit of coughing, which only had him more mad. Setanta took his cue and snapped at my ankle, so I kicked him, and Da gave me a belt across the head. 'Will you stop!'

Then Da stopped for a moment and took my hand in what amounted to a show of affection. My face was still stinging from the wallop. 'Is that what you're going to make me do to you as you walk out of here? Jasus, can you stop yourself for even a minute?'

I said, 'I can.'

He proceeded. 'I don't forget them SRA cards, and you shouldn't either. Father Tom says to me back then, "Your Liam is a genius. Are you sure he's yours at all?"' Da laughed for a moment, remembering. '"Genius," that's the word he used. "Genius!" and Father Tom knows what he's talkin about.'

The barman winked and butted in, 'It takes discipline, though.'

Da scowled and said, 'We ordered sandwiches an hour ago. Where are they?' The eejit slunk off and barked an order and came back in this simpering manner to wipe down the counter. Ah, yes, once upon a time I was number one man on the SRA cards, this fancy American reading series where you advanced by colours to more advanced books based on getting the answers right to these brain-teaser questions. I was up in the stratosphere of magenta, a non-colour, a nuance that represented the level of sophistication I'd achieved. I got the classic American A+'s and the shiny gold stars. But that was a long time ago, when I gave a fuck about life, before all this shite.

Da was hidden in this chimneystack of smoke. His face was destroyed with drink, the eyes swimming like oysters. He had an ally now in the bartender, whom he asked for an opinion on the six hundred eighty quid. The ol foxy-faced bastard said, 'There's no greater love than what parents bestow upon their children.'

I scurried off through Duty Free when the Bean Counter went off to relieve himself. I saw him through the glass looking around for me. Setanta followed to harass me, to keep me for Da, but customs turned the bollocks back. 'You have to have a passport, Bollocks!' I laughed, and gave him a boot as a parting present, right in the snout, that sent him skidding across the floor.

'Adios amigos,' I shouted out to Da when he came back. What a portrait of bemused despair. The dog, as befuddled as Da, licking its snout, sniffed the air and barked. Da was in a rage. He raised his fist to me through the bulletproof glass. He'd only been getting started with his what-he'd-done-for-me routine. Martin and Pat gave me the thumbs up, like Jackie Stewart at the races in Monte Carlo. But it wasn't all fun and games. I saw the good half of Ma's face was contorted with expression. I'd never see her alive again.

Metamorphosis

It was all in the recesses of my head now, the Great Escape. I looked like I'd been hosed down with fatigue when I stared at myself in the mirror. The motel was on the edge of a highway near the George Washington toll booth. I got this unceremonious welcome from a Galway bogman looking like Frankenstein's monster. 'Tom O'Connor's the name,' is all he got out of his big horsy mouth; he said fuck-all to me after that. We drove off into a series of tunnels, a slur of light and noise. I was mesmerised with jet lag and anticipation. The ear had nearly blown up mid-flight with the build-up of pressure. I survived by munching on a load of hard sweets from the hostess.

Immigrations took a dislike to me, but I had a visitor's visa, all official, from Eddy McDonald's cousin Thomas McDonald, a bank manager, who had sworn and signed as guarantor on my behalf that I was gainfully in his employment. 'I am vacationing in the greater metropolitan area,' I said, and so began my odyssey in America. They took back three of my bottles of Jameson, saying I was over the limit.

Grunts were all I could get out of Boris Karloff. Then we got to the motel. Total isolation. It looked like the cardboard stage of some film prop, the cheap crimson lights giving off an electric hiss that tasted like metal. He said, 'Somebody will be by Sunday night to pick you up for work.'

'How about eating?' I said to him. 'I don't have batteries up my arse.' There was nothing around except this highway, no town. New York loomed beyond the toll bridge, and the only way across was by car. Typical America.

'There's a diner over there,' he said, and off he went into the night to his car.

I might as well have been Robinson Crusoe, marooned. As a parting comment, Boris drops this one on me, 'You walk out there onto the highway and the cops are only waitin to kick the fuck out of you. You stay put and learn.'

'Stay put and learn, my arse!' Course, I didn't say anything to him. Already I knew I was going to give this country about six months of my life, and then I'd bail off to another continent or something.

The bed in the motel room shook for ten minutes if you inserted a quarter. The lads would have loved this shite back home. I inserted a quarter, and the bed jerked alive. It groaned in this nightmare way. This was the kind of contraption I'd like to have strapped Setanta onto to sort him out. The bed moved in the direction of the door, like it wanted to go out and die somewhere with dignity. At least the bed had some common sense. It had been totally abused by sexual maniacs. The whole thing smelt like spunk. And that wasn't to mention the porn on the telly, which I thought was free until management came by three days later to warn me I owed them eighty-eight dollars so far. Jasus, that cut the habit quickly. But the state of what I saw left its impression. I was in this indoctrination room of deep throat porn, a slug in a shell of exhaustion jerking off the anxiety of jet lag. I'd never seen the size of these pricks shoved up the arses of these birds, double penetration, gang bangs, massive dildos, birds fuckin other birds with big black strap-on pricks, birds shaving their boxes and shoving bananas up their fannies. I'd wake up to shots of spunk flying across the screen. Jasus, it was a long way from night vespers in the old school back home.

I was to work the night shift at this meat packing dump, but the skin disorder set that all back a few weeks. I wasn't there four days when the rash flared up on me. First this furious itching. Then mosquitoes had a go at me. I had zero immunity to these flying needles. I went around like an albino Zulu, in my underwear, swatting everything that moved. I was in the throes of depression as the itching progressed, and I began to bleed from all the scratching. I had a go at the bottle of whiskey with a vengeance, down the hatch with the eyes closed in that small motel room. I thought the sun would clear things up, so I went out to a swimming pool the size of a teacup. A graveyard of smashed bottles and discarded needles littered the pool area. Off in the distance, New York jutted against the sky, a fortress of concrete and glass. I had the bottle of whiskey and a can of coke and took a swig of one and washed it down with the other until there was nothing left. Then I flung the bottle against a wall. The pool water looked like shite, boggy brown. Broken glass gleamed underneath, cesspool. So I just lay out on this smashed-up deck chair and fell asleep, passed out is more like it. That's what really fucked me royally. We're talking skin that hadn't seen the light of day. Ever.

The ground trembled all the time with the shudder of pneumatic brakes in the aftermath of my sun poisoning, in the post depression of porn withdrawal. I'd lie awake and wait for Frankenstein's monster to come by and take a look at me.

'Sun sensitivity compounded by alcohol poisoning and immune reaction to the mosquitoes,' that's what Boris came up with after he looked me over and came back with a report from some phantom doctor. He said to me, 'You owe us for this. In the United States Army you can be subject to court martial for sunburn!' I got the message loud and clear, totally incapacitated and laid out in the bed of spunk. 'You think you own me?' is what I wanted to shout. I got the message, but I said nothing.

I thought the sun had affected my brain. I concentrated on taking an inventory of my senses, like a NASA flight check. I repeated the alphabet out loud, counted backwards from a hundred, did the maths time tables up to twelve times twelve. All systems go. I was still normalish. The Bogman sat and smoked and looked off at New York and said fuck-all until he erupted as I began the alphabet again. 'Shut your trap for fuck's sake, will you?'

I was stretched out and on fire. The Bogman looked at me, and there was disgust in his face. He gave me this medicated cream and some gauze that I was to use. I struggled to the bathroom, this hole of stinking shite, and worked to turn myself into a scary looking creature. My whole head was a welt of rawness, a swollen boil on a set of shoulders. It was the most disheartening sight I'd ever stared at in all my life. A small naked bulb exposed the grim spectacle of my body, casting darkness around my eyes and under my chin. The cream was some sort of silver-based medicine, and as it dried my face took on this strange phosphorescence.

The Bogman watched at the door, looking to the East for night to descend. He had a flask of tea in his hand and sipped at the steaming hole, blowing gently. He said to me, 'You look like the Mummy in *The Werewolf meets the Mummy*.'

I was furious. I walked like a zombie in slow torturous movement over to the bed.

'Jasus. I should get a photograph of this,' the Bogman said. 'This is one for the books.'

'Fuckin leave me alone,' I said half-heartedly, but it was good to have someone there, even if they were only there to spy on me.

'With a face like that, you're not going to get yourself a woman any time soon.'

Getting a woman to marry you was the key to American success. 'It'll clear up,' I said to him in a conciliatory manner. 'It's not that bad, is it?'

'I've seen worse,' is all he answered, and took another long drink of tea from the flask. 'I'm getting too old for this racket,' he began, and then stopped himself. I stared at him through the web of gauze. The Bogman stared back at me. My eyes were moist.

'You'll be fine, don't worry.' He waved his hand in the grey light, then he went off and came back with a brown bag of beer and a carton of cigarettes, some sticky buns and two egg sandwiches, which he gave to me without a word. He flicked on this Zenith telly and turned his back on me. He went for the porn. I heard the moaning in the background and closed my eyes.

The Bogman was stalking me in the silence as he slurped

the beer and ate the buns. I stretched out in the cool gauze, feeling the soothing effects of the cream seeping into my skin. He'd given me a powder for the pain. I felt oblique memories of the old days stir in my head. It was hard to reconcile that I was now in another country, that I was a hostage, a refugee, abandoned. I thought about going out to the airport and roaring my head off that I was an illegal immigrant and getting thrown out of the country. But there was no going back.

Sleep descended like a curtain, and I was adrift of this motel, out in the cold wetness of home, slinking to the back door to watch my Da and the dog getting ready for work. I shouted, but my father didn't hear me. He was eating a big breakfast and reading the newspaper. The dog turned and grinned at me and then turned and rubbed his leg up against Da's leg. I was shouting, 'You dirty bollocks dog. Da, it's me! It's me!'

The Bogman shook me by the arm. 'Wake up for God's sake.' He told me I'd been screaming. 'You have to forget all that behind you.' He pointed off into the distance. 'You're here now.'

Some bird was leaning over a huge prick, making this slurping sound. The prick was disappearing down her throat and reappearing. I felt the dissolution of my body from my mind, until I felt nothing. I'd damaged myself in the sun.

The Bogman left a few sandwiches, a bag of chips and two bottles of Coke by the bed. 'Keep up with the liquids.' He raised his big hand in this pre-emptive way and stubbed his cigarette into the deep shag carpet. 'You've fallen from grace,' he said quietly. 'There's people that think you're not worth keeping. You just stay put and recover fast is the best thing you can do for yourself.'

'Did they send you here to watch me?' I whispered.

He didn't answer, but he had an old paternal look, the laconic kind of man who bears witness to events in silence, forms opinions and keeps them locked in his own brain. 'People disappear in this country. Remember that. You're not their only concern, if you get my drift.'

I felt the effects of the powder I'd taken, the lolling sensation of sleep pulling me under again. My Da and the dog waited on the edge of consciousness. The dog was sniffing for my return, anxious to drive me from my own dreams. 'You're talkin like they'd kill me,' I said with a vague laugh.

'There are concerns here that live off a complicity of silence. When it was told what you did, the general consensus was that you weren't worth pissing on. You're still breathing only because of who got you over here.'

'You mean McDonald?'

'You see that now there. In this business you forget names.'

I lay flat on the bed, stared up at the ceiling and felt my heart racing.

'I'm letting you in on things so you don't go missing is all. Everybody deserves a second chance.' Then he ended things with the macabre but trite, 'This conversation never took place.' He shook my hand in this ominous way, then shut the door leaving me in the dark.

The days and nights were a blur. I brought myself to the window in a chair and sat behind the thin curtain and listened to life outside. Most of the inhabitants were refugees of the highway. They hesitated at the edge of New York. New Jersey was some sort of psychological reprieve on the edge of a promised land. It was total industrial limbo out here, the shudder of trucks coming in to settle for the night. Men mingled in groups in the lot, drinking into the night, a constant slur of life drifting in and out of the motel rooms, doors banging, a woman screaming, a languid life of sex and frustration and exhaustion. It smelled of sulphur mostly in the thick of night when the factories belched their toxins amidst the settling sleep. I stared into the night, struggled out into the hallway to walk off the effects of lethargy and boredom. Prostitutes squatted in the hallway and watched me with suspicion. Their perfume mixed with the awful odour of sulphur. It smelt like one of them stink bombs the lads used to set off in the study hall to get us out of school. But this was like every stink bomb in Ireland had been set off at once.

I had to keep the curtains drawn to keep the glare off the

television during the days. The hibernation continued in the twilight of tropical heat, the slow moult of past into present, the translucent peel of skin tearing away slowly. My new skin had a hard roughness, more scar than skin, the armour of prehistoric survival. The swelling never really left my face. I stared from eyes that recognised the metamorphosis. I had fried the left side of my face to a ruddy scar. It was hard to reconcile what I'd done to myself in that aborted attempt at suicide. That's what that drinking must have been, in retrospect. Something had been transformed deep inside me, a ganglion grown in the dark, etiolated strands of creeping nerves colonising old memories. I longed for the relief of pelting cold rains, for the crackle of the fire, for the pull of wind through the house, for the whistle of the kettle, the taste of burnt toast. I felt this procession of the past collapsing in a melancholy requiem.

In the dark I felt the unconscious process of the brain sifting through new sound, cataloguing meaning, registering smells and sounds, wearily threading a matrix of meaning in this new world. It was a draining process, my writhing pupa of transition pulsing and turning into something else. I had an informal education before the lord of all meaning, an indoctrination at the altar of the telly. I watched these ancient programs on the telly, *I Love Lucy*, *Lost in Space*, *Leave it to Beaver*, *My Three Sons*, *I Dream of Jeannie*. I got a good sense of the shithole I'd arrived in from the telly. They had these commercials for low-life fuckups who hadn't a high school education, GED training classes complete with cassettes, secretarial courses, mechanical institutes with smiling graduates brandishing soldering guns, now in good jobs, who said it was the best move they ever made, 'so why don't you make that important call and begin your new career today?'

Numbers streamed across the television. Confetti and American flags fluttered down at second-hand car dealerships, where fat men in suits thumbed through wads of cash and dared you to make them an offer they couldn't refuse. And cheap car insurance deals regardless of your previous driving record. You could be blind for all they cared. There was so much, cheap carpet sales and liquidated inventories of furniture at never-before-seen prices. Everything must go. Salesmen were screaming for their lives. It was fuckin hell out there in sales. I felt the buzz of insanity, the television hissing, the picture grey dots, like something beamed from a distant planet.

Sometimes I turned the sound off and watched the flailing arms, the faces thrust into the camera. But mostly I went back to the porn, just stared at the endless penetrations, the rawness of animal lust, and despite everything I always got an erection.

I was amazed at the regenerative powers of the physical body. I had begun this macabre project of peeling away the skin on my body and rolling it into this organic cocoon of dead matter the colour of a brain. It was a good way to see how far I'd come back from the dead. New skin grew in the dark as I wasted time watching the TV. I seeded this growth with Coke and these family bags of Tayto cheese and onion and Mars bars and Crunchies I got at the Duty Free, half a case of all that stuff. And Jasus, wasn't I glad of it. Sometimes I went over to the diner across the lot and got a few egg sandwiches.

After a week I was on the mend. One evening the Mexicans were getting hammered on bottles of Tequila and beer. They came by my room and saw me standing there. They looked me up and down, speaking in their broken English. They started a game of football with a beer can out in the lot. They wanted me to join in. I did. The lot boiled with dust. They were screaming and roaring.

Their women came out and sat in the back of a pickup, small and dark-skinned with long black hair. I stopped playing and went over to the pickup. I took a swig of Tequila and let it burn my throat. It eased the tension. The New York skyline emerged in the dying evening.

I drank some more. I saw the shrivelled worm in the end of bottle. I said to this Mexican standing beside me, 'That looks like me in there,' but he didn't understand me. I was getting drunk quick. I was trying to say something to one of the

Mexican girls but it wasn't working out. She had her chin resting on her tanned knees. I could see the white of her panties under her dress. And then the game ended when a cop car came into the lot. The Mexicans just disappeared. I went back across the coming dark and went into my room and waited until the cops left.

While I recovered I sat at the door and watched America. Trucks belched blue diesel smoke into the searing days of my recovery, backed up for miles, slouching towards toll booths. I'd never seen such a collection of cars. It was all about movement. It was an insanity of mobility, America. It inflicted a sort of insomnia on the brain. It gave me the jitters. Fuck, did I miss the immobility of back home where you'd stretch like a cat before the fire, eating toast and drinking tea and waiting for the rain to clear before doing fuck-all. I needed this long attenuated beginning, this slow process of adaptation, feeling the immensity of America seep into my head, losing my island consciousness.

Angel and Sandy

There was this one girl, Angel, or that's what she called herself, beautiful, sixteen at the most, showing the first signs of pregnancy under a dirty red print dress. It was what Mary Magdalene must have looked like back in the Bible as a young one, a real ride who dredged through a mire of mortal sin and spunk. She needed redeeming by the looks of her. This Angel was a total American tragedy situation. It was a sad country that let someone like her roam the country in her condition. She was everything I'd seen on the porn, that drugged look of deep penetration. But I suppose that's the latitude of freedom and choice Americans are always on about. Illimitable space and freedom to arise out of anonymity into stardom, to suck off men for an audience of millions.

I could tell she had the beginnings of a pregnancy, this slightly distended belly. 'Jasus,' I said to her. 'Don't you have any religion at all?'

She said, 'Fuck off, freak!'

Angel did a daily ritual, walking through the hot sun in her bare feet, knocking on doors, saying she was trying to get money to get home to Georgia. She pointed to an old Dodge up on blocks and said softly, 'Some niggers done robbed our tyres.' She curled her dirty blonde hair behind her ear. 'We's tryin to git money to git tyres. I got to git home. I'm havin a baby, sir.'

'You all alone here?' this man said, big trucker, metal buckle reflecting in the sun.

'As alone as the day I was born, sir.'

'You got to be here with someone,' the trucker said.

'Ain't nobody's business what I do exceptin my own, sir.'

'I saw you with some guy.'

'Oh, he's only my brother.' Angel played with her hair.

'You sure?'

'You sayin I don't know my own kin?'

'How old are you?' The trucker looked all cagey, like someone had the video camera on him.

'Older than I looks.' She was up to the game, a real whore.

A door closed, and she was gone into a room.

The sun burned in the blue sky. Total madness. I went back to watching television and minded my own business. It was the most desperate and lonely place on earth, this dump where people could inject poisons into themselves, where women sucked men off for drugs, where you felt compelled to curl up and touch yourself. Fuck, was I a depressed bastard with that skin condition of mine and the ear driving me demented. I was a freak among freaks. Even with my eyes closed, my eyes moved under the eyelids watching this new cathedral of despair named Motel.

The first money I earned in America was from selling my piss. This drug fella saw me at the door and said, 'You into drugs, man?' He was going to give me a hit cheap. I was standing there with the skin condition looking like a space alien. I still had red welts from where the epidermis had gone on fire, so to speak.

I said, 'Like fuck I am.'

We got to talkin, and he had this theory on high tension power lines. He said that's what fucked me, cosmic radiation that the United States Government had being subjecting its citizens to since the Korean War. He was a scary bollocks. He kept touching me, taking me by the arm with this earnest way of a nutter. The next thing he said, real candid, is, 'I'll buy your piss.'

'Are you jokin me?'

But he wasn't joking. Drug-free piss was worth something to the drug community. They went down to this clinic and had to give a sample to prove they were clean to get themselves methadone. They'd drink the methadone, but not swallow it, go on outside and spit it into a jar. They sold this regurgitated stuff and still came out on top with the money they paid for my piss.

There wasn't much for me in America, not that I expected much of anything. But this was shite beyond my wildest dreams. It was the kind of sadness that made you philosophical. Eighteen years old, and here I was in a New Jersey motel, lost to the world, an illegal immigrant. Jasus, it wasn't like I didn't have a brain in my head. If I hadn't got into trouble with the law back home, I'd be down in Central Tennessee hanging out with rich college birds. I said to myself, 'You better get fit before it'll all be over for you.' It was hard to keep things in perspective. I banned myself from the porn for once and for all, a sort of forty days of Lent to try and get some moral decency back into my head.

But this Angel is all I could think about most days of the skin disease. She was a sex machine and beautiful. What the fuck was she doin? She was like one of them English birds you'd see in the porno mags the lads hid back at the reformatory, real young good-looking birds with this drugged out look, saying in this cartoon balloon, 'I like it in the arse!' and there'd be this big black lad with his prick shoved up her arse.

Angel had some deal with the cook in the small diner. I watched her eating biscuits and eggs in the small grease hole, this prefab room up on blocks. Sometimes the cook would put up the 'Closed' sign in the middle of day and pull down all the shades in the restaurant. I saw the flight of her butterfly legs and the cook standing over her. I had my face up against the window. Angel had her mouth on his little sack of dog balls. I'll tell you it didn't make you want to dine there, that was for sure.

'I'm sorry for troublin you, but you see that car out there?' It was the Dodge Angel went on about. This eejit's name was Sandy, into the drugs in a big way. He was associated with Angel, either a brother or boyfriend. It was hard to tell. He smiles at me with this ugly-toothed smile. 'How come your skin is like that?'

I could see the cogs behind the bulging red veiny eyes. They looked like he got them in one of those novelty machines at the fair.

'Only fellas been in prison looks that white. You killed somebody or somethin? You hidin from the law, mister?'

I stared blankly, 'Who isn't?'

Sandy looked real serious, 'Isn't what?'

'Isn't hidin from the law.'

'I ain't.' Sandy's brain turned an idea and then it got lost somewhere in his head. Trucks shuddered and bucked out on the road, the grind of gears downshifting. The motel shook with this subterranean nervousness.

'What's wrong with yer face?' he said to me.

'Can you keep a secret?' I said to him.

He leaned toward me with this quizzical look. 'Yeah . . .'

'Plastic surgery!' I said out of nowhere. 'I'm changin my identity.'

'Jezus! You in with the Mob?'

'International terrorism. IRA, you heard of dem fellas?'

Sandy had this vacant stare of bewilderment. 'You for real? IRA? Shit, man. I heard a them.'

'This whole place is staked out. You make a wrong move, and you're fucked.' I prodded my finger into his chest. 'I'm trusting you to keep your mouth shut. I've taken you into my confidence, and now you're implicated. One word and you're dead.'

He raised his hands slightly, like he wanted to show he was unarmed. 'I got this policy that I don't get into other people's business.'

The next day I saw him again with Angel. I was at the door. The face was looking better. I put my finger to my temple and pretended to pull a trigger, then put the same finger to my lip to signify silence. Then I pointed at him. It was the kind of thing you'd wish you could leave your body for so you could see yourself.

Sandy nodded and looked around. He and Angel came over

to me. Sandy said, 'I want to show you something.' Sandy gave Angel some coins from his pocket. She tipped her head back and ate the money. I just watched as she made this jingling sound deep in her throat. Sandy said, 'Shit awmighty. You hear that?'

I just nodded. Her eyes were staring at the sun, her mouth half-open. The wind was blowing through her hair.

'How bout makin me change for a quarter?' Angel made some movements with her throat, and slowly her tongue came out with two dimes and a nickel. 'Shit, you ever seen anything like that in all your goddamn life?'

I said, 'No.' It reminded me of them grotesque-looking Laughing Policemen contraptions at the seaside carnivals that ate the pennies and roared laughing at you.

'How bout change for a dime?' Sandy said.

The tongue withdrew into the mouth, and there was that jingling sound again. I could almost see the coins coming up out of her throat. Then the tongue emerged with two nickels. Sandy placed the wet nickels in my hand.

It was another day before Sandy arrived again. 'We done got robbed,' he said. 'I ask you, what kind of world are we livin in, I ask you?' There was true disgust on his face. 'Niggers, I figures, done robbed us.' He pointed at the Dodge. 'I ain't about to ask for charity. Ain't like we don't all got our problems, but it's like this. My car needs fixin. I heard they're givin twenty dollars for plasma over at this clinic, which I'm aimed to give, but ya gotta have money to make money. Ain't that the irony of life. Ya gotta have money to make money. Ya gotta have money to get over there to where the money is, and, I ask you honestly, how is you supposed to make money when you don't have money?' He stopped dead. He was out of breath. 'Tell me?'

I said, 'Why don't you get your girlfriend to cough it up?' but he didn't laugh. He just stood there.

I gave him ten bucks in silence. It was part of the piss money I'd made.

Sandy's attitude changed when he had the money. He tried to look into the dark interior of the room. He was a sneaky bollocks, the kind of fucker who'd sell you out in a minute. The television flickered in the background. He leaned forward, trying to see if there was anybody else in the room. 'You ever killed anybody?'

I didn't answer him and said, 'You know anybody wants to buy clean piss?'

He smiled and said, 'Maybe we can come to some financial arrangement.'

Prisoners of War

One midday this smoking Volkswagen van pulled into the motel lot and set out displays of paintings and towels with Confederate flags and horses running wild on black velvet prairies. A bald eagle perched on a mountain peak on one blanket. This man selling the stuff was wearing a POW shirt, and POW flags hung still in the dead heat. He kept spitting tobacco juice into a cup. He called everyone who stopped, 'My fellow American.' Vietnam lurked in the consciousness of America.

The heat was rising in a wavering swelter of mirage in the mid-nineties. I came to the door and listened to what was going on in the parking lot.

'The name is Sergeant John. I did two tours in Nam. Ain't sayin I didn't do things I'm ashamed of, but war is war. Jesus Christ. I'm an American. I was over there, two tours when people here didn't give a shit if we lived or died.' He opened up with that remark to everyone.

The cook came out wearing a mesh net to hold his graying hair in place. He said in his defence, 'I was too old for Nam and too young for Korea.'

'You don't look that old.'

'I'm older than I look.' The cook wiped his forehead with his stained apron.

A trucker standing beside them smiled. He said, 'You got a licence on you to prove it?'

'I don't gotta prove nothin to you. Who the hell are you anyway? This here is private property.' The cook had this look of desperation. The sun beat mercilessly down.

The trucker and Sergeant John exchanged meditative spits, heads rocking in concurrence.

Sandy strolled over. He was smoking a joint. He smiled because he hated the cook.

'A man's got to live with himself,' Sergeant John said.

The trucker said, 'Ain't that the God's honest truth.'

'You plannin on sharing that?' Sergeant John said to Sandy.

Sandy took a deep pull and held it in his lungs. He passed the joint on to Sergeant John, who passed it on to the trucker. They did that three times in a circle until their eyes looked like they were going to pop out of their heads.

The trucker said. 'I want to show you gentlemen something.' He took a step back and pulled up his shirt and showed a tattoo with his name and his parents' address written into his heavy white belly. It said underneath, RETURN TO SENDER, C.O.D.!

Sergeant John seemed mystified. He pulled a face like people do when the national anthem is played. 'Ain't that somethin.'

Sandy, the eejit, mouthed the words and then looked at the trucker who gave a rolling smile that revealed his teeth.

Sergeant John's voice choked until he spat and cleared it. 'You mind if I get a picture of that?'

'Shit no, I don't mind. I wasn't goin to trust no dog tags. No sir!' He looked directly at the cook. 'No sir! I wasn't goin to trust no dog tags. I got a fear of the Army but trust in my fellow Americans, least I did once upon a time. Ain't that right?' The trucker looked at Sandy, who moved his eyes up and down and from side to side like he was testing them for the first time.

The studded rhinestones on the trucker's denim shirt flickered in the brilliant light as he held up his shirt. 'There weren't nothin else in that joint, was there?'

Sandy shook his head, and saluted with his right hand. 'No, sir.' I could tell Sandy was screwed up from the drugs.

'I like you,' the trucker said.

Sergeant John rummaged for a camera in his van and found it, saying, 'You stand here by my van, Henry.' He said Henry, because that's what it said on the trucker's belly.

'I tell you what. How bout I stand by my rig?' The trucker's belly was a mass of white flesh.

'How bout I take two shots? And how bout if cook here takes the picture of us?' Sergeant John said.

'How about if he don't.' The trucker made this long face of disdain.

Sergeant John said, 'Suit yourself. But how bout the kid takes a picture of us by my van here?'

'OK.'

'You know how to work a camera, kid?' Sergeant John asked.

'Shit, aim and click. I ain't dumb.'

Sergeant John said to the cook, 'OK, then, so was there something you was interested in, my fellow American?' He said it real sarcastic.

I came across the lot and looked at Sergeant John. 'Howdy,' he said to me. 'I'll be with you presently.'

The cook bought this print of howling wolves and said, 'Keep the change.'

'There weren't no change for you.'

'You worthless piece of shit!' the trucker shouted. His eyes watered from the searing heat and the pot. Wind created eddies of swirling dust.

The cook walked an eternity to his prefab metal diner. He was a miserable bollocks.

Sandy said, 'This man here is a POW.'

Sergeant John looked at me. 'You been in what war?'

'IRA,' Sandy said, looking at me. 'You see his face? He's hidin out here cause he got this plastic surgery so nobody will know him.'

'It's a murderous world,' Sergeant John answered. 'Why is it our heroes, our goddamn war heroes, are reduced to the scumholes of society?'

The trucker looked at Sergeant John and seemed bored. He paid me the attention of a disinterested cat. 'We takin that photo?' is all he managed.

'All right, I'm gonna say cheese!' Sandy said. He took a shot. The camera made a winding sound.

Sergeant John took the print and hid it from the light.

Then Sandy took another shot. Then he said, 'You mind if I get a shot?' He gave the developing print to Sergeant John.

'Sure,' the trucker smiled. 'You got film, Sergeant John, right?'

'I ain't got much film left, but what the hell. Ain't everyday a genuine American hero stops my way.'

Sergeant John held the prints close to his chest like he was playing a close game of poker. He said, 'Now that I think about it, I met a guy out in Montana who shows me this gook pinkie finger he carries around in a box. It looked like a dried up root. Offered him two hundred bucks. He wouldn't sell. That's when I knew he was for real.'

The trucker interrupted him. 'You got somethin to keep me awake on the road?'

'Sure don't. You know this country has really got me down. Seems like when a man says he's proud to be an American, people look at him funny. You know what I'm sayin? Like that man is hidin behind the flag. I've been drivin on the road towards towns where the sheriff pulls me over and says somethin like, "I hope you ain't plannin on stoppin anytime soon. We don't like your kind." My kind, I ask you both, what is my kind? Ain't it my kind that saved this nation's sorry ass?'

The trucker looked at Sandy, who looked around anxiously as he reached into his pocket. The trucker said, 'This is the best damn country there ever was is all I know!' The trucker bought himself a POW flag.

'Don't get me wrong, partner. I laid my goddamn life on the line for this country. But I ask you, what the hell is happening when there is people in Detroit who have given their lives to a company, and now they're getting canned like they don't mean shit?'

The trucker climbed back into his rig and hung the POW flag over the entrance to where he slept. 'Unions! That's what done us in to those damn Japs. We got a nation bloated on the fat of unions. Shit, who the hell is worth eighteen bucks an hour to screw a goddamn bolt into a car door?'

'That's pure Reagan hogwash. Jesus, dismantling America with the goddamn flag wrapped around you. What the hell is people supposed to live on?'

'I work my ass off for myself. Ain't that what this country is about? Independence? Unions is another name for Communism.' The trucker pointed at himself, let his finger circle the extent of his life, his truck, and then he pressed his own heart. 'You got to look after yourself, is what people got to understand.' The truck hissed and began its long drone of gear changes as it pulled out onto the highway.

Sergeant John looked bewildered. 'You ever get the feelin you wish you was dead?'

I bought a POW flag as well and headed back to my room. Even in the short time I'd spent in America, I was learning fast. I felt its solitary effect, the strange individualism Americans went on about. Watching the telly all those lonely days made you feel worthless. The powers that be lambasted the fuck out of you, not by calling you a wanker, where you could shout back at the telly and tell how hard you had it. No, they didn't give you the opportunity to form a sentence of revolt. What the telly people did was celebrate the success of others, offering you the opportunity to learn the secret to their success. In other words, the problem was you, if you happened to be sitting on your arse, not the system. I was hanging the POW flag and staring at the telly, which was all I ever did, with my door open, when I heard Angel outside. I got up and looked at her.

Angel came out of a motel room. 'What you doin, Sandy?'

'None of your business.'

Angel put her hand up to protect her eyes from the light and the dust from the truck as it turned and snaked out onto the road. 'He got any sparklers, Sandy?'

'You got money for sparklers?'

Sergeant John stared after the truck.

'How much you have?' Sandy said to Angel.

'Enough for sparklers.' She turned her bare feet in the gravel.

'Well come over then. This man don't have all day to talk.' Sandy turned. 'You got them sparklers, Sergeant John?'

'My fellow American, do I ever.'

Sandy giggled and scratched his head, 'All right, my fellow American, gimme ten sparklers.'

Angel came over and stood beside Sandy, giving him the money. Sandy frowned, counting the crumpled bills. 'How much for that towel there?'

'You don't have enough.' Sergeant John stared at Angel. 'What's your name?'

'Name's Angel.'

'Angel, I'm Sergeant John Bailey. It's nice to make your acquaintance.' He took her hand and kissed it. It was pure cinema, Jesus Christ.

Angel giggled and turned her toe in the hot stones of the lot.

'What do you mean, I don't got enough?' Sandy grumbled. 'How do you know I don't got enough?' but then his voice trailed off when he saw what Sergeant John wanted.

'It sure is hot,' Sergeant John said, smiling at Angel.

Angel looked at Sandy, who nodded.

A hot wind swept up dust in the lot. It pulled the red print dress close against Angel's body. Anybody could see she was pregnant.

Sergeant John hesitated and looked at Sandy.

Sandy smiled and said, 'I sure like that towel.'

'You got a bathroom I could use?' Sergeant John looked around the lot, anxious. He moved the tobacco out from under his tongue and spat. His face turned awful in the hot sun. He saw me in the doorway and looked at Sandy.

'You ain't got to worry bout him.' He gave me the thumbs-up. 'How're you doin, Mr Kennedy?'

'I don't know,' Sergeant John said, shaking his head.

Sandy faced him. 'Angel, you go on and show this man where he can relieve hisself.' Sandy nudged Sergeant John, smiling, 'I sure like that towel.' It was a towel of a girl in a bikini bending over a Harley Davidson chopper.

Angel said, 'What you got in yer hand, Sergeant John?'

Sergeant John showed her one of the pictures.

Angel looked at it for a moment. 'That's some kind of address. What the hell someone got that there fer on his belly?'

'That there is a soldier from Vietnam, Angel. He wanted people to know who he was, in case he was killed. Seems like a girl like you should have a tattoo like that.' Sergeant John spoke in his sweetest voice.

Angel looked him in the eyes. 'You gotta have a home to put there first.'

I watched Angel walking across the hot tar. She looked over at me for the first time with a detached stare, her hands spread out over her small rounded belly.

Slaughter

The routine became permanent after the skin condition went away. I was up to my gills in debt to Mr O'Connor, alias Frankenstein's monster. At 3 a.m. every morning, he came and took me across the George Washington. He already had other illegals from a Howard Johnson's down the road stuffed into the car. They were from Poland and didn't speak English. They smelt like stale socks. 'They sew monograms into the shirt cuffs of Wall Street brokers,' the Bogman told me on one of his more talkative days.

The car drifted into the warm morning air across the bridge. Weather patterns stuck for ages in New York, not like the blight of intermittent showers I'd lived through all my life. In the silence I'd stare ahead at the brownout of the New York city horizon. Sometimes the Bogman would yawn, and it was contagious. He'd have us all yawning after him.

The Poles were all related, or at least they all looked the same, dressed in clothes from their homeland. Now, I could see some justification in their being here. They came from a political dump where you could get killed as soon as not. Political insurrection and guns. 'You are family?' I said one morning in this broken English, but they only smiled, their heads bobbing in the grey light of the city's glow. Poor fucks. I noticed over time that their hands were dotted with tiny spots from where needles had run over their flesh. They never said anything though, not even to each other.

New York was a great machine that ingested and digested matter. I watched garbage barges move silently up the Hudson in this early morning dead hour, cutting steel grey lines in the calm water. Down the other end, the Statue of Liberty was only a vague outline against the night sky. Nobody coming to America saw the Statue of Liberty any more. There was nothing to signify a new beginning. You got in on the sly, ran for cover and stayed low in the Bronx or out here in New Jersey. Nobody seemed to give a fuck about us.

I worked on 9th Avenue and 13th Street, in the slaughter district. The gay bars were tucked in down here as well. It was Sodom and Gomorrah come to town. I saw things no Americans saw, passing the leather jacket gays, the S&M bars thumping with music, a trickle of neon light leaking into the street, the cesspool bathing houses, men as thin as rakes kissing, some bald, some with distended stomachs and fat arses, hybrid transvestites on stiletto heels in a plumage of pink feathers, like exotic birds making squawking mating noises. Needles littering doorways, the smell of stale piss on old newspaper. You didn't have to be a genius to tell they were incubating plague down here.

Jesus Christ, but the meat business was competitive. Warehouses opened and closed, changed ownership. Gay bars sprang up in the shells of old warehouses, sawdust sprinkled to absorb the pervasive odour of invisible meat. Only a month and half in New York and the change from back home was unbelievable. The worst thing was that there was nobody to tell this to. The scenes passed into my skull in total isolation. I saw this kid sucking off a fat man in tight leather trousers in an alley one morning. The fat man was running his hands through the kid's blond hair. I could see it all in this small bowl of light from a street lamp.

I worked at Shamrock Wholesale Meat Packing Company, under a picture of a pig playing a fiddle. By half-four in the morning, I was pushing carcasses of meat along an overhead system of rails with hanging hooks. A freezer door breathed into the dank humidity of the August morning air. I worked in this margin of warmth and freezing cold, shivering constantly. It was only a matter of time before I'd die of something.

There was no solidarity among the men, an alien workforce speaking different languages, grunting and roaring into a sleeping city. You learned by observation, not by being told what to do. Dare you ask a question down here, they'd tear the head off you. It was pure insanity.

'What da fuck are you lookin at? Am I payin you to look at me? Move, do SOMETHING!'

In the glass booth above the whine of saws and swirling blades, the owner banged phones on the table, shouted and cursed. A skinny blonde in a tight red skirt chewed gum and typed orders into a phosphorescent green screen. The boss called her Lamb Chop, but her name was Miss Barbara Wright. She wore perfume so strong it lingered in the cold vaults of meat, scenting them. Sometimes she rubbed the owner's neck, and when his head was on the desk she'd look down at the men working and smile.

The thud of cleavers on heavy blocks of wood filled the air as master butchers cut meat for upscale restaurants, boneless sirloin strips, prime rib fillets, London Broils, king cut, queen cut. Trucks backed up to warehouses by half-five, smoking in the blue dark of early morning. Buyers in limos arrived in Armani suits, viewed tables of meat, making faces, looking at one another, figures going in their heads, looking for deals.

The owner, Mr Frank Pitello, this small Italian, wore a press-on tie with a knot as big as a noose. 'You're insultin me with an offer like that. Jesus, fuck, what the hell do you want? Do you want me to bend over and let you fuck me up the ass, because that's what you're doin to me. I gotta work within margins and this ain't goin to work. Why don't you get back into your fancy motherfuckin limos and get the fuck out of here? I ain't gettin out of bed to go broke. How the fuck am I supposed to live? Lamb Chop, get me a pill. Get me a glass of water. This guy is doin a number on my ulcers.'

It was a speech which sent me running the first day on the job. I thought guns were going to fire, but it was the same shite every few days. Deals were as raw as the meat over which they were waged.

Mr Pitello saw me one day and said, his Italian arm around my shoulder, 'You think that nation of yours will ever be free?'

'Will I ever be free?' is what I wanted to say, but I smiled and said, 'I want to thank you personally for what you've done for me, Mr Pitello.' I said that, because that's what I'd been told to say if this bollocks ever asked me anything. Mr Pitello reeked of aftershave. The cuffs of his shirt were monogrammed. 'I came to this country with nothing,' he said to me.

'Is that a fact? Aren't you the man,' I said.

Mr Pitello didn't like that and took his arm from my shoulder and squinted at me.

Lamb Chop stood behind him, the cold of the freezer door smoking. 'We have an appointment,' she said, ending a stalemate of silence.

I watched the staged fights out of the corner of my eye every day as I swept up disgusting scraps of meat from the master butchers' work. This was where the real money was made. Mr Pitello had deals with discount supermarkets uptown which sold the crap to welfare mothers. The scraps of different animals and chipped bones were fed into a monstrous steel-mouthed creature which squatted in the corner of the warehouse. Gallons of lard and spices were poured to add weight and life to the meat. As long as the machine was fed, it sat content all morning long, trembling and shitting into translucent socks that went by the name of Uncle Tom's Traditional Breakfast Sausage Links, or Aunt Esther's Southern Pride Sausage Patties.

I came home one day to find Sandy had broken into my room and was sitting there, as cool as you like, watching television. Before I could say anything, Sandy smiled, 'I didn't touch nothin. You can check if you want.'

I rubbed my face, exhausted and drenched from the job. I was definitely coming down with something. The sun beat down on my back. The mercury was near a hundred. 'You have to get out,' is all I managed.

Inside the motel, the air conditioner frothed through a vent like an exhausted animal. Outside it was an inferno.

Sandy just stood there. 'I don't mean to bother you, but right now I need some piss.'

'Christ.'

Sandy rolled his eyes. 'Hey, things is tough all over.'

I sat up in the bed and rubbed my face.

Sandy was half-smiling. He said, 'You ever hear of organ donors?'

I said, 'Yeah. What about it?'

Sandy squeezed his arms and nodded his head. 'Well, I want to run this by you, see what you think. These donor transplant programs is all wait listed. Don't matter if you is rich or poor, you got to wait like everybody else. You can see how that pisses the rich off, right?'

I said, 'Yeah, so?'

'Well, you ever hear how down in Mexico they got these doctors who do operations for the rich who don't feel like waitin?' He didn't let me answer. He came close to me. 'You know how much a kidney is worth on the market these days?'

I said, 'Listen, I don't have time for this shite,' but Sandy said, 'I'm talkin twenty thousand for a kidney. Shit almighty, you hear what I'm sayin? Goddamn heart just as much. You never thought about it like that, right? People is a cash crop these days. A guy like you might fetch fifty thousand on the open market.'

I had this sudden halting sense of fear. I said, 'Are you threatenin me?'

Sandy made this face of disgust. 'Hell, you got me all wrong. I was just thinkin is all, thinkin about people was all. We got people here that ain't worth shit, nobody would miss em at all. Kind of scary when you think about it like that, ain't it?' Sandy shrugged his shoulders. 'All you need is a goddamn cooler is all. You get a kidney and them doctors send someone to get it from you. Now I been thinking, you must be getting pretty damn good with a knife down at that Meat Packing Plant of yours. You think you could identify a kidney?'

I peeled the plastic off a pack of cigarettes and offered him one. I'd taken to the smoking down at the meat plant. I said, 'Sure I could identify a kidney. No sweat. But it seems like you're talkin about murderin people.'

Sandy said, 'Hey, I was just talkin is all. Just puttin things into a certain perspective is all.' Sandy blew rings. 'I can spell my initials. You want me to show you?' He changed the subject just like that.

Sandy curled the hot smoke in his mouth and looked real serious, then he curled and fanned his unseen tongue until a stream of thin smoke rose into the air and spelled out S B. 'Sandy Bridges. Thank you, thank you very much.' He took a bow. Then he spoke. 'I got to get down to the clinic, but I got something to ask you first.'

I inhaled and let the smoke out through each nostril in two tusks of smoke. 'What?'

Sandy picked up three limp fish from the floor. 'I've been fishin down on the Hudson. Ain't this somethin else?' He slapped his leg with his free hand while holding up the shining fish in the other. 'I was thinkin about invitin you over for somethin to eat this evenin. Yes, I am,' he said, getting all serious. 'Course, we goin to need corn and some bread.'

I took the hint and went into the toilet and pissed the money for dinner.

Later on I lay out on the bed exhausted, a web of humidity drenching me. The lying around in bed was fucking me when I got home from the Meat Packing. I was making zero progress with getting back into shape. It was crucial not to slack off. The distance running wasn't like the football training. You had to have a solid foundation of miles behind you in the running or you'd be useless. I had the old training shoes from home with me stuffed into a bag, caked with old mud from the mountains. It was probably the first time I cracked a smile in nearly two months. Home, fuck sake, who'd have ever thought I'd miss the rat hole.

I laced up the shoes and headed out in a pair of old shorts, going off by the Hudson, down this embankment of rock onto this trail that headed off towards upstate New York. I ran under the skeleton of the George Washington Bridge, graffitied foundation pylons covered in an exotic infection of colour. Across the way, on the New York side, a mountain tunnel excreted a snaking commuter train. Life went on in all its normality while I slept the days away in the motel.

Not used to the baking heat, I was drenched after a few minutes. But it was good to be free of the stale odour of sex, despair and cigarette butts. I felt the stink coming out of my pores. The sun burned down from a cloudless sky. It made my eyes squint. My feet were on fire in the shoes. I could feel the sand grains from the old mud cutting into my feet. Still, I dug in. I kept on the narrow trail of hard brown dust. I came up on these two girls who had on shorts halfway up their arses, their legs long and tanned, and halter tops holding in their wobblers. I went by, collected my stride and gave them a big, 'How's it goin, girls?' and the thumbs-up.

They gave me this show of white American teeth.

The breathing was ferocious a mile or so on. I had these shallow gasps, like a granny. 'Come on, bollocks!' I started shouting. This is what I was built for, this running game. I was parched dry after three miles, nearly on my knees, totally humbled by the heat and from the smoking. I felt the suffocation of heat in my lungs, the lead weight of my legs. I stopped at about four miles out at this outcrop of rock that jutted out over the Hudson, totally banjaxed. I retched off to the side of the trail, coughed up bile. A whole year wasted at the reformatory and now this shite hole. I was a physical wreck.

The first pang of homesickness really set in. I had a look down at the rocky decline and thought about taking a dive and ending it unceremoniously, smashed by the rocks and then drowned. But this bollocks in shorts and a headband and carrying a water bottle jogged by on the trail, and said, 'Get tough, guy!' His wrist gleamed with a gold band. I went into a fury, 'Fuck off, homo!' and lashed off back towards the motel, leavin him in the dust.

I was reduced to walking back to the motel, famished and exhausted, beaten and sweating like a bastard. I should have waited for the sun to set, but it wasn't just that. The sickness and the jet lag had never left me. I gave myself a good thrashing. There's nothing like a sense of physical decline to shake the hell out of you. I was freezing by the time I got up the embankment. Dehydration, heat exhaustion. I had these little pimples of cold, goose bumps, and it was in the nineties. The internal thermostat had gone haywire. I got back to the motel and drank from the tap, guzzling the cold water, letting it run down my chin and stomach. I put on a heavy shirt and got into bed and curled up. The room was this grey box of depression. I knew I was on the downside of existence, alone. All I said to myself was, 'Fuckin Central Tennessee State! Fuckin Tommy Flannigan, that bollocks!' but it wasn't their fault. It was mine. I felt my scrotum turn up into the warmth of my insides, a sorry migration from the filthy bed sheets.

Hours floated past. I must have gone unconscious or delirious in that shitehole. I woke up still cold, sweating in the heavy jumper. I emptied my bowels in the toilet, a runny mud of liquid splash. Oh Christ. Another illness. I was famished but couldn't keep anything inside me.

Outside it was dark and warm. Thunder rolled in the sky, the smell of rain coming in. I heard the crackle of mosquitoes getting electrocuted in the sizzling blue neon of the mosquito-killing contraption, stared into that nauseating country of mindless death and insects and transience. A train trundled off in the distance. The room was invaded by a dull sour odour of my body. I was miserable, with a headache from hunger, alone, illegal, a nonentity. The sweat from the run had dried to salt on my body. I kept a blanket around me and shivered.

The dark cracked in seams of jagged lightning. The crimson flow of lights bled VACANCIES. A husk of bone-white moon smoked in fast moving clouds. Moths gathered under a yellow bulb lighting the road to the highway. Birds swept into this margin and ate silently. I took a deep breath, felt the soreness of exercise in my shoulder blades. I stared at the pantomime of slumped figures in the toll booths, exiles of the highway. There wasn't much traffic. The night had settled in for storm. Everything had an abbreviated stillness, crouched into submission, awaiting the skies to open up in fury and rain. It was all slow motion. I felt the deadening silence of anticipation. Next door to me I heard some people sitting on chairs with their door open. I waited and said nothing, listening to the wheezing rasp of a lifetime smoker. The people sat there in a heavy silence broken only by some insignificant remark or spit. I heard a tinkle of bells. Pale gray eyes emerged from the doorway and shone. It was a cat. 'What you see, Marmalade?' a woman's voice whispered. 'You get back in here.' It was a soothing voice of contentment.

A chair scraped and a giant man appeared and said softly to me, 'Looks like a storm is comin.' The man smelt of sweet whiskey and smoke. The cat curled around his leg and disappeared. 'Seems like this storm has been followin us up out of the Gulf of Mexico.' Then the man turned and went back to sitting, whispered something to his woman who said, 'I still got that cold chicken wrapped up if you want, Frank.'

When the rain started hammering down they closed their door. I went down by Sandy's room to see what was up with the dinner. I had the blanket wrapped around me like an Indian. The rain fell from the dark sky in long stinging needles. Sandy's door was shut, but the curtains were slightly apart. I put my face against the glass, felt it tremble. 'You in there, Sandy?' I said softly. A fork of lightning burned away the dark inside. Angel was on her back, her arms and legs spread, writhing like some overturned beetle in distress. I heard the cook scurry from her legs and hide behind the curtain. 'I need something to eat,' is all I managed. 'I want two egg sandwiches.'

I went back to my room and drank water out of the tap. The parched ground drank the rain. I felt the wind wrap around everything. Things whistled in the pull of night rain. I stood by the window staring at the cook's diner. I was starving. A car parked in the lot and an old man and this skinny homosexual got out and ran through the dark for the security of a room next to mine.

Things had begun to take cover, to fold in on themselves with the approach of the storm. A sign outside creaked and groaned in the wind. I shut my door and sat shivering in the dimness, the strange porthole of grey light coming in from the bathroom. The coldness had settled around my shoulders and crept up my neck. The new skin stretched like something alien on me. I felt trapped in this cocoon. It didn't have the elasticity of skin. It was hard, cracked open at the edges of my lips, cracked in the squint of my eyes around the temples. Maybe it was the fact that I'd done this to myself that made everything worse. My ear had this ringing soreness, swimmer's ear or something.

Next door the porn was on the telly. I heard the bed shaking. They were feeding it quarters. I mustered the scrap of religion left in me and said a Hail Mary. I felt my insides betray me again. I went to the toilet and felt a burn of emptiness. I wanted to vomit, but there was nothing there. I turned on my telly, and Kojak was sucking a lollipop. He said, 'Who loves ya, Baby?'

Back in bed, I got a pen and paper and wrote down, 'Day 1 of the Rest of My Life: Eight miles along the Hudson. Nearly died.'

I turned off the light in my room then and went to sleep under the stale covers. The cook knocked on the door and said, 'You owe me three-fifty plus room service.' He left, and I crept over, took the two sandwiches into the bed and ate voraciously with my eyes half closed, then settled back into unconsciousness.

Lightning tore open the room. I braced against the reverberation of sound. A thunderclap shook the foundations of the motel. I felt hell was opening up under me.

I was tortured by the earache until I somehow fell asleep after God knows how long, only to find Da and Setanta walking around the dark corridors of my brain. Da was explaining the finer points of football to the dog, who was looking up like an attentive pupil. Da wasn't too steady on his feet. He'd been drinking. I knew the walk of him. I called out his name, but he heard nothing. I felt sorry for pissing off on him back at the airport the way I did. Da had the collar of his coat upturned around his neck and a paper stuffed under his armpit. I followed Da along this maze of tunnel to where my ear was killing me. He gave the sore part a big scratch with his walking stick. Oh, Jasus, I felt the relief. 'That's it Da, right there.' The dog dawdled and sniffed at my brain up around where my head was splitting from the headache. 'Hey, fuck off Setanta!' I shouted. Da shouted, too, at him to cut the shite out, and Setanta came up along Da's side. Da took a turn, and suddenly we were out in the train station in Limerick into this gust of cold wind. Da was having a smoke and a cup of tea in the little shed he used for his personal belongings. I said, 'Da, it's me, Liam!' but he said nothing to me because he was deep into Spot the Ball in the sports page. He folded the paper into quarters and muttered away to himself. He used a little bookie pencil like a dart and spotted the invisible ball with an X. The dog twitched in his own dog dreams at Da's big booted feet. Da got up, because some eejits were outside, arsing around on the platform, and shouted, 'Hey, you. Yes, you! Get up here this minute!' The lads made a dash for it. Da roared to the dog who was off like a shot after the thugs. 'Hey, you Corner Boys!' Da shouted and ran down after Setanta. It went on like that through the night. I was on the plane to America, and Setanta shows up next to me drinking a vodka tonic and munching on peanuts. He barks some shite to me, and then Da looks back at me from the seat and says, 'Stop kicking my seat, Bollocks!' I must have been going round the bend or something. I awoke each time into utter darkness, shivering.

I was under the bed by the time the Bogman was outside. I stayed still and said nothing. He banged so hard the glass trembled in the window. The cook was really pissed off when he came back with the Bogman. They saw no sign of me and they left.

I must have slept right through the night and into the next evening before I awoke again. Mosquitoes buzzed the stillness. Cockroaches waited patiently, antennae reading the air. I was sweating like a bastard. Sandy was standing over me. He said, 'The cook was tellin me you're a dead man.'

I let my eyes adjust to the light. 'What?'

'That's right. There was a man here lookin for you last night. I was thinking maybe one of them organ donor gangs got you. A guy like you could fetch big money real easy. There's men on ventilators just waitin for the human harvest.'

I felt this surreal edge in the sweat of the new evening, the globular amber light of a sunset outside settling into dark once more. I was thinking of the Meat Packing District, had images of me strung up on a hook, men bidding on my liver, my kidney, my eyes, my heart.

Sandy must have seen something in my face because he said, 'Shit, but you look scared for your life.'

I said, 'I am.' I was finished with New York City and the Emerald Underground. I'd take my chances.

Escape

It was later that night, when the world had closed in on itself, hidden away from the pull of another lashing rain, that Sandy wheeled four second-hand tyres out one by one into the parking lot. I was up drinking a cup of water, looking at the rain, the traffic, the night sucking meaning from everything. My ear was killing me.

Sandy came up to me. He said quietly, in a whisper, 'I figure we head down to the Appalachians, back down home. Ain't nothing left here. These veins ain't worth shit.' He held out his arm, showing two black cuts that looked like a vampire had feasted on his veins. 'Collapsed,' he whispered. 'Infected. I ain't worth shit no more here.' He just shook his head. 'And that bitch ain't nothing but trouble now. Got herself pregnant if you don't mind.'

I looked off towards the road. New York was like some galactic vessel amidst the dark.

'Course you gotta have some gas money. You got money, right?' Sandy shrugged his shoulders. 'Ain't like I'm lookin for charity, but . . .'

'I have some,' I conceded.

It was as good a chance as any to disappear. I still had unfinished business in America. I had to give the running a last chance. That's what could turn things around for me. I had my first run under my belt. Getting the mileage up, that's what I needed to concentrate on. The Appalachians, what the fuck! It was a better prospect than the Shamrock Wholesale Meat Packing Company. I was going to give myself six months to make it in America. I would get myself into shape to show up and redeem myself and get that scholarship. It was only late August. Guilt had besieged me. Da and the dog were there in every sleeping moment. It meant something. I had fucked my family over.

Sandy had nailed the towel of the girl in the bikini and the snap of the trucker to the frame of the window. They hung as a strange disembodied dream. The chopper was out in the middle of the desert. There was a cactus in the background. I knew this was where Sandy went at night when he closed his eyes.

'You got everything?'

Angel gathered the blanket and pillows from the bed.

The night roared in a fury I'd never experienced before. It was like someone was throwing stones at the window. We were forced to sit together in Sandy's room for an hour as the sky opened up in a downpour. Rain streamed in through the doorway. Sandy had the door open, giving everything a mist of cold rain. His wound had begun to bleed again. He squeezed his hand and flinched as he tore a sheet into thin strips and exposed the wound. 'Goddamn it.' I stared into this black rectangle of the doorway and waited silently, not wanting to get drawn into anything. 'You hold this, Angel.'

She tied a knot around Sandy's arm. 'You got to let a scab form there, Sandy.'

Sandy went and sat at a table and counted the money I'd given him. 'Ssshit,' is all he said, like he had a slow leak. He had his one good hand to his temple. His hair was all matted down and flat. The flesh had honed itself down around his skeleton. 'This ain't shit!' He drank from a bottle of duty free whiskey I'd brought over with me. He waited, mixing the strength of the whiskey with water, wasting time until his patience ran out.

Angel lay on the bed, curled away from the cold rain, and said nothing, but she looked at me with a look of cold sadness. I stared back at her.

Thunder opened up a seam of jagged light, illuminating the room for a moment in a brilliant flash. And then Sandy said simply, 'I got to pay a visit to someone.' He looked at me. 'You come with me.' He took something from a box.

'You ain't goin to do anything stupid, is you, Sandy?' Angel turned. Her eyes were visible in the dull light. 'Just hold me, Sandy,' she said softly. I could see it was a ploy to hold him back. 'Sandy,' she whispered again, 'don't do nothin stupid.'

'I already done somethin stupid. I got stuck with you, bitch!' A crash of thunder broke over his roar. The wind sucked the curtains into a dismal flutter.

Angel sat up. 'Leave him alone,' she said with a fatigue of dull indifference, like she wanted to die. 'I need you for this baby, Sandy. Please, leave him alone. You don't have to do this. You hear me, Sandy? Why don't we just leave now?' She sat up and placed her hands over her small stomach. It was like looking at something out of *Rosemary's Baby*, It scared the shite out of me.

Sandy held a series of photos in his good hand. 'Maybe I can negotiate a settlement. I got a right to get what I deserve.' He didn't look at Angel. He looked at me. 'You see this shit that motherfucker done?' He slapped down instant photos like he was dealing cards. The cook had his cock in Angel's mouth in one of the photos. The cook's face was staring at the camera.

'You see that shit-eatin grin on him, like he don't know I been photographin him? Motherfucker wears women's underwear sometimes. Ain't that right, Angel? He likes when she sticks her finger up his ass when he comes.'

'Don't, Sandy,' Angel said.

'Old-fashion blackmail. Ain't nothin complicated about that,' Sandy laughed. He was trying to play things out in his head.

'I hate you,' Angel said quietly. 'I hate your guts.'

'I wish you'd shut up,' Sandy's voice quivered. 'You don't get it, do you?' He moved the photos around on the table. 'How bout this one?' He tapped at the photograph. The cook's face was beet red, in a grimacing look of ecstasy as a thread of mucus hung from Angel's tongue. The cook's prick was bent like a banana. 'Ain't it fucked what the camera sees?' He said it with an excited anger. His fist clenched, and he banged the table.

'He's got a gun,' Angel said. 'You go over there, he'll kill you.'

We slopped across the dark lot, the transient cars penitent, facing the shut doors of motel rooms. In the falling rain, Sandy stopped and looked at me. 'You let me do the talking. I just want you there, just in case.'

'Just is case of what?' I said.

'Just in case,' he said wryly.

We were soaked by the time we were halfway across the lot.

There was nobody in the diner. The sky flashed in the slashed bars of the blinds. The formica counter caught the glint of lightning. 'What you lookin for?' the cook said from behind the counter. 'I ain't fixin anything more this evenin.'

Sandy trembled with the cold from the rain. He was drenched, in only a tee-shirt and jeans plastered to his thin legs. 'I come to negotiate,' he said with a sudden seriousness. 'I come to negotiate your freedom.'

'Look punk, I ain't in the mood for you. I thought I told you to move on.' The cook put down a small toothbrush on the counter and wiped his hands on his apron. He'd been scrubbing down the grill. A scent of pine filled the small diner.

'You shut that door,' Sandy said to me.

I stayed by the door and shut it. My eyes moved between Sandy and the cook.

The cook suffered from goitre or some glandular disorder. An ugly sack of inflated flesh spilled from his chin and spread down to a red swell of distended neck. This bloat of flesh moved independent of the cook's head, like a hot-water bottle.

Sandy held up a photograph and said, 'This, my friend, is what lawyers call incriminating evidence.'

The cook said very civilly, 'You got a case against me, I'll see you in court.' Then he moved to go by Sandy and said, 'Now if you don't mind,' but by that time Sandy had locked the door from the inside. Things took this ominous turn. The cook's eyes began to look around for a weapon, for an escape route. 'You ain't plannin on doin somethin foolish, cause right now there's nothin done yet.' His skin writhed in its loose creases, giving off a doughy odour of a fat infant.

'We doin nothin but talk is all we doin here.' Sandy held the photograph at arm's length, stepping into the path of the cook. 'You recognise anybody in that photograph?' Sandy persisted.

'You don't have shit on me. She consented,' the cook fired back. 'You come near me and you're going away for a long time. You hear me?' The cook directed his attention at me. 'I ain't done nothin to you. Aiding and abetting a criminal is what you're down for now if you don't open that door. You hear me?'

Sandy laughed and moved a step back from the cook. 'Don't listen to this shit.' Sandy raised his voice. 'There ain't no consent when it comes to minors. "Statutory Rape" is what they call it. And I got the proof right here.' He flicked the edge of a photograph.

The cook laughed and turned and went back behind the counter and took a tip off the counter. He flicked a dime at Sandy. 'Tell you what. I'll pay for the call. You go ahead and call the cops. Maybe you didn't know, but distribution of pornographic materials of a minor is a Class A felony. Ain't like everybody don't know what you two have been up to. I got a list of witnesses. You go ahead, Mr Law-Abiding Citizen.'

'Two hundred bucks,' Sandy said, moving towards the cook, but the tide had turned against him. He began in an aggravated, but conciliatory way. 'You don't want the trouble I can bring you. I'm tryin to do the fair thing. Shit, ain't like two hundred bucks is goin to break you.' He stomped his foot. 'Shit, two hundred bucks and you got no troubles. Seems like a goddamn bargain if you ask me.' Sandy looked at me.

'Fuck you!' the cook said. 'Go ahead. Call the cops. You got nothin. You think you goin to hustle shit out of me, well fuck you, LOSER. You porn-peddlin LOSER. You hear me, LOSER? You got nothin on me! NOTHIN, LOSER . . .'

I gathered LOSER was one of those expressions that cuts deep, like BOLLOCKS, because Sandy was literally shaking. The word LOSER flew back and forth like a Chinese star in a Kung Fu film. 'I ain't no LOSER!' Sandy shouts. 'I ain't fuckin around here. I don't know what kind of fool you take me for, but I'm gettin that money one way or another, you hear me?'

The cook looked at me and said, 'I think it's about that time you decide if you want to remain a free man. This is the last time I'm goin to tell you to get out of here. You don't need friends like this LOSER!'

Sandy let out this primordial scream and dived at the cook, knocking him to the ground.

'Jesus Christ!' I shouted. 'Sandy, hell!'

I never saw exactly what happened, but I knew when fortune was against me. The cook gave a squeal of pain and disbelief, then this grunt of pain. 'I ain't no LOSER. You're the LOSER!' Sandy roared so loud I thought he was going to bring people over from the motel. Such déjà vu, like when I'd done the granny back home, total loss of control. Everything spiralled out of control, these yellow and black spots of total shock floating before my eyes. I could hardly see. My balance nearly went out on me. I heard the dull thud of punches, the grunt of spent effort, the wheeze of exhaustion in Sandy's voice as he pummelled the cook. It seemed ages before Sandy emerged, with blood on his shirt.

Sandy panted and held his bad arm. 'I only wanted what's mine . . .' His voice trailed off, a warbled voice of horrible fatalism, like he knew there was no turning back. 'Turn off the goddamn lights. You hear me? Turn them off.'

I managed to get the lights off and set the CLOSED sign against the window. My head was spinning. I crouched and put my head between my legs. 'Murder . . . Christ Almighty!'

'Help me!' It was the cook. Jasus Christ. 'Help me!'

I scurried over to where the cook was lying on the ground. He was still breathing. A splotch of blood soaked his shirt. He grabbed at my arm.

Sandy was on his feet, shaking with exertion and madness. The outside lights made the small diner glow in this soft blue. Sandy went at the cash register. 'Where's the money?' He pulled at the register. It made the sound of a child's bicycle bell. The register was empty. Sandy shouted, 'You ain't goin to do this me, LOSER!'

I grabbed Sandy by the ankle and knocked him to the ground. 'He's alive! You hear me, you stupid eejit, Sandy? Stop before we're fucked!'

Sandy breathed hard, flopped and turned away from me, growling under his breath. 'I was tryin to be reasonable.'

Blue pilot lights glowed on the grill. The rain still poured down outside, obscuring everything. The cook recovered enough to watch me. I could see the fucker was okay. He put his hand out to touch me. I looked at the cook, and thought to myself that this bollocks was going to get me done for murder.

Sandy saw the cook moving. 'Ain't like you didn't deserve what you got,' Sandy said in the dark. Then he said, 'Guess I'm goin to have to kill you all over again.'

'No,' the cook said feebly.

Sandy sat there and said, 'Shit,' lost as to what to do. He was coming back from the world of total collapse. He wiped his face.

I reached up and turned on a light under the cash register, this fake banker's lamp with a draw string. The lamp spread a rectangle of light down on the rat faces of Sandy and the cook.

The cook slumped as we took him out and sat him at a table. He had his hand over the wound in his stomach. It was obvious he wasn't really badly hurt.

'What did you stab him with, Sandy?'

Sandy showed me a small penknife with a three-inch blade.

The cook said quietly, 'I need a doctor.'

Sandy looked at the cook, 'You want to tell me where you got that money?'

A car turned into the lake of the parking lot. I was in shock, halted by the sudden swoosh of light. The cops came into the diner some nights to get free coffee and eat donuts. The car's lights washed the dark of the diner and then died and went back out onto the road.

'We have to get out of here now, Sandy. Come on.'

Sandy shook his head. 'Shut up! I gotta think. You think you can just walk the fuck out of here?'

The cook touched the wound and said, 'You goin to let me bleed to death?' He had this desperate look on his sagging face. 'I die and you'll be up for murder.' He said that for my benefit, like I could do shite for him. 'I gave you them sandwiches and this is what I get? Wasn't like I didn't know you was under the bed last night. I didn't give you up.'

Sandy still had the knife in his hand, with the blade still extended. Things weren't settled yet.

There was this sense of inevitability unfolding, a total sickness and remorse, and still this question, why do victims make us killers? Two hundred bucks is all Sandy wanted. I mean the cook had abused the fuck out of Angel, and now we were back to square one, except now we had this aggravated assault, attempted murder looking us in the eyes. I felt the way I did after a run, that coldness after exercise when the full effect of the elements comes down and robs you of heat, makes you shiver. You're vulnerable, sweat turning cold. It was all meaningless.

Back at the reformatory we used to go out after the heavy rains and find snails and use a pin to extricate them from their shells, tease them out until they squirmed and curled away from the cold and the light. An episode out there with the snails and the big black boots of reformatory schoolboys told you God didn't give a fuck about anything. That was the way I felt in that diner, waiting for the boot of God to stamp me into extinction.

The light from the banker's lamp burned on the counter, casting shadows on the walls as the trucks moved outside on the road. My eyes had adjusted to the grainy effect of slow motion we occupied.

The cook held his wound like it was something precious. He began crying, but you could see it was all shite. There were no tears. It was a whine from his chest. But you could tell he was thinking about what might happen to him. He was becoming humble now when it was too late. Sandy undid the wound around his arm, exposing a dark marsh of infected skin. 'You see that?' He held the arm before the cook, who looked at it with a miserable face.

'Ain't like I'm a millionaire. Ain't like I don't work my ass off,' the cook said in his defence, which was the wrong tack to take. 'We're from the same side of the track, you and me, and her out there.'

Sandy went wild and hit the cook across the face with the back of his hand. The cook slumped sideways in the booth. Sandy held his wounded arm again. He said to me, 'You ever think that I was once a small baby?'

I said nothing.

Sandy held the arm and said finally, 'There ain't nothin left but to finish this motherfucker off.' His eyes had the severe look of hopelessness.

The cook collected himself enough to say, 'A man like me is willing to say he was wrong, and I was wrong, and you was right, and now I think there ain't no real harm done between you and me, no hard feeling or nothing, because you was right and I was wrong . . .'

Sandy's forehead beaded with grease and sweat. He had this ongoing dialogue with himself, saying out loud to me, 'I don't really give a fuck if I go to prison, just as long as I know they got him in there too. And that's the truth. Motherfuckers will rip the shit out of his asshole. I'll just be in there thinking of his asshole bleedin and these guys all lined up.' He sat there in the glow of yellowish light and said nothing for a few moments.

'You gotta be reasonable is all I'm sayin, Sandy. Me and you and her and him is all the same, and we got to stick together cause there ain't nobody really gives a shit about us, except that we take care of each other in this world, and that's the way it's got to be, cause I don't hold no grudge against you or nothin . . .' He was panting when he finished saying this.

Sandy said, 'You gonna shut your fuckin face, or am I goin to have to kill you again?'

The cook sulked and mouthed, 'I was just sayin . . .' when Sandy waved the knife at him.

'Shut it!'

I knew at that stage that the cook wasn't going to die.

'Sandy, you in there?' It was Angel.

'Jesus Christ! We goin to charge admission to this show?' Sandy shook his head. He opened the door, and Angel pushed by him. 'I can tell you done something stupid. He dead or somethin?'

Angel looked at the cook sitting in the booth and then at Sandy. The light from the lot loitered at her back, mixing with the dark. I could see the relief in her face. Angel was completely ragged, the thin dress clinging to her body. Rain had soaked her. Her small hard nipples showed under her dress.

I turned on the light and shut the door. I looked outside and saw the lights in the motel rooms, half of them empty and dark.

'I think you owe us somethin,' she said to the cook. 'Ain't like I didn't do things for you.' Her voice seemed on the verge of tears. 'You know I did.'

The cook raised his shirt and smoothed out rolls of fat and showed his own wound. It was a thin sliced opening above the navel, deep in folds of skin. The fat had saved him. The wound had stopped bleeding, dried to a brownish rust color. The cook looked down and seemed almost disappointed.

Sandy rocked perceptibly, still the thrill of anger wandering aimlessly in his brain. He was over by the register again. 'Ain't shit here! He got some kind of drop safe or somethin?' Sandy had the befuddled look of anger. He hadn't even the competence to kill a man he hated. 'I came to negotiate fair and square,' he said flatly. He held his damaged arm and stared into the empty register. 'I say we tie him up and set fire to this dump.'

Angel came over to the cook. She had one of the pictures of herself on her knees. It was a picture taken from the side.

Angel had her head turned in this awful grimace, looking back at the cook. The cook had his prick buried inside her. 'You see this?' It was obvious from the photograph that she was pregnant, the rounded mass of her stomach showing. 'Ain't any jury goin to see it your way, Marvin.'

'Marvin?! Shit, if I ain't heard it all now,' Sandy ridiculed.

'Why don't you shut it, Sandy.' Angel looked hard at Sandy with a frankness that showed exactly what she thought of him. Sandy dropped his eyes and wiped his mouth. 'Burn this dump. It's the only way out. You with me on this?'

The cook's face was already taking on a deep bluish swelling, like a jagged outline of a map. He said, 'I ain't a millionaire. I ain't, Angel.' He tried to get out of the booth to touch her. 'Honest.'

Angel drew back from him.

'I want two hundred bucks, Marvin!' Sandy shouted.

'I ain't a millionaire,' the cook said again. He ignored me and Sandy, and that was the way I wanted it to end. 'You gotta be reasonable with me, Angel.'

'I'm running this show!' Sandy shouted, but it was all melancholy boredom and sickness.

I stood like a zombie and said, 'I want a hamburger and chips.' I don't know where that came from, but Angel looked at me and said, 'Now that's the first sensible thing that's been said in here.'

Angel looked at the cook and then at me. 'Marvin makes the best milkshakes, with a cherry on top.' Her smile settled everything there and then. We left the door locked. I looked outside and the rain still poured out of an obscured sky. I was shaking something terrible. It was the kind of day that feels like a life, a day that makes you age, gives you the dull feeling that life is total shite, and there's nothing you can do about it. It's the kind of thing that has happened to every adult, every married man who doesn't have the money to live a decent life. Nothing as dramatic as stabbing a cook, of course, but the feeling is the same. Goodbye youth, goodbye good looks, goodbye dreams of respectability. Hello forty thousand children, hello council house, hello pub. Now I knew why my Da done my mother until she was a walking wound. He was stabbing her in his nightmares, spilling out his frustration. But at least all them bolloxes had a soft landing into their oblivion, not like me in this dump, totally isolated, alone. I knew the feeling of my father, knew the sick hatred and despair he had for having a bollocks like me. I was so close to a scholarship, nothing there to stop me giving him the satisfaction of picking up the paper and reading about his son, letting him have his brag down at the pub with his pint and that bollocks, Setanta. That's what he wanted, and I robbed him of any dignity. Fuck! I robbed myself of any dignity.

The cook went behind the counter, and soon the hiss of meat filled the night, replacing the dull static of rain outside. He cut an onion, and his eyes watered. I was struck with the hunger. Everything else left me, only to be replaced by total starvation and headache. Starvation came back and took its rightful place in the hierarchy of self-preservation there in my head and screamed for food.

The cook's face was a deflated sack of patchy bruises. The cook took a cold pickle from a jar and cut it down the middle and gave it to Angel. She said, 'Let me see that stomach.' She took a bottle of vinegar and a napkin and dabbed the wound clean. The cook made a wincing sound, but I could see he was enjoying Angel touching him. Smoke rose from the meat sizzling behind him. I licked my lips and wanted to eat.

Sandy took advantage of the situation and took two fruit cups and a bowl of hardening custard from under a glass case. 'Don't mind if I do,' he said, as he made eye contact with the cook, who had his white belly exposed. 'Medium rare on them burgers, Marvin. I like to taste blood in my meat.'

I could only roll my eyes. It was hard to believe that the cook was there with a knife in his hand and we'd just stabbed him. But that was the height of things, insanity, misfits, everything contained in this greasy box, all contained by the sexual sadness of a sixteen-year-old prostitute.

Me and Sandy ate at a booth, burgers and fries,

institutional string beans laced with a buttery salt. I stuffed myself with three hamburgers and went up and poured myself an icy glass of Coke. I got a rice pudding from under the glass case then had a custard. I felt the food traveling down into my stomach, filling it for the first time in nearly two months. The ebb of sleep was almost instantaneous. My whole body wanted to hibernate, to shift into some corner and let this night pass. I looked at the cook, who seemed genuinely content that he had prepared the food. He was talking with this earnest manner, like he wasn't that much of a bollocks. This is what he was made for, simple as that. He drew a long deep breath of pot and held it, passed Angel the joint. 'Ain't like I'm goin to stay here the rest of my life. I got places I got my mind on, real nice.' He used his arms like he was going to point, but the sting from the wound broke through the effect of the pot. He winced and showed his teeth. I knew it was time to get the fuck out of the diner.

In the end, the cook counted out two hundred bucks and gave them to Angel, who said, 'How much we owe you for dinner, Marvin?'

'You jokin me, right?'

'Ain't no such thing as a free meal. How much, Marvin?' Angel counted the bills. 'Twenty cover it? Six burgers, dessert . . . You charge for refills, Marvin?'

The cook nodded his head. 'Shit, yeah, I charge for refills. This ain't Burger King.' He put his hand to his temple as he spoke. 'Angel, you goin to leave them photographs, right? And the negatives, too?'

'Jesus, Marvin! Ain't no such thing as negatives with Polaroids, dumbshit,' Sandy laughed, then got up and looked out the window, shaking his head. He turned just the once and said, 'I don't feel right not killin him.' He stared at the cook and then winked. He said, 'I want you to see me in your nightmares, asshole.'

I just had to shake my head. A blue smoke drifted through the diner. The heat of the fryer made the windows fog and weep with the humidity. The reek of onions burned my eyes.

Angel laid a row of photographs down on the table and

curled her lower lip like she had a fish hook stuck in it. 'You thinkin about gettin the car ready, Sandy?'

The cook waited for me and Sandy to move towards the door.

'That all of them?' the cook said as we began to leave.

'I got some for insurance is all,' Angel said softly. 'You can trust me, Marvin.'

'Ain't you I'm afraid of,' the cook answered. 'Shit. I'm the one with a hole in his stomach.'

I went out with Sandy to get our stuff. Everything smelt of the Hudson, a dank odour of decay. I gathered the canvas bag of gear and was about to go when I saw the ball of dead skin beside my bed. The skin had turned a greyish colour, a hardened mass of dead matter. I took the ball in my hand, pressed against its sweating doughiness. I remembered this special on the telly back home about the dung beetle, this creature that mixes its saliva with the shite of animals into a food ball it nudges off to its burrow where it descends underground to feast on excrement in the dark. I put the ball into my bag.

I put a quarter into the bed and it hopped mercilessly against the floor. It was like looking in on the set of *The Exorcist*.

I went over to the window to see how things were progressing. I saw the shadow of the cook pressed up against Angel. Sandy saw it, too, and said, 'I should have killed that motherfucker long ago.'

I wasn't sure who he meant, the cook or Angel. I didn't ask him.

Sandy had a needle stuck in his arm, stuck into the black wound. I couldn't look at him. 'You comin, Angel?' he shouted from his doorway.

The Dodge was a huge boat of a car with a two-by-four for a front fender. It didn't even need a key to start. Sandy kept the lights off until we were out on the highway, going south.

Highway Driving

I sat up in the front seat, slumped against the door. Christ almighty, what an episode of despair. My head throbbed, the effects of the disastrous run still on me, and the ear was beginning to resurrect itself into a pinprick pain. Thank God we ate. The food settled deep into my body. I could almost feel its nourishing effects. I wanted to eat like a whore and sleep for a year, that's how tired I was. The time of hibernation still held me. The delirium of the night-shift had kept me in that world of illegals, slinking through the dreams of Americans, cutting up their meat, a sullen participant in the service industry. No wonder Immigration didn't really give a shite about deporting any of us. I knew some Irish birds who worked as seamstresses, abandoned for days, forced to complete wedding dresses for upscale Park Avenue women. And the poor old eejit Polish that I'd met with the Bogman, working in the New York garment district, paid fuck-all to sew monograms for Wall Street brokers. And not to talk about who built New York, an invisible army of Irish, locked into a world of work and drink and no mobility, unless you call climbing scaffolding upward mobility. That was what immigration meant these days, an existence of shame and falsehood, lying into the phone, telling them back home how great things were, but the truth had seeped through the lies. I was under no illusion what America meant. None of us were. But the lie lived on, as it usually does in the Land of Double-Speak.

Sandy yawned from the effects of the long night, pressed in the coil of the cigarette lighter and waited for the soft click. 'I thought we was all dead back there.' He kept his head straight forward. 'I did,' he whispered. He had a cigarette behind his ear which he took and put to his lips.

I listened to the slur of the car pushing through the night and felt the shudder of exhaustion beset me again. The ear was killing me. I poked at the pain. The eejits back at the reform school had done me in bad, all those times I got my head stuck down the toilet, held there with the water flushing around my ears. What diseases could you get from toilet water?

Angel slept in the back seat, curled up in a blanket. I smiled to myself despite the ear, looking at her small sleeping figure. She had saved all our lives. There was something powerful about her. She wasn't the whore I'd copped her for back there at all. There was something deep inside her besides that baby. She hadn't abandoned hope or love or forgiveness. I felt human again for the first time in ages just to be near her. Maybe there was light in this cesspool.

The main thing was, I was out beyond New Jersey.

I closed my eyes, and the pain resurfaced in the silence, because this is where the pain lived, in the silence of my cranium, coiled up in the ear canal. Sleep won out, though, in the end, and I must have been out half the night I suppose. When I awoke, a river meandered below the rise in the highway, barely visible in the night. Sandy was there at the wheel. The pain seemed to be resting in the ear. I stayed still, keeping it at bay.

Sandy was something else all right. He had a scavenger's consciousness, trotting at the edge of disaster, slinking through darkness. He was talking to himself, muttering more like it, the eyes searching the road, staring into the universe before us. I averted my eyes and looked out at the darkness. We had climbed into a dense growth of trees, up high. Lights glittered in the distance down below. At this height the air was cool and damp, trees holding the night humidity. I felt a coldness at my shoulders from the sleep. I went to straighten myself, and the ear pain awoke, and holy fuck it burned in this spasming vengeance, like the ear was going to blow up. I let out this moan, stuck my finger into the canal and went deep into my cranium. I'd have used a drill bit, it was that bad.

Sandy caught sight of me twisted and turning. 'If that ear's still bothering you, why don't you use one of them straws?'

I couldn't speak or nothin. I leaned my head and palmed the bad ear, trying to get this suctioning effect to draw some wax out. It was like there was an army of ants on the march. Oh, it was bad. I groaned and moaned. The pain unfurled itself, like some primordial slug probing slowly with its antennae, coming out of its shell. I felt the movement, the protracted recoil of pain, and jammed my finger into the soft membrane of my ear. I didn't give a shite what damage I was doing. Jasus, the pain was colossal, primal. Out the window went four billion years of evolution. My eyes rolled back into my head. I gave this bawling cry of pain.

Sandy slowed the car down. 'Ain't supposed to put nothin smaller than your fist into your ear, you know that?' I took this straw from the stale drink, no hygiene or nothing. I was dying. I bent the opening on the straw in desperation and inserted the stabbing point deep into my ear and went to work, digging away at the warm wax, heading for the centre of my brain. My hand sweat and trembled, but I kept scraping against the lining of the ear wall, digging into the soft wax build-up deep in the ear.

'You gettin any relief?' The car picked up speed again.

I said nothing, leaning sideways into the door, working with the long probing sensation, the deep scraping excavation inside my head. I was moaning in half relief in this atavistic pleasure, like a dog after an itchy spot. I kept my eyes closed, concentrated on the straw, guided it with my trembling hand. A hot baste of wax clogged the straw. I pulled it out slowly, smelt this warm basic odour of wax. The car was filled with the smell. I squeezed out a thin pinch of wax from the straw. The ear was on fire with pain, a hotness that felt like blood. The centre of my universe converged into this vortex of ear as I invaded the canal again. I winced and mined the old burrow of the previous attempt, the slow process of invasion, feeling each centimetre, the scraping advance into my head. And then suddenly I arrived at an impasse deep in the dark canal, this hard nugget of wax. I took a deep breath. My whole body was shaking. I shifted against the door, trying to prepare for an assault of pain, working up the courage to stab into the heart of this hardness. The straw bent against the force. I knew I was doing damage, but I didn't care. I was drooling with pain.

Sandy had slowed the car down. 'Shit! You's liable to go right clear to your brain.'

I pulled on the earlobe, tried to open the deep canal further, wedging the straw further into the impasse. I worked for God knows how long, scraping into the hard wax nugget, feeling everything by the sensation of pain alone, blind, watching with my mind's eye, digging away like one of them outer space soil-gathering machines that edge across alien landscapes. And then, Jasus Christ and Holy Fuck, pay dirt and salvation, a long funnelling relief, this warm exodus of wax erupted in a volcano of waxy shite. The thickness disintegrated into this warm flow of wax and blood. I felt the ear throb in relief, all that stuff that had gotten into my ear back at the reformatory. It was a humiliation that I would never forget, and now this legacy of pain, Jasus, no telling if it was only gone to sleep again, gone dormant.

Sandy shouted, 'You're goddamn bleeding! You busted your eardrum, Jesus Christ!'

I slumped there, and I cried to myself. I grabbed his arm, shaking. I opened my eyes for the first time in ages.

Sandy shook off my hold. He wiped his face and said, 'Shit, if that don't beat all.'

A dark trickle of blood and wax ran out of my ear. I had ruined my hearing forever, but I didn't give a shite. I sat there in the dark as the car sped through the night. It sounded like putting my ear to a seashell, listening to the sea. Sandy was speaking words, but it was drowned out. I was shivering cold, trembling in the aftermath of violence, in shock. A hollowness of an empty corridor replaced the pain, a strange darkness inside me, this cold expanse of silence. I drifted into sleep with my hand to the ear, curling into the passenger door. I moved amid this vastness of darkness, looking for some sign of religion, some artifact of God or some avenging angel sleeping with wings folded, awaiting instruction. I shouted inside my head, 'Is there anybody there?' and wandered through the dormant labyrinth where the pain had lived. I passed the sin of the granny-bashing incident. The granny was in there at the proceedings against me in the court dock, her little claws in plaster of Paris, a bowl on her head to keep her brain from oozing out. The policeman who'd nabbed me and the lads for hocking the stolen goods on the train up to Dublin was sitting off to the side. I was there with counsel, not as myself, but as this mound of pulsing blackness, pure regret just throbbing like you'd see on Dr Who, a cheap-looking prop of psychological pain. I knew Da was in there, somewhere, and that dog of his, and Ma was probably there hiding and crying and saying a few decades of the rosary for me. I woke from time to time, freezing cold. I got a coat from the back seat, withdrew into its warmth, and had visions of motels passing through a blur of night, the hush of sound cold and sad.

Da was waiting as usual on the other side of consciousness, this manifestation of shadow, draped like a druid. He was looking terrible. He had his head bent over a boiling bowl of menthol and a towel draped over his head. He was at his usual ritual of loosening up the night's congestion in his lungs, coughing up phlegm from the years of smoking he'd done on them unfiltered Sweet Aftons. He came out from under the damp skin of towel for air, and his face was a boiled ham. He looked like a deflated balloon of skin, the double chin and the massive belly. He looked up and gave a brooding sardonic grin, but then he coughed, and his eyes closed in a bout of hard choking coughs like the sharp bark of a dog. 'It's you,' he managed, but tried to wave me away. 'No call or nothin, and your mother on death's door.' He took a gasping breath. 'But what could we expect, I ask you?' His voice wheezed. I could smell whiskey the way he always hid his drinking, diluting it in his tea. A pack of cigarettes was set out by the table. He was going to smoke himself into the grave.

Setanta came into the work room and sniffed around and

barked with that vicious head of his. Da gave him a slight kick, 'Shoo, son.' Then he hid his head again and drew in more of the menthol. He came up again and took off the damp towel and raked his fat hand through his wet hair, pushing it back on his pink pate. 'Have you ever seen such a self-centred bollocks in all your life? There's been others who left home and made a job of things for themselves, but I'll guarantee he'll get in with the wrong crowd over there. You mark my words.' He took the basin of menthol towards the sink. The menthol had begun to congeal around the edges of the bowl.

Setanta wagged his tail and went into a sitting position, curling himself around Da's big boot and licking it as Da swabbed the bowl clean. Now that was the kind of shite Da really went in for, boot licking. Da leaned forward and placed his hand on Setanta's head. His belly poured out before him. Da had one abiding genius. He knew how to pick the meanest dog in the land. He could see viciousness in a week-old pup.

Da looked up and directed his attention at me, but he was addressing the dog. 'He'll call when the money runs out, I wager you that, son. I know the bollocks won't come of anything now that he's gone into hiding, run out on another job that I got for him. Do you know, Eddy McDonald came down by the house the other day and said he wanted due compensation for how that bollocks ditched them over there in America?' Setanta licked Da's other boot. Da gave this bewildered look of desperation and banged the table, and Setanta withdrew his coarse purple tongue and growled. Da looked up at me and nearly doubled over with a renewed fit of coughing. Some glob of phlegm broke free and threatened to choke him. He gathered this spit and launched it at my face. 'You good fer nothin bollocks!' he roared.

I shivered and came around slowly. Like an eejit, I checked the back to see if Da was in there. Of course he wasn't. Outside two beams of light illuminated a thin lane of highway. The pain in the ear was gone, which was something, though. Anything was better than physical pain. I moved tentatively, making sure. A preacher spoke in a hiss of static and Sandy was laughing to himself. I thought the hiss was something in my ear, until Sandy played with the dial. I checked the ear. No pain, thank Jasus.

Sandy looked at me. I watched the thin angular face, saw that look of exhaustion in the glow of instrument lights, the eyes watering with each fatiguing yawn. He rolled his neck to ease the tension and said softly, 'I was thinking you was going to die right there on me.' He was silent for a few minutes. 'Guess I should sleep soon. We got enough distance from trouble, I figure.'

'You think that cook's goin to do anything about that stab wound?'

'We got a state line between ourselves and him. We're in the clear. They ain't goin to haul my ass across state lines for some aggravated assault charges.'

Distance assuaged memory and pain. The life at the motel was over. I let out a long breath, tipped my head and made this cracking noise like I was breaking my own neck.

Sandy pointed at a sign. 'Figure we got another hour and then we rest.' The car pushed through the dark, up through the rise of hills, into the deep veined tracks of highway.

Dark archipelagos of cloud sailed against a smoking white moon. I felt the creeping dampness of vegetation outside. We were still within an ocean of storm, the distant rumble of heat lightning making the sky flicker. The preacher came drifting back through the radio with his monotonous droning salvation. The injured ear was dead, just a dark tunnelling stillness.

'So you got a legitimate plan or what?' Sandy said matter-of-factly, but then he raised his brow and said, 'Well?'

'Same plan I've had since I came here. Get myself back into shape and get a scholarship down to Central Tennessee State, where I should be right now.' Then I went into the long story of my demise, and Sandy said, 'So you ain't no IRA or nothin. Not that you had me fooled . . . Well, let me tell you this, then, cause it might just suit you fine. I'm headin for the hills is what I'm aimin for. I figure, why not go back into hills and regroup, as it were, take stock of things.'

'That suits me,' I said.

We passed a motel snug against the trees, the VACANCY sign branded into the dark. It had the feel and look of a fifties movie. It was sinister, to tell the truth, this oasis of light. I could imagine the silvery flicker of a TV screen, the insomniac at his telly waiting for some loser to turn and eat up the gravel and bring the car to a stop, exhausted and needing the comfort of damp sheets.

We were in darkness again. The exhaust leaked its poison. There was a hole somewhere in the car sucking in the fumes. It must have added to the tiredness. We came up slowly on the crimson lights of a banjaxed old truck. And then suddenly from out of the darkness came this blizzard of feathers.

'Jasus Christ!' was all I said, and Sandy swerved, 'Shit!' It was a huge hutch of live chickens caged in wire, this Auschwitz of fowl strapped to a flatbed old truck. Jasus Christ, it was horrifying what Homo Sapiens did in the name of hunger. Sandy cursed and slowed down and yelled, 'You motherfucker!' The smell of droppings invaded the car. The pale ghosts of those poor chickens laid eggs in fear. Sandy hit the horn with his usual malevolence, and the truck swerved slightly. The invisible driver's hand emerged and waved us by frantically. 'What I wouldn't give for a goddamn chicken right now,' Sandy said with the sneer of a predator. I thought he was going to run the truck off the road.

In the stark light of a State Information centre, Sandy drained himself into a urinal trough, pissing onto the small blue mint sanitiser. It floated past me in a tide of dark yellow piss. Sandy looked at me with jaded eyes, his mouth half agape, shivering. I saw the pale skin of his penis, a fat hose with a big rubbery head. He was turned sideways to me, so there was no helping looking at the thing. 'We made it,' is all he said, massaging the head with his thumb, squeezing out droplets of piss. He smiled obliquely, still replaying his salvation, his thumb lingering on the head. 'I thought we was done for back there. I swear to you, I did.' His eyes watered with tiredness. 'You see, I ain't afraid to die if it come down to that. I got principles to uphold, but hellfire, I didn't mean to lose my life over some piece of shit like him back there.'

I nodded gravely. 'You showed great control back there, Sandy.'

'Control. There weren't nothin but the hand of fate directin that knife. Fuck if fate ain't a runaway train. You can't rely on fate no how.'

'We made it is the main point.' It was hard to believe that me, the fuckup of all fuckups, was giving a pep talk.

I stood there watching him in this eternity of mindlessness, literally shaking to get on the road again. The lights overhead buzzed with energy. Then Sandy took hold of my arm. 'I got a little somethin to keep me goin.' I could see the wound needed feeding again. 'Ain't no point wastin it. Once this is done, I'm goin clean, finished with this shit. Ain't like I need it, but why waste something when you got it, and, shit, it ain't anything but the end of things . . .' He stopped abruptly, a thin veneer of mucus on his lips. 'You go on out.' He turned for the abandonment of a stall door and locked himself away.

I went over to the mirror and washed out the dried blood from my ear. I looked bad, physically altered by the sunburn, and now the ear was dead. It was a sad realisation, a defeat. I was literally only months from the time at the reformatory. The sullen acceptance of immigration set in like the blood in my shirt as I had a good look at myself. I had a look of mild deformity, the dry skin coming away in a translucent peel of flaking skin. I had lived a rat's existence. I had to put everything into the training now. It was the only thing left.

These dark blobs of exhaustion passed before my eyes as Sandy let out a moan. I listened to the scrape of his feet on the cold floor as he shot himself up.

I shuffled off out into the main hall, into this meeting place bereft of emotion or homeliness, erected solely for the purpose of alienating and making people want to continue with their journey. Brown moths wandered in aimless trajectories in the stark light. Truckers drank coffee and smoked in a buzz of mindless sleep.

The truckers had their names stitched onto their flannel

work shirts, their hats with the names of the companies they hauled for. They were a morbid clan with no arses, their thumbs in their belts, eyes squinted in a crow's foot of wrinkled insomnia. The monotonous rumble of their diesel engines had ruined their insides, shaken organs loose in seeping haemorrhages. The road had altered their genetic structure or something. Some of them took off their baseball hats and wiped their brows before setting the hats back on their flat greasy hair, making simple statements of fact, talking directions, talking weather, talking about the loads they were pulling, about the pressure of time, about exhaustion, but mostly about women they loved, a soliloquy of plaintive cadence, the CB handle of whispered yearning spoken into airwaves, into frequencies of desire and broken hearts. I felt the tiredness of their mobility.

Sandy came out of the toilet and stood beside me. He rubbed his arm and squeezed his hand, showing his teeth in a nervous jitter of abysmal sublimation. His eyes were swimming in a delirium of drugs. His head bobbed perceptibly. It was the relief I'd gotten from the straw in the ear, the same stunning numbness of abatement when silence registers and there is no sense of longing, only peace. It's the silence of animal ignorance. Sandy was smiling to himself. 'We don't got to mention anything to her about . . . Well, you know? This one was for the road, to get us where we got to go.' He was slowly getting hyped, an undercurrent of satisfaction and meaning crawling up from the slime of his brain.

We fed a vending machine and hoarded bars of chocolate and cans of Coke and went out into the night. In the cool mountain air Sandy shivered and went down on his haunches, his hand between his legs, and drew a long breath. 'Kind of knocks you, this air.' He recovered, waving me away, cradling the food in his other hand, and breathed hard, shaking his head. 'Things is goin to change. I'm tellin you, I got this feelin inside me. I feel like Lazarus raised from the goddamn dead. I tell you I got this feelin, this sixth sense, I'm tellin you.' He squeezed my arm tight, in a sudden jolt of energy. It was the false feeling of drugs.

I couldn't get the thought of Da out of my head. It was everything at this stage of the game, but still Da was stalking me in my dreams. He was that Greek muse we used to hear about in them Shakespearean tragedies that I hated back at school. You didn't have to be a Freudian psychologist to know that I was a mental train wreck. I tried to stop this dialogue of gloom. I wanted to drive my head into a wall, smash up the cranium, and concentrate on getting myself on track.

I got it into my head that I was going to have it out with that fucker Da once and for all. By my reckoning, he was getting up to meet the 6:45 a.m. from Cork. I'd put a call through to the station and tell him what a miserable bollocks he was. I'd exorcise the demons once and for all in a roaring match. I'd ask him why the fuck he let me be born in the first place, because that's a question that should be put to every eejit that reproduces. As far as I'm concerned, you should have to apply for a licence and state something other than, 'Bored out of my skull lookin at my wife,' to have any hope of being allowed to mate. I'd say something like, 'Da, you sexual grunting pig, it's your wayward son, the first of your grunting litter wanting to ask you, if you please, why the fuck was I born, not in the metaphysical sense, because I know you have sawdust for a brain, but how were you capable to reproduce with that swill of Guinness and sperm you shot forth all them years ago?'

I blurted out to Sandy, 'I have to make a call back home to Ireland this minute, do you hear me?'

Sandy looked at me suspiciously. 'How much is that goin to cost me?'

'Maybe twenty dollars or something, and I chipped in on this trip, do you hear me? I'm no hostage, you bollocks.'

Sandy scoffed at me. Only the edge of highness kept him calm. 'We don't got that kind of money. And besides, where you goin to get twenty dollars in change?' But he acquiesced a little and said, 'Maybe I got five dollars.' He gave me the money. 'Either speak twice as fast, or say half as much.' He put his hand on my back and leaned into me. 'I ain't bein cheap, you hear me? There ain't no amount of money I wouldn't spend to be able to speak with my father again . . . That's the God's honest truth.' It was a quiet, plaintive expression of submission and humility, even if it was only drug-induced.

Sandy went off to the car. 'You give your father my regards.'

I might as well have been calling the planet Jupiter. The operator finally got me through, and the stationmaster answered in his thick accent. I asked for Da. The stationmaster recognised my voice all right. I hadn't hello out of my mouth when the phone wanted more money. I shouted into the phone, 'Will you ask Da if he got the ten thousand dollars I sent home last week?'

'The what?'

'The ten thousand I sent home last week!' I shouted.

'Holy Jasus. Have you struck gold?' The stationmaster roared into the phone.

I said, 'Sorry we're breaking up . . . I can't hold her . . .' I made this hissing sound like at the beginning of *The Six Million Dollar Man*, when Steve Austin loses control of his plane, before he becomes the Bionic Man. Then I ended with a crackling, 'God Bless All!' as the real icing on the cake. I stared off at the dark scar of the highway snaking off into the night, and the phone wanted two dollars for the extra time, but I said, 'Fuck Off' to the operator and left the phone off the hook. That would sort Da out for a while. I was on another continent, and I could still reach out and fuck his life up. Jasus, but you had to hand it to the man who invented the phone all right.

I got back to the car. Angel was still in a deep sleep in the back, obscured in a blanket. Sandy looked into the dark sky outside, 'Guess we ain't seen the last of this weather.' Sandy set a Snickers and a Three Musketeers and a can of Coke in the small curl where Angel's arms cradled her pregnancy. 'She got a sweet tooth like you wouldn't believe.' He kissed her on the damp head. The car trembled slightly with the dull shake of Sandy's body. Chemicals moved deep in the labyrinth of his head, roaming into cavities of want, satiating longing with numbness. Outside the sky opened into blue flashes of lightning and rain. I was thinking about Da and Setanta, listening to the roars of him at the stationmaster trying to figure out where the money was. Sandy said softly, 'They all doin well back home?' I said nothing. I leaned into my door and Sandy into his, and we drifted into sleep in the hills of Pennsylvania.

The Campsite

We slept until the light of dawn was beginning to cut through a steely mist. I felt the abrupt catch of gears before realising we were moving again. Sandy was agitated and squeezing the wound again. I kept quiet. We were into our second day on the road, and Angel still hadn't moved. The candy bars were gone. Only the wrappers remained, which gave me this weird feeling.

Sandy leaned forward, looking out at the land. The sun was still below the horizon, rising up out of the East. 'That there is the Promised Land,' Sandy said. He winked at me. 'I ain't jokin, if you think I'm jokin. That there is Amish country, the forefathers of this great nation. Quakers, Shakers, Mennonites and Amish, they is all down there. You know what they are?'

'What?'

His hair was sticking up in horns. 'Shit, man. That's what America meant once upon a time. Freedom of religion, escape from persecution from kings and lords. Ownership of your own land, my friend, the right to pursue liberty.' Sandy looked at me. He liked telling me things. 'You think I'm shittin you?'

'No, no. I believe you.'

Sandy had the look of one who truly felt sorry for his fellow man's ignorance. America was going to open up through his consciousness, so I let him have his way. I had no real choice. I became a silent sponge and soaked up his cadence and hatred, I let his rhythm flow through me.

'Let me say this short and sweet,' he began, and I looked at him and nodded, and he said, 'I ain't got time for the history of this nation, but let me tell you short and sweet. Them people down there is what was the persecuted, and they came on boats, the *Nina*, the *Pinto* and the *Santa Maria*. Well anyways, them people got the Promised Land when they got here. It was just lying here for them. It was as simple as that, all ordained in the Bible by God hisself. They been livin the same way since the day they come here, too. They do nothin but pray and make furniture is all. Best furniture in the world, is what they say. They brought their skills from the Old World, and they passed them from generation to generation. And mind you this, they don't use no machines, no tractors, no chainsaws, nothing but horses and the strength that's in their backs and hands. Don't abide by television neither. It's like they drew a line in the sand one day and said to themselves, "We ain't goin to let sloth render us indecent and sinful in the eyes of the Lord." They get out of the day what their physical bodies will abide, no more.' He stopped talking and went by a convoy of trucks labouring through the mountains. I looked back and saw Angel's eyes wide open. She put her finger to her lips and smiled.

I looked off at a simple unadorned steeple, a lean economy of Amish spiritualism. We'd learned all about the mental head cases of the Reformation, Luther and Calvin, the nutters who abandoned statues and indulgences and gave the Pope and Holy Mary their walking papers. I was in the Promised Land of the persecuted. Jasus Christ, I'd come a long way from the reformatory. Maybe that was the whole thing about this journey, the reality that there were other worlds out there, other lives being lived in different continents, small towns that I'd never heard tell of in Africa, in Australia, in South America or who the fuck knows where.

It made me feel insignificant and worthless. It made everything arbitrary, meaningless. There were no old memories to fall back on here in America, no transition into a new life, just this abrupt change, this realisation that the old life was gone for good. It was hard to take, nobody to fall back on, no retreat, no easing into life like I'd seen back home. I mean, that's what I knew, not this. It's like when you start getting old. It comes slowly, the fat belly, the eyes getting tired and sagging. You scrap doing sports and just read the paper, take your drink long and slow. A few strands of grey here and there appear, but it's gradual. It sneaks up on you. That's how evolution has handled the matter of our demise, with creeping resolve, nice and slow. But what if you were like Rip Van Winkle or something and you fall asleep and the next thing you know you're old and everybody is dead and you spend your remaining days looking backwards at the past because there's no comprehending the present? At least when the old immigrants came over, there was some collective struggle, some identity, a passage through Ellis Island. Bad as it was, immigrants brought their old world with them. They went into their Irish slums and continued with the old ways. They went through a transition together. Fuck! They were at least legal. But what about me and my kind, what about the fuckups like me all right who came at the end of that trail of tears without even the right to be in America?

We lived in a terrible age where the rate of birth was outstripping the ability of nature to come up with a disease to slay us. Oh, sorry times that there wasn't a war to send us off to die in or a plague to lay us low. There could be no nationalism, no dirge songs of grief. We disappeared, refugees taken down to the airports, down to ports for ships to England, individually kicked out, but at least you were legal there. I was just a superfluity who'd escaped disease and famine and war, and the country was bewildered by the sight of me roaming round the place. I was an ignorant bollocks, a physical menace back there, staring at old grannies, leering at the black gas money box in their hallway, wanting to go in there and get the tenpences. They used to have these images of Ireland as a Sean Bhean Bhocht, The Poor Old Woman with her four green fields and all that garbage. She was our mother Ireland looking off across the ocean at her children dead and gone, the ground heavy with her corpses of famine dead, and it was the English bastards that were to blame, or that was the party line anyway. I say, well and good and all due respect for the burden that was on us once upon a time. I'll grant history that and sing and cry for the old dead. Don't get me wrong, we were starved and murdered. But we're talking different circumstances now, things of our own doing.

To be honest, I felt scared in the car, tired, lonely, embarking on a hard future, trying to resurrect some decency in my life. I was outside the domain of New York, and, bad as it was, at least I was an inconspicuous illegal back there. Now I was at the mercy of a drug addict and his pregnant girlfriend, and who knows if the law was after us for aggravated assault. I'd aligned myself with the worst element, but beggars can't be choosers. Drastic action had been called for, and I took what I could get. I was on a high wire without a rope. I knew that, but there was no turning back. I was already damaged. I would rather have killed myself than go back to that factory. I'd rather be a martyr to underground immigration, slice myself up or blow my head off before I submit to a dead existence of shite work in this America. I said it there and then to myself in the car. If I don't make it on this running gig I'm checking myself out, suicide.

Angel whispered, 'I need to go.' Her voice broke my train of thought and brought me back to some level of sanity. She was the only beauty I'd seen since I'd landed, defiled and all that, but still something worthy of being saved, the Mary Magdalene of my life. I looked back at her, and she smiled at me, and I knew why I was here, drawn to be near her, to be close to her was the reason. It came as a sort of shock, but it was the truth. I needed to fixate on something beautiful. The hardness of the motel wasn't in her face now.

Sandy stopped the car. We waited at the side of the road. I turned and looked at her. She was an obscene egg of pregnancy, like something you'd see in a Humpty Dumpty sex book, if there was such a thing as the daughter of Humpty Dumpty. I knew barely anything about the human female reproductive cycle. Frogs, now I was your man there, spawn and tadpoles, but this stuff . . . We'd gotten a bit of sex education back in the reformatory. This nurse came in with an anatomy model with the green and red and yellow guts exposed and this big hairless bliff looking at us. We'd learned about the humiliation of the female species, the bleeding and all that stuff.

Sandy was going on about something. I watched him lick his wound with the sullen earnestness of a cat. He was silent for a few minutes, looking back from time to time to see what Angel was up to.

Sandy pointed off into the distance. 'I hate the goddamn Amish. You know there's something about people who got too much religion. When I was real young we learned all about Pennsylvania. You know this here was all part of the Underground Railroad, all them niggers from down South sneakin up through here. Them Abolitionist assholes used to put pies in their windowsills and hang sheets out the window to tell the niggers the coast was clear. You look around here, my friend, and what you is seeing is where America went wrong.'

I looked off into that underground, the furrow of trees spreading into the distance. I was deep within it now, hiding inside America in the late twentieth century. I took a heavy breath.

Sandy said, 'Shit! I want you to listen. I got this contingency plan, so I have. You want to hear it?'

'Sure.'

'I'm swearing you to secrecy. You go on and swear.'

'I swear.'

'All right. We got these goddamn salad bars all over the country, these goddamn troughs where people gorge themselves. It's what keeps this nation existing is the way I look at it. Wasn't it some general that said, "An army marches on its belly?" Well anyways, what I'm proposing is a letter of warning to the President of the United States tellin him that there's this potential situation just waitin for some enemy of the people to kill literally millions of American citizens. I don't tell him shit in the letter. I write it like I'm advising him of the situation, but I don't mention the situation. You see what I'm driving at?'

'No.'

'Jesus H. Christ. I'm talking about taking out the Salad Bar, the All-U-Can-Eat Restaurant.' He raised his eyebrows and looked around to see if there was somebody listening to us. He took hold of my arm, squeezed it, rubbed his chin with the other hand. He was literally trembling. 'Change the goddamn face of America is what I'm talking about. How much you think it would cost to keep something like that under wraps?'

'I don't know, Sandy.'

'How bout thousands! And it could be done all legal and everything, cause I'd be bringing up a situation is all. I ain't threatenin nobody or nothin. We don't even say All-U-Can-Eat or nothin. We just hint that we's talkin big, something that, how should I say it, "Somethin that might compromise the food supply of this great nation." You see the beauty in a plan like that, don't you? We ain't kidnappin no rich kids. We don't need no goddamn hideout or nothin. Jesus H. Christ. It would be the easiest twenty thousand bucks you ever make. You think about that. We'd say, how bout if the CIA just puts the twenty thousand bucks in unmarked twenties in a suitcase in some hotel and then drop off the key to the room in some trash can. We go get the key, and we live happy ever after.'

Sandy nodded his head to himself for a while and looked at me and kept grinning.

Angel seemed like she was gone for ever. Sandy breathed hard and drummed his hands on the steering wheel. 'You know, I want you to forget we ever had this little conversation, okay? It wasn't nothing but talking shit was all.'

'Sure.'

I could see he was sorry he'd told me about his plan to poison the All-You-Can-Eat buffets. He was thinking of retractions, ways of making me forget it. This was his secret.

It seemed our collective destiny was the backwoods of the Appalachians. We passed through a normal town and found an outfitter's store. We decided upon a rainsheet instead of a tent. Sleeping bags were beyond our means. We bought ourselves a set of tin pots and a propane burner and three containers of fluid, some blue enamel cups and a set of cutlery, a jug for coffee. Sandy eyed a rod. He cast across the shop and caught hold of something on a shelf, and something broke, and the salesman said, 'We got a "you break, you buy" policy,' but Sandy laughed and ignored him and said, 'I'll take this rod, cause, as the good Lord once said, "Give a man a fish and you feed him for a day, teach a man to fish and you feed him for life."' Angel smiled at Sandy, and he said, 'I ain't makin this shit up, Angel.' We bought an inflatable airbed for Angel because the salesman felt sorry for her and said he'd do us a deal. We bought rice and grain, dehydrated soups and reconstituted meat packed with soy.

Angel wanted greens for the baby inside her, so Sandy bought two strings of drying green beans and a head of cabbage at this stall where the man was closing up for the evening. He was in the mood to deal. He didn't want to die was more like the truth. Sandy had that marauding sense of affability you'd expect from a lunatic who was just trying to get a rise out of someone before he plugged them. He manhandled the sales clerks in the store, the eyes set deep in his head and the spirited sense of impending doom behind his greatest plans. They watched him for weapons, trying to keep a distance which he shored up in an instant. I liked the manic way he went on most of time. He was the most dissatisfied poor fucker I'd ever met in all my life. I might have had the ups and downs, but he had some genuine philosophical underpinning governed by fate, collusion and fraud and violence. You could tell he would either die or kill or end up in the electric chair.

We loaded the trunk with bags of roots, parsnips and potatoes and squash. Sandy priced a rifle for hunting rabbits, but it was more than he could afford, so he settled on a trap the salesman suggested could provide a man with enough rabbits to keep himself in meat. We watched the salesman pull back the jaws of the steel trap. It could hold a deer if you were lucky enough to get one. Sandy dropped a cabbage head into the trap, and it snapped and savaged the cabbage. Sandy got a kick out of that and wanted to drop a bottle of milk into the trap, but the salesman talked him out of it. I watched

Sandy survey the store, rubbing his chin and picturing some idyllic life unfolding. We bought a provision of canned goods. Sandy said to the salesman that he was going to peel off all the labels, and 'When you open a can, it's goin to be a surprise. Might be meat, might be dessert.'

Angel moved on her thin legs. Sandy helped her, taking her by the elbow gently. 'We are going to live amidst the hills!' he announced to a few of the customers who kept their distance. When it came to paying for the stuff, Sandy laid down what he said was all the money he owned in the world, and the salesman rubbed his face and said he couldn't let this stuff out the door at Sandy's price. Sandy went back and looked at the gun again and looked down its barrel and pointed it at the salesman and said, 'I got your head right in the cross hairs, I do,' and he pulled the trigger. The gun made a clicking sound, and he went 'Pow, Pow, Pow,' and the stuff just sat on the counter. No matter where the salesman went, Sandy trained the gun on him, saying 'Pow, Pow, Pow,' until Angel slipped the salesman another twenty when Sandy wasn't looking. Then things were settled on Sandy's terms, or what he thought were his terms, and he shook the hand of the salesman and said he knew he was a good man all along. He said he was coming back for that rifle real soon.

Out in the car Sandy laid out our life. Sandy was going a thousand miles an hour. We were in this huddle of complicity, led by this eejit, but that was the height of things for that day anyways.

'A journey of a thousand miles begins with the first step,' Sandy said to me. 'We're goin to return to nature is what we're goin to do. That's a goddamn American tradition, that is. You ever hear of Thoreau or Walden? They were Americans that went back to nature to get their heads straightened out. That's right, we all got internal rhythms inside us, things that make us function. We goin to find what's inside us out here.'

Angel smiled. 'That's what I love about him. Every day is a new beginning.'

Sandy said, 'Shit, once a man stops believin in the future, it's over.'

I was in no position to laugh or roll my eyes. The dementia of a drug addict had its poetic quality. The mania of hope and longing was heightened. It was the same psychosis I was under, I suppose, the need to change, the self-hatred.

'I ain't sayin I know all the shit that goes into trainin, but I can help you, if you want.' Sandy nodded his head at his own suggestion. 'That's right, maybe we can be an inspiration to each other. I know you're goin to think that shit is corny and all, but we got to pull together, all of us. We're pack animals. Why go against our goddamn nature?'

I extended my hand without malice or irony, totally crippled by emotion, and I was saying to myself that we just might make it. We had escaped into nature, into the backwoods. We had that volition to get away from disease and poverty, from that mindless existence. I said, 'I only have you two. Thanks for what you've done for me.'

Sandy squeezed my hand hard and said, 'Shit, we'll help each other out, and we're goin to make it all right. I feel good bout this.'

Then Sandy left us in the car as dark descended. He went into a liquor store and had some dealings with a man inside. Angel said, 'I love him for the times when he's like this, when I see he wants to do good.' It was a remark filled with qualifiers, and then out comes our friend Sandy with raw marks in his arm and a brown bag filled with beer and whiskey he said was to keep out the mountain cold.

I looked at him there beside me. He fought a terrible battle with the chemicals in his system, that long yearning of addiction pulling him under. I saw the change in his body, the eyes glazed and the mouth half open. I braced for the inevitable, for the violence. I wanted to trust him. He wanted to trust himself, but I knew in the end things would derail. I imagined violence and madness, screaming and murder in the end. I was travelling with a time bomb. The secret was to know when to leave, to crawl from the wreckage of his life before it was too late.

On the outskirts of town Sandy pulled over and kissed Angel deep in the mouth. The drugs wanted some flesh. He said, 'I want to taste your pussy,' and I flinched, because some animal mania dragged him under. The windows steamed, and I just sat there like an eejit and waited and the car puttered and rocked, and he was leaning over the seat kissing her. 'I love you. You know that, don't you?' He reeked of beer. He was on his third bottle in less than twenty minutes. He had some drugs left. There was a mark on his arm, fresh and bleeding. I hated the wound. The sun was gone. The sound of crickets filled the night air. I focused on that.

Sandy said, 'I just want to fuck you so bad.' It was just pouring out, lust erupting from deep inside him. 'I want to eat your pussy.' He stopped kissing Angel and retrieved his tongue and said, 'Shit, are you still here?' like I had any fuckin place to go out in the middle of nowhere. 'I want to see just how goddamn fast you run,' Sandy shouted.

Angel's face was red and blotched. Her face was eaten more like it, like something had savaged her. 'I want you to go out there and show us what we're dealing with. In fact, I just might have me a go at this running. You don't look much if you ask me.' We both got out of the car, and Sandy ran like a mad fucker down this long dirt road. He was out ahead of me by fifty yards with a bottle in his hand. 'Come on, you son of a bitch!' I passed him a moment later bent over with spit hanging out of his mouth. He waved me away, trying to catch his breath. 'You go on! This here . . . is the culmination . . .' He was gasping, 'the culmination of a lifetime of inactivity, and I am ashamed, I tell you honestly! Go!' He drew in a heavy breath and pointed. 'Go!'

I ran on with the apprehension that this was the end of our association. I kept turning, seeing the lights of the car far behind, until they weren't there at all. Then there was a sound of dogs barking and a farm up ahead, and I wasn't for getting myself attacked by some vicious dogs. I slowed and looked back again and still no car lights. Fuck! I turned back and ran as fast as I could along this narrow road, crops off at each side of me. I stopped and cursed at the top of my lungs. I roared,

'Sandy, you bollocks!' I ran like a madman again. I'd been duped by that bollocks. All the money I had was with him back there. I came up hard onto the main road, the rush of blood in my head, the sky glowing with the passage of each minute. The whole universe was lighting up before me and I felt only more lonely and stupid.

And then there was the car, up on the main road with the lights off and Sandy in the back with Angel. I waited outside, listening to him moaning and speaking the kind of indefensible shite men speak to women when they want them to do something for them. I was on the verge of tears. It was going to be like this with him, the violence of mood swings, skulking in his wake, watching for the signs, letting him feel he had me under control. It wasn't in my nature to suffer that coercion. If I were somewhere else I might have laid into him, stabbed him or beat the hell out of him, drop a brick on him when he was sleeping, because I wasn't the sort that was going to take it. But that's what I did, there in the dark. I took it, because all the big-man talk of juvenile bravado was over. I was a prisoner whether I liked it or not. I ran a half mile down the road, and my insides were trembling, but I went away from that car with the conviction that it was going to be there, because that bastard needed someone as hapless and messed up as me to be his effigy. I was serving a purpose for him, a sounding board, a loser who wasn't even legal. He was a small-time tyrant. Each relationship has that dominance, I'd seen it all my life. I was something to despise now, something worse than him, as far as he was concerned. He needed to roar into my face, erupt in madness, fuck his girlfriend before me, demean me and send me off into the night.

I did a series of high knee lifts and sprints, forced myself to do them because it was going to be like this from now on. I'd have to make myself focus on the running, not let this shite distract me. I breathed hard and dug in and did those useless sprints, because they weren't useless at all. It was absurd to be doing them out here, but that didn't matter. Let him fuck her for the night, as far as I was concerned. I'd do high knee lifts and sprints until the sun came up if that's what it took. And fuck, yes, I was nervous that he was going to start up that car, and I looked at it in the distance, but I had to get it into my head that he could do that any time. If I was going to be around him, I had to learn to live with unpredictability. There was no point anticipating disaster. What I had to do, and do it quickly, was to work in the margin of his benevolence, to stay with him until I was back in shape. I needed to believe in my ability to get back into shape, to get myself that scholarship. It was as simple as that. I ran there in the dark, the universe twinkling overhead, and it was grand and limitless, and that's what I had to believe in, the vastness as liberation, a means by which I could become a different person, where the past life of fucking around ended. I had to work towards what America had to offer.

I was eighteen years old. The future was there before me. 'Don't fuck it up!' I said out loud to myself, 'Don't fuck it up!' I came back up and waited patiently, away from the car, and, yes, it was cold and humiliating, but so what. I had a secret understanding that I was using him, and not the other way around, and, when I got my break, that would be the day to laugh, but for now, it was to be silence and subservience.

Sandy came out and threw a bottle into the dark and shadow-boxed and chased me until he was exhausted and lay stretched out, breathing hard and holding his stomach. He had the remnants of an erection. He actually touched the thing against me through his trousers when he got up and put his arm around me and breathed his breath of alcohol into my face. 'Shit, but you is fast! I take my hat off to a man who has the goddamn volition to get his ass out there and live like man was supposed to goddamn live!' He shouted into the night. 'We was all a nomadic people once upon a goddamn time.'

I let him maul me, let his erection stick through his clothes, his trousers stained, and I took on the impervious resolve of a saint as I saw the miles unfolding out there before me. I was literally shaking, because I wanted to smash the bastard's head in, but I didn't. There was this thrilling sense of anger there in me, a wave of blinding pain, but I said nothing.

Angel turned on the small interior light. It was like

watching something at one of them grottoes where they have candles burning for the holy. Sandy put his arm around my shoulder and righted himself, and we came back in that embrace, approaching this small shrine of pregnancy, this car stuffed with camping equipment and dark vegetable roots growing eyes in the pitch black of the boot.

We spent another night sleeping in the car and drove slowly into the mountains, and it wasn't until the following afternoon that we came upon this unnamed campground of shadows high up in the mountains. The lateness of the afternoon made us tired and want to rest. The car moved slowly along a gravel road among lines of trailer homes where children played on creaking swing sets and in boxes of sand. They all turned to stare after us, as did a small man sat out on a garden chair getting his hair cut. An exotic gaudiness of plastic pink flamingos clustered in the confines of a white plastic fence. A painted sign advertised fresh venison, ice, soda, live bait and work. 'Now that has possibilities, work,' Sandy said, pointing to the sign. Cut out oil drums and picnic tables demarcated the perimeter of camp spaces. It was darkish in the interior of the campground as the road curved and meandered. Sites were sporadically populated. We moved in silence, the brittle blue of the sky breaking through a shroud of cloud that portended eventual rain. A fire burned in a bed of ash at one site. Men drank from bottles, gathered around two old pickups threaded together by the red and black tentacles of jumper cables. It was a conspiracy of machinery in a blight of poverty. The men were shaking their heads, and then the dead engine roared, and a plume of smoke billowed and broke the silence.

Our car ate into tall weeds and came to an abrupt halt. 'It ain't much, but I call it home,' Sandy said wryly. Sandy left it at that and sat there with his arms folded. He looked at me. His face was in shadow. He took a cigarette from behind his ear and lit it. He said, 'You think you might want to find a hose and wash yourself off, cause you is stinkin to high heaven.' Then he qualified his remark and shook my hand with the cigarette throbbing in the centre of his face. He meant no offence.

This was the extent of our resources, the reprieve until something else drastic happened to us. Now, if this had been any other country there would have been war, I mean bloodshed and revolution, but not here at all. Some presiding sense of national pride still beamed on these poor bastards' faces. I couldn't really believe that this was where I was now. I mean the New Jersey motel was a dump and all, but it approximated civilisation. I got out and regretted that I'd ever given up the hundred and sixty dollars to Sandy. Then I said to myself, sure, isn't this what the Africans live like who win all the medals, tribesmen from the hills, spending their days running in search of food. Yeah, that was right. Endurance was the name of the game, constant motion. It was a total dump, but maybe I could recover here.

I had no choice.

Things seemed to sweat in a warm damp fog rising from the earth. I went off down a passage of trees and found a primitive shower contraption fed by some subterranean spring. I went into a stall and sat on cold metal and breathed in the smell of chemicals. My breath fogged in this box of shadows. Literally hundreds of flies hit against the plastic sides of the toilet. I put one hand to my face and waited and used the other to swat away the flies. I felt the pinch of my insides pushing things along. A long coil of shite fell from me down into a pit with a melancholy splat. I felt a cold emptiness inside me.

The water was warmish, held in a reservoir of rainwater heated by the sun. It tasted metallic. I found a shard of old soap in a rusting soap holder and lathered it under my armpits, scrubbed the remnants into my scalp. The slab of stone was thick with mud that oozed between my toes. I was shivering in the sullen gloom. The sun was falling fast and so was the temperature. A radio played at some site. A man scraped open the toilet door behind me and exploded in a hollow echo of farts. I went out into a clearing in my underwear and just stood there and let myself air dry, swinging my hands like windmills. There was this river heading off down the mountain and these men fishing. The sun dipped beyond the horizon, breaking into a streaming sea of warm orange and purple light. It was magnificent really, changing shades with each passing second. I said to myself I'd better ease off with the cursing, let go of the past and get on with living, which was easier said than done. Children shouted in the distance. I watched their shadows skulking in the coming dampness. A car with its headlights on beeped and proceeded into the campground, a station wagon filled with kids. The station wagon was burning oil real bad. A kid gave me the finger from the back seat, and I did nothing about it.

When I got back, Sandy had the tarp draped over the car and a fire set in the oil drum. Night was settling in on us, a blue inkiness mixed with the smell of burnt oil and campground smoke. The wood split and wheezed, a thin smoke and pale yellow flame stark against the stillness. Sandy sat on a tree stump and peeled potatoes in a pail of water. He rose and shuffled towards me and spoke softly, 'We goin to eat somethin good for once.' Flies landed silently on clumps of dark venison he had purchased. Sandy withdrew a hand and slapped the back of his neck, the hand blanched from the cold water. Angel was on an air mattress beneath the tarp, and she said, 'Ain't this something?' It was something all right.

It wasn't long before it rained in a wrathful blackness of warm fat rain that smoked and made the trees whisper above our head. I thought of that song, 'A Rainy night in Georgia,' that this priest used to play in his room on a record player late at night. The record had that scratch of rain and distance, and it felt strangely comfortable back at the reformatory to hear a man singing of love and regret. It showed us there was something out there beyond our fields of rain and shite. Now I was standing in the mood of that song, in America. I stood and watched Sandy at the fire and let my nerves ease. We were going to eat, for once, something decent. The campground was desolate, with families all inside their tents and rusted out old Fords, waiting patiently for the storm to pass. An exhaust pipe blew grey smoke into the air. A child cried, and a man spoke roughly, and there was the slap of flesh on flesh and renewed crying, and it made me think of home. Life within the camp took on the compactness of provincialism, shaped and defined and identifiable, and I felt myself smile for the first time in a long while. It was night, and humankind had retreated as in prehistoric times.

Sandy had a small flashlight pointed at the ceiling as our only source of light. It threw shadows around our eyes, giving us a dark conspiratorial attitude. Angel had her long legs outstretched on Sandy's lap. He was in the back seat with her, massaging the slight swelling at her ankle joints. She held a bowl of stew and blew gently into each spoonful. 'Right there, Sandy,' she whispered. I went outside and poured coffee from a tin. The rain had stopped. The aroma of coffee penetrated the cool aftermath of rain. Life stirred in the campsite, voices speaking to one another, the smell of food heavy on the air. I drank the coffee black, felt the dampness gather around me, felt night rob the day's heat. I moved from foot to foot and felt the animal within me, looked into the tall stretch of trees and set my mind to getting on with life. I got back into the front of the car and ate another bowl of stew, and Sandy took his coffee black. We all slept well in the cradle of the mountain.

I wasn't out long when up resurrects this dream in my head. I could see dust on the horizon like on *The Lone Ranger*. There was Setanta wearing this Stetson. He kicked in the swinging doors of a saloon and said, 'I'm lookin for the man who shot my Paw!' He was holding up the paw. It was the oldest joke in the book, but Da broke his arse laughin, and Setanta held his miserable paw and grinned, and Da said, 'Tarnation, but don't I just love that one.' Setanta and Da bellied up to the bar and knocked back whiskeys. Da was dressed in a Stetson and covered in trail dust. He lit a cigar by flicking a match off the heel of his boot and lit Setanta's own cigar. Da puffed away and blew a ring of smoke.

It was typical form all right for Da to think of the obvious, with that skit and all. It showed he didn't know fuck about America. I shouted, 'Da, you're in over your head, you stupid fuck! It's not like this at all over here! I'm in a campsite is all,' but Da didn't hear me or nothin.

Da scraped up some phlegm from his lungs and spat it with the acrimony of a two-bit cowboy and wiped his lips with the back of his sleeve. The coughing got worse and Da held the bar and fell over. His tongue came out of his mouth.

The next thing, Da was waking up in his bed, and I was standing there over him and Ma in their shoebox bedroom. Da sat up and coughed in a fit.

I felt this vertigo, removed from a dream in a dream. I stood there and adjusted to the grief inside Da's head or Da in my own head. Jasus Christ.

'I'll get you water.' Ma got up and wrapped herself into her dressing gown. Da was at the edge of the bed, recovered, and looking up at me with them watery eyes of his. 'You'll not plead this sort of melancholy shite with me. Fuck off out of it! You're gone from us, insufferable bollocks that you are.'

I just stood there.

Da was down to his fishnet undershirt and I could see the deep purple scars on either side of his back down along the shoulder blades. When I was young, I stood there one evening when Da was dying sick and spitting up all that stuff, and I saw the scars, and my Ma hesitated and put her finger to her lips. Later that night she told me this secret that Da had wings once, that he was an angel up in heaven that had come down to live on Earth.

Da knew what was going on in my head. He wheezed, 'Get the fuck out of my room!'

I opened my eyes, and the fire was burning softly. I heard Sandy in the back. I stayed quiet, listening, and slowly closed my eyes again, not sleeping, just remembering home.

Da was there again. He was tired and staring at the floor. He looked up, then dragged something up from deep inside him.

Ma came back and gave Da the water. He drank it in a long gulp. Da stood up and breathed deep. He took off his shirt, sat down again and leaned his torso forwards.

'Do you know what hurts the most?' Da said in the dark of the room.

'What's that?' Ma used the heel of her hand and rubbed Da's back.

'It's the sickness I had. From the time I was a lad and had them operations on my lungs, I couldn't do the sports. When the other lads were out playin, I was standing at the sidelines, taking it easy, afraid the lungs would burst inside me.' Da stopped and caught his breath and looked at me. 'The insufferable shite you come up with, your shite pantomime of grief! I lamented fuck-all about sports. Don't make me into your pathetic father! "It's the sickness I had. From the time I was a lad . . ." Jasus, where do you think of it at all, you self-servin bollocks?'

Ma used her hand in an upward motion to help bring up the congestion in Da's lungs. She heard none of it, allotted to be the ghost of innocence with her hair gone grey and in that pale cotton nightshirt, an apparition of sadness. She stopped rubbing Da's back. She sat in a slump at her side of the bed.

Setanta came into the bedroom and stood there like a grim sentinel against the night, watching Da's pain. He sniffed the bowl of menthol.

I opened my eyes again, shivered, the spool of memory turning slowly inside my head waiting for dark to trundle again in a slow requiem of longing. It was unnerving, the dreams and memories. I hated home, but it was there with me.

Life was still going on, even with me gone off. I remembered the headboard banging at night and the suppression of coughs and Ma up getting Da his medicine and boiling the kettle. That's what punctuated my early years, a fear of Da dyin. I'd go down there and look at Ma, the light of the moon coming in the kitchen window. Faithful ghost in her nightgown and bare feet. She'd warm milk for me and say nothin, just a soft touch of her hand, the bleeding heart of Jesus above the kitchen table. Jasus, she had it hard. The hard truth of it was that Da was going with Ma's sister Eileen. But Eileen went off to England for a long weekend and never came back. Da just couldn't break the habit of going over to the house after Eileen left, and so they gave Ma up as a consolation prize. They were a perfect match, though. Funny how things work that way. Chance has some handy work all right. Ma thrived on that quiet power. She wanted to be taken for granted. That's where she got her power, slowly seeping into our lives, boiling kettles of water, heating saucepans of milk at night.

Jasus, what I wouldn't do for a feed of her cooking. I was thinking of how we got the breakfast set for us downstairs, before we were even out of bed. You'd wake up to the smell of sizzling bacon and eggs and black pudding. The toast would be slathered in melted butter. The jug of milk would be out there, along with the Weetabix. If you were sick, a tray came up with all that stuff on it, and a little glass of orange juice if it was the flu. Maybe that was the worst of it. From now and for ever, the simple things were lost to me. There was no more breakfasts in bed, no more listening to the hiss of tyres out on the main road, knowing it was lashing rain. Gone were mornings of waiting for the jingle of the milkman's van, no more listening to Da's radio playing in the background. I just waited in the dark, stared at the embers of the fire at the campsite from where Da and Setanta had emerged, from the memory of boyhood cowboy films where men drank around fires when the land settled in utter blackness and coyotes howled in the distance.

I got out of the car and went over by the toilet, and the air was warm. I could hear men talking in tents, playing cards. A smell of whiskey lingered in the air, along with the smell of roasted meat. In the dark it was like the settlement of a wagon train hitched to the night with dreams of a better future, everything loaded and stored and carried with them. I stayed still and listened to the quiet laughter of men and women, the snore of somebody sleeping and thought to myself, I'm not the first man that's ever ventured away from home. All them dirge songs of grief stored in my memory were of emigrant life, the drifting dreams of emigrants gone to America who never saw home again, Irishmen blown to kingdom come on railways out across the plains or Irishmen fallen from New York's skyline. I walked around and let the tension leave me. I felt Da putting away the cowboy uniform, settled in for a night of dormancy, him and the dog, like a cancer of guilt that would wait on the other side of consciousness, ready to come and assault me for the things that had been left unsaid, for what I did to them back home.

I came back and lay under the tarp and pulled the horsehair blanket around me. Insects chirped in the darkness, and I felt a certain security that I was away from New Jersey. No matter how bad the campsite was, it was reprieve from the road and the past for me anyway. I was on my way to succeeding. I had found a way into the heart of America. I closed my eyes and awaited that haemorrhage of guilt and said, 'Goodnight Da,' but he didn't answer, and so I slept without dreaming.

Bill Hayes' Wife

There was this mountain man, Bill Hayes, like something I'd seen on the telly back home, a monstrous form with a big belly and this long beard, who became our friend. He had lived in the hills all his life and worked at this lumber mill which gave jobs to most of the men at the site. He had a small trailer, a gorgeous young wife and three children. Bill Hayes had engineered some system where long electric orange cords were hooked up to invisible heaters inside two old cars, and this is where his children slept.

One evening Sandy went and introduced himself, and Bill Hayes invited us over for supper. His trailer was strung with smoked meat and long threaded lines of beans hanging from the roof. We were like sardines in a can, all of us packed around this small table with Bill Hayes's wife pouring out stew for all of us. I'd never seen anyone so beautiful in all my life. I could only stare at the food to make sure that I wasn't caught staring at her. The inside of the trailer smelt of vinegar and feet mostly, because Bill Hayes had his shoes off, and his feet were immense, as were his hands. I looked at the hands when Bill Hayes spoke, and then I thought of them hands on his wife, and it was eerie that a man like him could have a wife like that.

Bill began talking about three guns on a rack over the doorway. It was hard to turn our heads, because we were that cramped, but we saw the guns all right, and Bill Hayes went on to explain each of them to us and told us the kind of bullets he used and what each shot could do to an animal.

Sandy was all interested in the guns and said, 'You ever have occasion to use that on a man?' and Bill Hayes was sweating, because it was boiling there in the trailer, and he wiped his head with the back of his arm and said, 'Can't say that I have ever.'

Bill Hayes' wife had small breasts, and the nipples showed through her shirt as she served us and leaned over us and put bread on the table and put glasses of water down before us. I could have sworn she was looking at me sometimes, and I caught fleeting glimpses of her arms and legs and her smile out of the corner of my eye.

It was Bill Hayes who got Sandy a job up at the lumber mill, and it was Bill Hayes' wife who set Angel at ease and told her that she was carrying her baby low and that she needed to lie out as much as possible to let the pregnancy take its course. She told Angel that she carried low on her first pregnancy, when she was fourteen. The two of them became close friends, and I felt glad that Angel had someone to help her. For the first time in America, it seemed somewhat normal.

We were all eating by the fire one evening when Sandy was onto his usual shite again. We'd seen this camp called 'Camp Yogi' on a run I'd taken, and Sandy said to Bill, 'Let me run this by you, Bill, if you don't mind?' and Bill just eased back in his chair as Sandy talked utter shite.

'What you know about Camp Yogi, Bill?' and Bill answered, 'I guess I know they got kids in that camp from the cities.'

Sandy said, 'They got police down there or anything like that?'

'They got counsellors is all, I guess, college kids mostly, watching the kids.' Bill looked at Sandy and said, 'What you drivin at, Sandy?'

'Maybe a little kidnapping is all.' Sandy raised his eyebrows and said, 'You think bout that now, Bill.' The fire was going strong, and the wind was going through the trees, and it made a whistling sound.

Bill Hayes shook his head. 'That ain't my style. I think you got me figured wrong. If you had a child, I think you'd know what I'm talkin about.'

Sandy put up his hands and said, 'Hey, I respect that. I was just thinkin it might have been the easiest twenty thousand you'd ever make is all, that is if and you was in need of money. I wasn't sayin like I was thinkin bout it serious or nothin, just thinkin bout what if.'

Bill Hayes turned a rabbit on a spit, and it looked horrible and glazed without eyes. He sat there and smoked and looked into the dark.

Bill Hayes' wife said, 'Maybe these children need to be in bed?' and Bill Hayes said, 'I figure it is about that time and all.'

Sandy waited while Bill Hayes kissed each of his kids, and then Sandy said, 'We is only wastin the night away is all, but let me figure this for you. It wouldn't be like we was goin to hurt the kid. Send a lock of hair in the mail to show them we was serious. Ain't no family going to fuck with their kid's safety. Patty Hearst, you heard of her, Bill? Point is simple. A family is goin to pay to get their baby back. And shit, camps like them have insurance policies on all them kids. Ain't like they not goin to want to co-operate. They get a reputation they ain't safe, they is out of goddamn business.'

'Maybe if and whenever you get yourself a kid, you'll understand, Sandy.' Bill Hayes shook his head. 'Anyhow, what you tellin me for anyways?'

Sandy shrugged his shoulders and was quiet for a few moments. The meat hissed and fat dripped into the fire. Sandy touched it with his small knife, the knife he'd used on the cook and to cut into rabbits, but Bill Hayes said, 'How bout we let that cook a while longer?'

Sandy said, 'Sure Bill.' Then he said, 'I figure no cops is ever goin to suspect a man who has got three children of his own is all I'm saying.'

'I thought we was finished with that discussion.'

Sandy smiled and said, 'We never did begin, really.'

It was amazing, the mind of the demented, the rudimentary genetic sense of survival, how it played itself out in the recesses of Sandy's brain, always dissatisfied, always yearn-ing, pecking away at half-truths, trying to survive on regurgitated shite. We were up in the hills, away from trouble, and there he was with his broken knife from an attempted murder, and he was at it again, thinking about crime.

A man named Lyle Carter drove in behind Bill Hayes' trailer, and he came and sat with us at the fire. He worked with Bill at the lumber mill. He was a small man, thin with a long face and rotting teeth. He was missing two fingers on his right hand which had been cut off by a saw, he told us. He used that hand when he talked, used it as a sort of indignation at what had happened to him, although I don't think his brain really knew that, but he did hold that hand up before his face, and there couldn't have been a person in the world who wasn't going to ask about the hand.

Bill Hayes said, 'Lyle, you got to hear this shit this boy here is on about. I reckon he's got this game of life figured, ain't that right?' and Sandy smiled and said, 'How do you do, Lyle?' and he introduced us one by one, and then Sandy said, 'Sometimes when opportunity knocks, you got to answer the goddamn door. Am I right?' and Lyle lit a cigarette, with the hand cupped like he was playing a harmonica, and said, 'What kind of opportunity is knockin?'

Bill Hayes' wife came back and sat in her husband's lap. I didn't listen to Sandy, because I'd heard the shite before. I looked at Bill Hayes' wife, and it was a depressing sight to see her there in his arms like that, her softness in the light and her long hair pulled back behind her ear and her arm around his neck. It made me feel inadequate, brought home the fact that I was abandoned to this wilderness until I got myself straightened out and in the sort of shape that would land me the scholarship.

Sandy was retelling his kidnapping story, and he said, 'What we do is kidnap us some guy off the highway when the ransom is delivered, and we make that goddamn son-of-a-bitch go get us the money, and if there is anything like someone followin him, we can see it, and we can hold onto the kid and lay down the law again. You see the beauty in using as many assholes as we can get our hands on? I was even thinkin of having the guy we get to bring us the money bring it to this other guy we kidnap, and then the cops wouldn't know what the fuck is goin on.'

'You gonna need a goddamn school bus for all the people you're thinkin about,' Lyle said.

Bill Hayes smiled and looked at Lyle and said, 'That is one persistent bastard,' and Sandy said, 'I guess I'll take that as a compliment,' and then Lyle said, 'Course you is goin to have to dig yourself a hole or something to hide this kid, something deep and hidden away down by a river or something and then you is goin to have to kill the scent of that kid and all, cause I know goddamn bloodhounds, and you got to work mighty hard to throw them off the track.'

Sandy looked at Lyle and said, 'How big a hole is you talking about? Shit! I wasn't figurin on no bloodhounds.'

Lyle squinted his face. It glowed against the fire. 'Ain't no point digging a hole really, but they got mine shafts up in them hills, abandoned and all. I know where they are all right, a shit load of caves that go on for miles.'

With that, there was a general silence, and we ate rabbit with salt, and Sandy and Bill Hayes and his wife and Lyle drank beer that Lyle had brought until they were pretty drunk. Me and Angel drank coffee and looked between ourselves and them, and Angel smiled, and you could see she felt safe for the first time in ages, sitting on the air mattress propped up against a tree. It was hard to reconcile the image of her with Sergeant John going across the lot. It was the sort of thing I just wanted to burn from my memory.

I smiled at her again. She was content to let Sandy's anxiety burn itself out in drunkenness and drugs, because we were safe, for the most part, because it seemed Bill Hayes was a match for Sandy. There wasn't anything really going to go haywire at all. When Bill Hayes said, 'I got this job up at the lumber mill,' Sandy took on an ease of drunkenness. He took Bill Hayes' hand and shook it, and then he took Bill Hayes' wife's hand and kissed it, but that must have triggered something inside Bill Hayes, because he pushed Sandy so hard that Sandy fell over the fire and screamed and nearly caught himself on fire. With the lateness of the hour, and because of the drink taken, the push was seen as nothing, and Lyle laughed so hard he woke the children, and they became the main concern. Sandy conceded he was pretty much drunk, and so we all retired to our beds. I knew there was something deep inside Bill Hayes' brain that said, 'Don't you ever look at my wife, you son of a bitch,' even if he didn't know that his brain was saying that.

Bill Hayes left early in the mornings for the lumber mill, and, because of my situation as an illegal, he took only Sandy with him to line up and see if there was any day work to be had. I got up from a blanket under the tarp tied to the car and made the fire, stirring the bedded embers by blowing on them until the crackling of kindling took hold in the fire pit. I had learned how to re-heat coffee over an open fire, sat there each morning waiting for it to bubble and spill down the sides of the tall jug while I got ready to go running. I lost the nervousness of regret and pain and became content for the first time in my life. I had some torment over Bill Hayes' wife, thinking about her when my mind was blank, but the running was beginning to take over my thoughts entirely. I ran through the canopy of trees in the early mornings, in my Emerald Underground of vegetation, deep inside America. I ran and thought of the meat factory, of that previous life, the hiding under the bed from the Bogman at the motel, that dark Emerald Underground of Irish immigrant slavery, that life in the margin of the American mainstream.

One day, after Bill and Sandy left, I was staring into the flames and thinking about the morning run when Bill Hayes' wife came out to a barrel of rainwater near her trailer and began washing her face. She said softly, 'May I join you for coffee?' and, before I could muster up the words to say anything, she took hold of each side of the barrel and dunked her head for a long time and then re-emerged with her face and hair dripping wet.

We sat together as she towelled her hair dry. Her nipples had come to hard points. She looked at her breasts and said, 'You want me to put on a bra? I will if you want me to, if and it's necessary I will, cause I don't want to embarrass you or nothin.'

I said softly, 'No.'

Bill Hayes' wife said, 'Good, because I don't got no bra except a training bra I got a while back that didn't even fit right. You see, before I had my children, I had nothing to show here at all. It was a pitiful sight I tell you. Just two nipples, here and here on a boy's chest.'

Angel came out of the car and plopped herself down in one of Bill Hayes' garden chairs and said, 'Morning, Alice. This might be the coolest morning yet, I figure.' Her breath fogged when she spoke. She didn't look much beside Bill Hayes' wife. Pregnancy kills something in some women. It was doing something to her face, changing it somehow, not making it ugly or anything, but making it different.

'I heard he runs,' Bill Hayes' wife said and blew into her coffee.

'He wants to go to the Olympics some day,' Angel said. She drew herself out of the chair and wedged her growing bigness against me, obscuring me from sight, and tried to get herself coffee. I said to her, 'Let me help you, Angel,' and she conceded and sat down and let me serve her. I couldn't quite tell who she was thinking she was saving, me or Bill Hayes' wife.

I warmed my hands and face and let the coffee warm my innards. 'He runs five miles every morning,' Angel said to Bill Hayes' wife.

She said, 'I used to run track in Junior High School. I ran the four-forty and the eight-eighty. There weren't even no boys that could beat me back then, and that's the truth.'

'What kind of times did you run?' Angel said.

Bill Hayes' wife said, 'There weren't no times. It was who beat who is how it was. There weren't no times.' I could tell she was agitated. The weak slant of morning light caught her black hair in a brilliant sheen. Her cheeks had taken on a pinch of red above her cheekbones.

Angel looked at Bill Hayes' wife the way women look at one another, and they said something in their own language of gestures. Bill Hayes' children began crying, and that was the melancholy end of that, and I wanted to ask Angel what the hell she was playing at, except that the question was, what was I playing at?

I ran, and the sun climbed up and heated the ground, and the dew evaporated, but it was getting to be longer each day before it felt warm. I had never experienced seasons before really, not the way it was going here anyway. I went down fishing, and it reminded me of how, once upon a time, my Da had shown me how to fish out by the Shannon Banks. The water was cool, but I edged out to the dark pools of still water where the trout wavered. I threaded the line through my fingers, spooling the line slowly, moving over the dappled pebble bottom, wading in water, edging out to the currents, to the boulders strewn across the river. The world was alive with grasshoppers and frogs and other insects and birds feeding. Cold-blooded turtles climbed out onto driftwood to warm their cold clammy shells. I looked up, and Bill Hayes' wife was standing at the water's edge combing her hair. I looked at her out of the corner of my eye, and it seemed for all the world that she wasn't looking at me, at least that is what I wanted to think, because Bill Hayes was a big, powerful man.

I came up and prepared the trout for Angel. I threw the wet guts of gore and fish heads to a cat which stalked us. She had the flaccid undertow of fat and swollen tits of a mother who had given birth. Angel lowered her window and said, 'I want to see them kittens.' We ate together, and the sun burned strong through the trees. Angel looked at me and whispered, 'Do you think I'm as pretty as Bill Hayes' wife?'

I said, 'Who says Bill Hayes' wife is pretty?' but Angel said, 'You don't make a good liar.' She ate a piece of fish and waited. Then she touched me with the fork and said, 'If I wasn't pregnant, do you think you could like me the way you like Bill Hayes' wife?' I felt sorry for Angel at that moment, because she was beautiful also, but she had that gauntness that had seen life close up. There was something in her face that told you that she had been damaged. 'I feel old,' Angel said.

'You don't look old.'

She touched my hand. 'I'm scared of what's going to happen to me.'

I had no answer for that, because I didn't know what was going to happen to any of us.

'I was thinking that maybe back there in New Jersey that, you know, that cook was kind of okay. I mean, he wasn't mean or nothin. It was Sandy being there that was the problem. You see what I'm sayin?'

'Angel, that was no place for someone as pretty as you. You deserve better than some old man who works beside the highway.'

Angel's eyes were teary, and her voice took on a shakiness. 'Sometimes it ain't what you deserve but what you can find. You don't think a woman like Bill Hayes' wife is really in love, do you?'

I said, 'Angel, you have to stop talking about her.'

Angel wasn't listening to me. She was pointing at her stomach, 'This here was never sposed to happen, I mean, not back there, like that. I got money from that cook so that I could end things at this clinic, but you know what Sandy did when he found the money? He took that money away from me, and he screamed that it was a goddamn sin even to think about somethin like that. He said he would rather see hisself dead and me along with him if I ever mentioned such a thing again, but I know all he was driving at was using the money for drugs. We went off together, and he roared at the junkies, and he told them that this here was blood money from some lovesick old man that had to pay for his pussy, and he shot hisself up, and then me up, and there weren't but a few days is all we got from that money. At the end of things I was still pregnant, and he says to me to go on back and tell Marvin that they made a big mistake there the other day and took out my appendix and not that baby and that I needed some more money for to get myself into a proper state where we could be together. And you know Marvin's answer, cause it's right here growin inside of me.'

I stared at fish bones on my plate. 'I think you are going to be even prettier than Bill Hayes' wife when all this is over. You see, she had three children, and she looks none the worse for it, now does she?'

Angel smiled. 'Maybe I need to wash myself in rainwater the way she does.' She reached for my arm and put her lips to my shoulder. I felt the heaviness of her breast sag and give against my arm.

'Do you want to go and find them kittens?' I slit open another fish and waved the entrails in the air. I threw them where I had thrown the previous gore, and the mother slank out from the trees, and we watched her retreat. We saw that she had her kittens in a small hollow in a tree where someone had set a fire. I had to get a fish head and feed the mother while she hissed and circled the hollow, trying to lead me away as Angel sat down and drew out two small kittens and brought them to her chest. Bill Hayes' children saw what we were doing, and they came and sat with Angel. They put their hands into the hollow of the tree, and the kittens scraped them with their tiny claws. The little two-year-old cried, and Angel kissed him on the hand. She said, 'You is fine. He's more scared than you. How bout you rub his belly, right there.'

The kid leaned up against Angel and rubbed the soft fur. I smiled at Angel. 'Looks like you're a natural with kids, Angel.'

She said, 'I get by, I figure.'

Bill Hayes' wife stood looking at us. She said, 'I wouldn't go through the pain of childbirth ever again for all the peaches in Georgia.'

I looked at her and just wanted to climb up into her uterus.

It went on in that skulking sexual tension at the site. Fuck, it wasn't what I needed at all. I was sitting with her and Angel and the children at this picnic table by the trailer one evening, writing in my running log and trying to figure things out, when this total fuckup in tight jeans and a flannel shirt came up to the table and asked me if I wanted to play cards for high stakes. I said, 'That's too steep for me,' and went back to the log book, but then the fuckup said, 'I'm talkin to you, hear? That's disrespectful, that is.' I looked up from the log, and the fuckup said, 'How bout we play for a kiss from your wife?'

Bill Hayes was inside one of the broken down cars, fixing an electrical wire or something, but he heard what was going on. He stopped work and came out from the car and said, 'That is my wife you is talkin about, and I want to hear how much you figure a kiss from her lips is worth.'

The fuckup was drunk, not out of his mind drunk or anything, but enough to stay and talk to Bill Hayes and not to know he should have got the fuck out of there.

'How much?' Bill Hayes shouted. The fuckup answered, and Bill Hayes was a bear standing there, but all Bill Hayes said was, 'You are way off with that sum,' and that was that. Bill said, 'I guess we ain't playin cards,' and he just pointed. There was no fight or nothing, and I didn't know what to think. The fuckup just walked off, defeated. He didn't even look back or nothing. I was amazed at the sheer power that Bill Hayes possessed, because right there, when I'd have been totally fucked, he solved the situation just like that.

Sandy came back from shooting himself up, and he stared into the fire and smiled and ate beans from a can and drank black coffee. He was pretty much a waste product all right, no self-restraint or nothin, but sure that was what drugs did to you. That's why you had to stay clear of them things.

Later in the evening, Bill Hayes said to me, with his wife in his lap, 'How much do you think a kiss from my wife's lips is worth?'

Sandy looked up like the question was directed at him and said, 'I ain't touchin this one, no sir,' and he put his hands toward the fire and let them warm. His arm was blackish and bruised again. 'No, sir. I ain't touchin that one.'

I said, 'Bill. I have no business answering a question like that,' and he looked at me and said 'Guess you ain't is right enough,' and Bill Hayes' wife said, 'What's this all about,

Bill?' and he rubbed her face gently and kissed her full on the lips, and then he did it again. Her face was lost in his beard. Then he said, 'I reckon a million dollars don't even come close.'

Sandy looked at Bill Hayes and said, 'Bill, where you ever get a woman like that?'

Bill Hayes looked at Sandy. 'At the laundromat is where. You can forget a bar. A woman who's washin clothes in a laundromat is in need of a man.'

Bill Hayes's wife said, 'You mean you stalked me?' She curled her hair behind her ear and smiled.

Bill Hayes squeezed his wife, but I could see his mind was on the fuckup who'd insulted his wife. His eyes moved back and forth from Sandy to the fire in the distance.

Sandy said, 'Speakin to you is like goin to college, Bill. I swear it is. But you ever hear of this one of how to get a woman to want you?'

Bill Hayes said, 'What?'

'This is surefire. You want to show a woman you ain't hooked up, you wear socks that don't match. Hell if it don't bring out the maternal instinct in em. They just want to take you home.'

Bill Hayes nodded his head, 'Maybe.'

'Maybe nothin. I was a non-believer once, but I tried it, and it works. Cross my goddamn heart it do.'

I rolled my eyes. I was on the verge of askin how a woman would get to see you were wearing different socks, but I kept my mouth shut.

At the card game going on a few sites over from us, cursing and shouting erupted, and bottles smashed against the night. We listened in silence until Bill Hayes yawned and said, 'What say we call it a night?' I could see his eyes in the firelight. He was looking over at that card game. There was something up all right.

I was in the car, awake. Sandy was snoring and Angel was asleep when I saw Bill Hayes getting out of the trailer, like a thief. It was dark, but I was able to follow his form in the dying light of the fire. He went in the direction of the fuckup's truck. I rolled down the window and heard the dull thud of flesh being dropped and the muffled sound of someone trying to breathe. I didn't get out, though. Bill Hayes was gone over twenty minutes. He took coffee from the dead embers of the fire and drank, and it seemed like he saw me sitting up in the car. He looked directly at the car, and I closed my eyes and expected him to come over and look, but he didn't. When I opened them, I could see him moving in the trailer. The light went off, and I spent the night thinking about what Bill Hayes had done.

In the morning I awoke because somebody was screaming at the top of their lungs. I got out of the car, and me and Sandy went over to where the screaming was coming from. There was a group of men standing around in a circle, and there was this figure lying flat on the ground and a deck of cards strewn all over and bottles smashed. Someone said, 'He's still breathin.' A pickup truck pulled up, and they wrapped the body in a blanket and lifted it into the bed of the pickup. The pickup left slowly, going around the campsite until it was out on the road down to town.

We went off to the toilet. A man said to another man, 'Shit, I don't know if he's goin to make it.'

'There was a card game last night,' the other man said. 'You find who lost bad, and you got yourself the man who done that.'

One of the men looked at me and said, 'You hear anything last night?' and I said, 'Didn't see a thing at all.'

The fuckup had paid the price for messing with Bill Hayes' wife, and now he was a mangled piece of meat on death's door.

Sandy said, 'I don't know how the hell I slept through something like that, I sure don't,' and I looked at him and at his arm and then into his eyes, and he looked away and said, 'You sayin I was out cold?'

I didn't even want to look at Bill Hayes, not because he was a bollocks, because everyone was a bollocks at the end of the day, but because Bill Hayes was getting on with living without flinching. He was doing what had to be done to survive and doing it with that easy disposition, covering his tracks. That was the way you survived this world. It was all collusion at this stage of the game. Now I understood when everybody back home used to say, 'Keep your trap shut. A shut mouth catches no flies,' and the way they moved around the place and didn't let the right hand know what the left hand was doing. That was the way it was down there at home, and here, too, seemingly. There was this man back home, Gerald Ryan, who poisoned Tom Martin's racing dog with weed killer. Everybody knew about it, but they didn't say. Gerald Ryan had asked Tom Martin to keep his dog out of this sweepstakes, because Gerald Ryan needed for his dog to win so he could pay for his son to go over to live in England. Tom Martin said fuck off, and so Gerald Ryan killed the dog, and that was that. Tom Martin pretty much knew he was blackballed, and he kept his trap shut, too.

We came back, and Bill Hayes had his hands in the barrel of rainwater, like a prizefighter after a scrap. Sandy went up to him and said, 'You heard what happened?' and Bill Hayes said, 'When you got three children, you sleep like a log.' Sandy, that ignorant bollocks, began to tell what he knew, which was shite. He just wanted to make himself important. I looked at him, and I saw myself in a former time, a mister know-it-all bollocks.

Training

We hardly used the car these days because Sandy didn't want to waste the money on petrol. Bill Hayes put him onto a scheme where they siphoned fuel from cars around the grounds and down in town. That's what got us out on the road for this run, stolen petrol.

Sandy shouted out a split at mile twelve. He was polluted drunk, holding the neck of a whiskey bottle. The absurdity of Sandy was funny at this stage. I was well into the running again, confident that I could make a go of things. His tragedy would make for a good story of a comeback. Just knowing I was going to escape made the difference.

Angel was in the back of the car, looking at me through the back window. She smiled when I got up close and waved. It was nice to see her there. It gave me a strange feeling of longing and family in a way. There's nothing as lonely as doing something by yourself.

'You was twelve seconds slower on that mile!' Sandy shouted. It had been into a steep rise on this dirt road humped in the middle. I ran in the groove of Sandy's tyre tracks.

We turned onto this twist of road, moving into an encroachment of dense forest. The trees formed this canopy over the road. I ran through the shadows and it seemed like evening had suddenly settled.

The car groaned and seemed to collect itself, the shift of gears deep in its guts knocking. Sandy put the car into a lower gear, and the car caught and climbed like a dark slug into the hillside. The road was littered with stones and runoff from the night's rain. I heard the car scrape something, and then there was this furious smell of burning oil. A billow of smoke poured from underneath the car. Sandy stopped and killed the engine and got out. He was going mad. 'Shit, I just hope we ain't bust a rod.' The car was burning oil bad. The smell was horrible, this bluish cloud of smoke extending down the road.

Angel got out. I thought the car was going to start on fire.

'Shit!' Sandy kicked the car. 'Fuck! Jesus, you got to lose this goddamn fear of dogs and shit. Look at this car for Christ's sake. I can't be out here protectin your ass. You hear me?' He began imitating me, ' "Sandy, come on the run with me. I don't like dogs, Sandy! Sandy, pace me. I'm afraid of dogs, Sandy!" Well, fuck you and your fear of dogs. Get over it, asshole! This is a nation of goddamn dogs! Now look what you gone and done to us!'

We were nearly vertical on this impassable rise of road. A wind of cool air funnelled down on us. I felt my bad ear plug with the pressure of altitude. Fuck if that started up again on me. I yawned, and the ears popped and the pressure dissipated. The unnerving silence remained, the three of us stranded on the mountainside. In a gap in the trees I could see the highway off in the distance, the slow procession of tiny trucks.

We waited for the oil to stop burning. Sandy started the car again and put it in gear. Things shifted and rolled as we continued up the hill. Sandy brought the car into the lowest gear, and it groaned and stalled and then bucked. Sandy looked out the back of the car. The oil was burning away. 'Fuck!' he roared. 'You fucked up the only freedom we ever goddamn had, you son of a bitch!'

We stayed there in silence. The smoke disappeared slowly, but the smell remained. Sandy got under the car. He pulled out a branch that was stuck. It was just an oil leak. 'We is goddamn lucky is all I gotta say. Here's what you is goin to have to do. Go on up there and get us some oil, two quarts to get our asses back down to the campsite, and maybe Bill Hayes will know what you do with blown gasket heads or whatever the fuck goes wrong with a car. Shit! I hate this shit!

I hate you! I hate dogs! I hate this life.' His echoes filled the bowl of the mountain.

Angel just sat on a stone off to the side of the road. She looked at me and shrugged her shoulders.

I followed signs advertising gas, home cooking, and The Gray Horse Honeymooner's Retreat. The road corkscrewed into the mountain, the ground hard from the night's frost now melting in trickles. A constant flutter of birds flew up from trees as I came upon them, merciless looking fuckers wheeling against the sun before settling again.

I was hobbling by this long rise. I stopped and got my breath with my hands on my knees. I was on a mission of mercy, out saving us. It was like the old running fantasies I had. We had this international jamboree on the Isle of Man, and I was chosen by the Irish scouts to run a secret parchment to home base, in a re-enactment of World War II war games. I spent the night out there with the other Irish decoys, poor fuckers who pretended to have the parchment. They got the shite beaten out of them when they got caught, beaten for their secrets. I could hear them as night fell, the rustle of tall grass, marauding bands of scouts. I was hyped up back then, listening to the comrades getting done. I hid in bushes, lashed down small lanes, crawled on my stomach, lay in rivers while these eejits looked for me. There was no catching me; even when they caught sight of me, I was off like a madman for the hills, off into the long grass and the trees, off by the cliffs as these fat toffees turned into windbags. If there was one thing that got me into the running, it was the feeling of bringing in the parchment before sunrise, lashing towards Command Central with these English and French tearing down on me. Up the Irish! I roared as these bolloxes ambushed me from this lane, knocked me down and beat the shite out of me. 'You Irish pig!' they called me, and dug in with their English black shoes. The rules were nobody could help me. I was a prisoner of war. I could see Command Central there, a quarter mile up the way, the lads roaring me on. But there was no hope. I struggled under the hits until the parchment was pulled out from under my shirt. This English bollocks grabbed my underwear and pulled it so hard it wedged up my arse, and they slapped me around. The Irish flag was lowered in surrender as I was led off to HQ for interrogation and torture.

And even at the reformatory, I used to go to sleep pretending I was with all the lads and the priests, and this shower of girls from Saint Bernadette's Convent for the Insatiably Gorgeous. We were lost out in the fields in this post-nuclear winter. The big puddings who did the rugby plodded slowly through the wasteland, crying like babies. They had no stamina, and that was the name of the game. The school was no more, blown to kingdom come, the town, history as well, all our parents dead. The priests were there, praying for a miracle in the grey light of perpetual nuclear night. They looked like death warmed up, tired ragged bishops in their druidic hoods, exhausted, at death's door, on the verge of packing in life. Then I'd come forward in the dream and volunteer to press on alone and find the lost city of Sligo, or wherever the fuck it was. All the young girls from the convent would be watching me out of the corners of their eyes, weeping because their mothers and fathers were all dead. I'd say something like, 'I'll be back for yous people, don't worry bout nothin. I have the stamina of a horse, Father. Don't yous worry. If there's life out there, I'll find it.' Then the girls would fall to pieces, and Jasus they'd have to pull them off me, cause they'd be wanting to hug me. And then I'd speed off into the darkness to save the day. That was the staple diet of shite I lived on back then. When you're out for an hour and a half every day, you make up these elaborate stories to keep your mind occupied.

I dug into the hill again, pressed on into the mountain road. I had a sense of pace again. The form was back, the steady breath and lean into the terrain. Browning leaves fell from the trees. The humiliation of the last year was going, slowly. I still had the secret inside me, the will to get myself out of this. I had my destiny in my own hands.

I saw a slow scroll of smoke in the distance, heard the distant whine of saw blades. There was that smell of cut wood, the sweet scent of sap and menthol taste of pine. Then an odour of smoked meat filled my nostrils. I turned a bend and was set on by dogs, a pack of mud-covered hounds who rushed out from the shade of crooked porches to tear into me. The dogs brought me to a sudden halt. Chickens scrambled into useless flight, an explosion of feathered anxiousness, disappearing into broken down cars. The ground had the odour of seed and chicken droppings, like out on the highway that one night.

Up on the porch sat this old man in dungarees and a heavy coat, faceless under a hat.

'Call them off!' I shouted. I felt this purgatorial stillness as the old man called the dogs off. The dogs seemed to ease into general apathy. A goat tied to the porch made a sound like a baby crying. It stared at me with its strange yellow eyes, that little billygoat scrap of a beard hanging from its chin.

I just stayed there, standing still. Puddles in the street reflected sunlight. The man coughed and spat into the distance between me and him. Above his head where he sat was this huge set of antlers that looked like they were growing from his head. The old man got up and unfolded himself like a knife, steadying himself. A small boy emerged on the porch in a dirty shirt and no trousers, crouched there on the steps and shat into a pot, keeping his eyes on me, and went back inside. The dogs looked between me and the old man, waiting pensively, whining among themselves. Everything was met with the same profound indifference.

The town was a ramshackle patchwork of huts, extension on top of extension, homes conceived in bits and pieces, slouching towards demolition, all off kilter, half caved in, held together by an armour of rusting corrugated metal. Long chimney pipes sent up long slow meditative puffs into the treetops. Everywhere about were cars in various states of disrepair, a species of immobility, the cannibalised progeny of mechanics, windowless trucks up on blocks, car seats torn to shreds where sleeping cats gave birth, the tentacles of distributor caps like alien aquatic creatures on broken tables, chrome fenders above doorways, tyres now in service as rope swings hanging from trees. It seemed as though these people had crash-landed from a distant planet, like I had watched on the telly back home, like *Planet of the Apes*, where the humans were on the run from the Ape Lords.

I walked on and heard the dim clang of metal being pounded out, the noise of chains and a winch, of things being wrought in a furnace. A young woman with heavy breasts opened her door and came out. Her hair hung in a long heavy rope that reached the small of her back. She emptied her washing water into the road. It spread in a hot steam of suds.

'They got a gas station here?' I said.

She said, 'What the hell you doin in your britches?' She turned and shut the door. I stared at the carcasses of stiff clothes already drying on the porch.

I kept walking up the hill. A dark ribbon of smoke issued from a long stone chimney. A man materialised from the foundry, fat bellied, with a heavy beard, in blue denim overalls and laced up work boots. He had a mallet in his left hand. His face was covered in soot. The man removed his hat and revealed a dome of brilliant white baldness. He looked like an egg with a beard.

I kept going until I got to the gas mart, this small dark store. A small old man with a chicken chest was behind the counter, with old-fashioned glasses on the end of his nose. He said, 'What the hell is you doin lookin like that?'

I gave him the short end of the story, and he said, 'Jesus, if that don't beat all. Livin at a campsite, and all, and runnin like that, and comin all that way from Ireland. That's a sad country over there, so it is. People killin people in the name of God. But I guess there's been more killed in the Almighty's name than in the Devil's name.'

'I just need the oil is all,' I said.

'That is some accent you got,' the old man said.

I stared at the worn wooden board, the grain polished by years of wear. The room was made of ancient dark-coloured wood hewn into big rafters. It seemed like some outpost from another century. Coffee hissed in a small jar like a round fishbowl. I stood there and waited in this warm light. And then my eyes fell upon this consuming hugeness of inhuman dimensions sitting back in this big couch off in the corner facing the cold light coming through a window. It was this monstrosity of human flesh, poured into a floral dress the size of sitting-room curtains. The creature had this massive beehive hairdo. I nearly died.

'Lemme get this straight now. You ran all the way up from the turn at Miller's Point?' The old man shook his head. 'That is some climb.'

I looked back at the old man, who was searching for something. Then his eyes turned, and he saw me looking between him and the giant.

The old man shook his head slowly. The skin on his forehead folded into deep lines, pulling his face upward, exposing the pink of his gums. He steered me away from her, so I couldn't see her and said, 'You wait right here and lemme see what we got here.' He disappeared for a few minutes.

The blob made a series of sucking sounds. I just waited.

I took the oil and headed off, down past the dogs. It was cold outside. I felt dark enclaves of people hidden away in these mountains, a total submission to fate. I was discovering that America was a place of dark secrets and abandonment, insular despair that was too ignorant to even feel sorry for itself.

Down below, Sandy was still drinking, sitting in the car. He looked awful with his hair greased back on his head in a slick mess of curls. He must have laid into Angel, because I could see she had been crying. He took the oil and opened the bonnet without so much as a word to me. I was about to say something to Angel, but she shook her head. I touched her hand. It was freezing cold.

Sandy said, 'You watch, and see if it's still leakin.'

The oil he put in just poured into the ground. My face got covered in oil. I was looking like a black and white minstrel. Angel burst out laughing. Sandy roared, 'Shut it, Angel!'

We got the car turned around and we rolled back down the mountain slowly, saying nothing. The engine wasn't running.

The car picked up speed on the decline. I braced and looked at Sandy. He had that defiance of a drunk. He took a swig at the bottle. The trees whisked by us in a blaze of reds and browns.

There was a house down the road which I hated because of a dog that harassed me. The dog ran out into the road and barked. Sandy never even touched the brake, just put the car into a swerve. I felt the soft roll of the wheels, and he hit the dog with a cracking force that rattled and tore at the undercarriage of the car. Angel whimpered. I turned and saw the dog in the rear window, still writhing. We turned a bend, and it was gone.

Sandy took a hand from the steering wheel and pointed with his index finger like it was a gun. 'You got to kill em one by one is what you got to do to the bastards. If you hate somethin, you got to eliminate it.' He went, 'Pow, Pow, Pow! One at a time is how you do it.' I could hear the tyres eating into the dirt road, that slur of sound and the engine dead. 'It ain't me that hates dogs. I ain't got nothin against them. You do! That's how come I don't got no goddamn car now.'

Angel was sniffling in the back of the car.

The momentum died on a speed bump inside the campground. Bill Hayes saw us and came over. He saw the blood on the plank of wood used as a fender.

Sandy said, 'Goddamn possums out there on the road is impossible.'

Bill Hayes shook his head. 'It's the season of death out there on the road awright.'

'I think it done something to my oil pressure, Bill.'

'Well, let's take a look then.'

I helped push the car over to the site where Bill Hayes had a hole dug like a grave, real deep and long, where he got down to work on his own cars. Angel got out of the car and went over to Bill Hayes' trailer. She had her hands to her mouth like she was going to be sick.

Another mindless week passed. The car was the centre of concern. I kept my mouth shut. I just ran is all, long fifteen-milers up by the old house where Sandy'd killed the dog. They had this sign painted. It said, 'REWARD! For the son-of-a-bitch that murdered our dog!'

Evening was falling and things were tense. The car had been patched up, but Bill Hayes said it wouldn't make it over thirty miles an hour or we'd blow the seal he'd put on.

Me, Sandy and Angel just crept along the roads at twenty miles an hour in the car with Sandy cursing under his breath.

Down at the doughnut shop, Sandy had a thing for the waitress named Darlene who was more than ten years older than him, divorced and with a kid. Everyone called her 'Nurse', because she wore nurse's shoes. She had blue eyeshadow and a doughy cleavage she liked to put before men like it was something on the menu. Sandy sat at the counter and smoked with her. She grew pot at home, and that was the real reason Sandy hung around her, scrounging for a bud.

Sandy bought a dozen of the day-old doughnuts for a dollar, and me and Angel sat like eejits and ate while Sandy chatted up Darlene, who had a pen sticking out her hair like it was an antenna. Angel suffered it and said nothing. Her face was tired. She ate the doughnuts methodically, without tasting anything, just trying to survive. She ate the soft yellow fillings and red jelly fillings and the doughnuts with the confetti sprinkles, the kind of colours you'd see at a birthday party.

I was tired. I had logged another long run of eighteen miles. Sitting there in the doughnut shop was what we did those days, wasting time mostly. I listened for the sound of rigs on the interstate, putting my good ear against the glass. I had been there, out among them. I remembered and shook my head. I was counting the time for an escape, but not yet.

Sandy said, 'Darlene, where'd you ever get such pretty eyes?'

Darlene laughed. 'You want somethin. I can tell when a man wants somethin.'

'Nothin but your company is all,' Sandy said softly. He was making the other people uncomfortable.

I yawned and settled against the wall. They had this

programme on the telly called 'Real People', about weird human phenomena around the world. It was Darlene's favourite. She said so and turned it up. There was this Chinaman with a huge head living off on some mountain. The Chinaman lowered his head, and an assistant parted the Chinaman's hair at the side. There was this tumour bulging out, and it had a face, a tiny twin head embedded in his skull.

Darlene let out this snort of disgust and said, 'Geeze awmighty,' touching her cleavage.

The assistant pointed out the disfigured features of the tiny face. The tiny head had teeth, not a whole set, but three little bits of teeth, and it had slits of eyes. It was fascinating. Everybody in the doughnut shop was staring up at the telly. A medical expert on the telly said it seemed there were Siamese twins originally, but that one had died off from the neck down before they were born. Then came this gloomy sideshow of tumours removed from women's ovaries. There were all these jars of dead deformity at this hospital, shelves full of them. The tumours had hair and teeth, like foetuses. The expert said it was rare, but it happened.

After the ads came the next spectacle, and we were looking at this grainy image of some kind of creature lumbering down a highway. It was shite footage, and the camera wobbled and rocked, and then it picked up the creature again, who was now lashing for the high hills. It was a hairy man, a Bigfoot, this mythical prehistoric creature who this expert said still roamed America's wilderness. They had a plaster of Paris cast of the creature's foot taken from the sighting. It showed five toes, proving it was linked to humans. The town out west was filled with visitors with cameras all along the highway edge where the creature had been spotted. There were shops selling tee-shirts of the creature and cups with the creature's face on it.

Sandy said, 'God almighty, but I think I might have seen that creature up by where we is stayin. Honest to Gawd, I seen somethin strange up there.' He held up his hand like he was giving testimony. The others in the doughnut shop drank their coffee, and one of them said, 'You could be right, cause every now and again some hunter comes on in and says he's seen somethin.'

Darlene said, 'Was he big, Sandy?' and Sandy said, 'I couldn't figure, really. It was up high and movin real fast, but, now that I think about it, the creature didn't look no bigger than a man.'

Darlene looked toward the door. It opened, and a rush of noise came in and then stopped, and a man sat down. Darlene was already there with the coffee. 'Maybe it was like a young Bigfoot you saw, Sandy.'

Sandy smiled. 'You know Darlene, I think you might be right about that. It just might have been a juvenile Bigfoot.'

Darlene went behind the counter and took out her purse and painted on a smile of cherry lipstick, looking into a small vanity mirror. She dabbed powder on her cheeks, and it was the same as the powder on the doughnuts. It sifted through the air. I watched it fall.

We went into the street, and life had settled against the hills, the soft street light leading down the main street bleeding against the encroaching dark. 'Indian summer,' Darlene said, and Sandy answered, 'A night for sitting on a porch and watching the stars.' I could feel that sentimental tug in Sandy, that need for home. He kissed her with his mouth open. Angel looked away and got into the back of the car. I looked at her and saw the growth of her stomach. It was getting scary having her like that now.

We were back in the car going up home when Sandy said, 'You ever seen anythin like that Chinaman, I mean all them people goin there to pray to him and all? I bet you that tiny twin head knows the future or somethin.' The car moved through the dark. 'Shit, some people get all the deformity.' He smiled and nudged me. 'I seen this picture in Health Class once where this woman had both sex organs in her. Could you image being able to fuck yourself? Sure as hell beats having to take someone to dinner and a movie.' Sandy banged his hands on the steering wheel. 'Shit!'

Sandy quieted for a while, then he said, 'So they got

themselves a Bigfoot here. I'll be damned.' He smiled, and I only saw the profile of his face, a strange malevolence of sad longing.

We pulled into the campsite. Fires burned the dark away in small patches of crimson light. It was an unusually warm evening, dry and clear, and the stars showed above the trees. Men were playing cards at some of the sites.

'Indian Summer,' Bill Hayes said as he let us into his trailer. 'Though I hear we is in for a storm later.'

Sandy said, 'It all balances out in the end, I guess. Bet we get a horrendous winter. I seen them brown caterpillars round here, and they got them big hairy black rings. That's how you can tell what kind of winter we is goin to have. Ain't that right Bill?'

Bill Hayes said, 'That's what the old people say, all right, and I been here long enough to figure they is right more than they is wrong.'

The trailer was tiny and hot. Bill Hayes' wife sat against an open window and blew her smoke out through it.

Sandy was shaking slightly. 'Bill, can I run somethin by you?'

'Sure.'

'You ever hear of a Bigfoot round these parts?'

Bill Hayes said, 'I figure this whole range is home to some kind of creature. You ask any of them old timers and they'll tell you there's somethin out there.'

Bill Hayes' wife said, 'Hogwash. Too much goddamn moonshine if you ask me.'

Sandy said, 'I don't believe I was askin you,' but Bill Hayes got that look in his eyes, and Sandy saw it and said, 'I mean, maybe you is right and all, Alice.'

Bill Hayes' wife ignored Sandy and looked at Angel and said, 'You doin awright?'

Angel smiled. 'I'm gettin by. We seen this show where they got tumours they took out of women with hair and eyes.'

Bill Hayes' wife tipped her ash out the window and said, 'I heard of this old woman back in Georgia who was gettin these pains real bad. They took her to the hospital and opened her up, and she's got this shrivelled up little baby inside her. Doctors figured it'd been there for years.'

Angel said, 'That happen much, you figure, babies dyin inside people like that?'

Bill Hayes smiled. 'You don't got to worry none, Angel. They's rare. That's why they got them on those shows.'

Bill Hayes' wife said, 'When I was expectin, I had dreams I was carrying a dog inside me. I don't know why. Guess the body goes kinda haywire with all them chemicals. You ever have things like that inside your head, Angel?'

Angel didn't get to answer because Sandy was shaking away, and the trailer seemed to rock with his nerves. 'Bill, if I could. I want to run this by you, if I might, if and when you is finished with your bullshit, Angel?' Sandy took a long breath, 'I don't know why I try sometimes. I really don't.'

'I don't see you tryin shit,' Bill Hayes' wife chimed in.

Bill Hayes said, 'I'm all ears, Sandy.'

'What you figure, if there were some sightings of this Bigfoot in these very parts? We get it on video or somethin and send it off to that programme, 'Real People'. But we have everything ready and all. We get us some goddamn tee-shirts for sale for when people come by to see if they can spot Bigfoot.'

Bill Hayes' wife breathed out a blue jet of smoke. 'Jesus Christ, Sandy. Of all the bullshit ideas. Where you plannin on findin yourself a Bigfoot?'

'I got me a Bigfoot right here in this trailer. Him!' Sandy shouted and pointed at me. 'This son of a bitch can run like an animal, I mean run real fast, and who the hell is goin to catch him? We get him into a costume and let him go. I've seen him run damn near twenty miles at a time. Ain't nobody goin to catch him up in them hills round here.'

I just sat there and laughed, and Sandy said, 'Bill, these shit for brains don't seem to see what I'm drivin at, at the cash cow I'm proposin here. How much you figure we can make, if and we were to invent ourselves a Bigfoot, and be there with the tee-shirts and cups and pens and all that stuff when the curious come waltzin in here?'

Bill Hayes puffed up his massive cheeks. 'Figure you got to drop a pretty penny before you goin to make anything.'

'Yeah, but think of the return on investment. I figure we can clear twenty thousand easy. This is a nation of people that wears who and what they are and where they been and what their politics is right there on their tee-shirts and on their car bumpers. You got to believe me on this one, Bill. It's a winner.'

Bill Hayes said, 'Twenty thousand some kind of magic figure with you or somethin?'

Sandy just got that crazed look. 'Twenty thousand some kind of magic figure? Hell yes. You ever see the Twenty Thousand Dollar Pyramid? Maybe that's the extent of my vision, Bill. Or how bout the Twenty Thousand Dollar Question and all that? I'm a goddamn idiot, Bill. That's what you take me for. I can see it in your eyes. You ain't no better than me, Bill. None of you is, cause at least I know what and where I am. I got a sense of just how fucked we all are. We are, if I may remind you all, the nation that fell for the pet rock!' Sandy just quit talking and seemed deflated. He held his arm. I could see the scars, and I felt sorry for him in a way. He looked at me. 'Shit, I could see you as a goddamn juvenile Bigfoot, I could. I thought you might just have been interested in gettin out of here.'

Bill Hayes' wife looked at me. 'You know, if you was up there in some Bigfoot suit and someone saw you, they is liable to plug you good. Alive or dead, it don't matter to no hunter.' She stared at me, and Bill Hayes turned his head and looked at me and then at his wife.

Bill Hayes said, 'What the hell is it to you if he gets killed?'

Bill Hayes' wife said, 'Gawd. We ain't goin to start into this again, is we?' She put her hand to his face.

Angel interrupted, 'That's right. There'd be a bounty on your head. It ain't as easy as Sandy thinks.'

'Shit, nobody's askin you, Angel. I was askin Bill in confidence is all. I was lookin at it as a financial proposition was all.' Sandy left, and I knew he was going to be outside drugging himself into submission.

Bill Hayes brought his big hands together. 'I kinda like him. He's crazy, don't get me wrong, but he comes up with a hell of a lot of ways to make twenty thousand.'

Angel nodded her head. 'You ain't heard the half of em, Bill.'

Cancer

Wanking became a problem up at the campsite.

I was living in a fantasy world with Bill Hayes' wife, and all was going fine when I was sleeping out under the tarp by myself. I could have a pull and no one was the wiser. But the rains of October started in for a season of floods. We were high enough up in the mountains to be out of danger, but the river brooked and roared with dead things rushing down into the valley. Sandy got Bill Hayes to make a flat board for the back of the car, and they took out the back seat and stowed it under the tarp. Sandy lived there with Angel in the makeshift bed, and I moved into the front seat because the ground outside was an ooze of dirt. This was when the trouble started.

I was sleeping like I was in a coma at night, but there was this issue of Bill Hayes' wife and the sperm build-up. I woke up with an erection one night. I was dying for her. I could see her trailer from my window. I felt the churn of useless sperm down there inside me. I listened, and Sandy and Angel were asleep. I began to go at myself, closed my eyes and thought of Bill Hayes' wife. It was like at the reformatory school, when the lights went out. Each of us in there closed his eyes and went to a secret place of longing, this collective stroking in the dark. You could hear lads trying to catch their breaths, cubicles only inches apart, and all of us going at ourselves. I got the image of Bill Hayes' wife there in that dress she wore in the trailer. We were off down in the town, and I was buying her ice cream, and she was on my arm. I tried to keep things quiet, holding my breath and not trying to let on anything, but the seat squeaked.

Sandy said, 'What the fuck you doin?' and I just froze and said nothing.

He said, 'Don't you fuck up that seat on me. Go spank yer monkey outside, you hear me? I know you're awake.'

Angel said, 'What's goin on, Sandy?' and Sandy said, 'That asshole is spankin his monkey is what's goin on. Jesus H. Christ. I feel like a goddamn father scolding his son! Shit's disgustin is what it is.'

I was humiliated and made this snoring whistling noise, a total giveaway that I was wide awake. The night settled, but the sea of sperm kept churning. I couldn't sleep or nothing. I waited for things to settle with Sandy and got out of the car. This humiliation of longing burned down there inside me as I dragged my carcass off to the toilet. I sat there and played with myself and kept my foot to the door.

It was utter blackness in there. But this dim margin of sleep and mental exhaustion was Da's playing field, and up he rises, him and the dog, slowly along this dark river brimming at the edge of my brain, this lapping sound of water against a shore. Da was already saying 'Could you have any luck when you're at that sort of shite at all? Didn't the good Lord say, "The body is my temple?"' I was inside the toilet and holding myself. I didn't want this. I had made peace with him back there in my dreams. I staved off his image, sayin, 'No, leave me alone.'

Setanta stopped and sniffed something, and Da lit a cigarette.

'What do ya have there, Setanta?' The dog whispered something to Da, and Da's eyes opened real wide. 'His first masturbation. Jasus fuck, that dirty bollocks.'

Setanta said, 'Of all the trite, dirty wanks, Charlie's Angels is who he was wanking off to, all three of them.'

Da rolled his eyes, 'Ah, the usual suspects, of course. Christ, does he have an original thought in that thick skull of his at all? Jasus, we're disgusting creatures.'

Setanta sniffed around the long grass by this ooze of blackness. 'I've the bionic woman over here a few times,' and Setanta grins at me from the dark, and he said, 'The eejit has himself bionic as well.' Da gritted his teeth and began to walk, and Setanta said, 'Watch out there, the neighbour's young one, Maureen Brady, has been ravaged right there, something about a picnic out along the Shannon banks.'

Da came and stared into the sticky mess of wank, and he could read each sordid fantasy. 'Self-gratifying dirty bollocks. God, can there be any forgiveness when the mind is as blighted and disgustin as this?' He prodded my head with his walking stick, and I had this shooting pain in my temple.

Then they came upon this mound of dirt and Da went at it with the stick, prodding to see what was in there. He stabbed at bits of a torn magazine. I watched him and waited in humiliation. It was a porn magazine I'd bought from Eddie Lawlor. But when I got tired of wanking to it and felt guilty, I tore it to shreds and buried the poor bodies of these women out in the back garden in the rose bushes. Da rutted around and came up with a harvest of tits and bits of fannies and decapitated heads. It was a graveyard of desire.

'Jasus Christ!' Setanta said.

Da stuck his walking stick into the cunt of this young bird. He just stared into this bleached-out looking pussy covered in mud and maggots and said, 'Jasus!'

'No wonder the rose took last year,' Setanta said and laughed his head off.

Da said, 'Jasus, Mary and Joseph, what the hell do I have on my hands at all?'

It smelt like a sewer there inside the toilet. I was humiliated, just holding my mickey, and there was nothing coming. The mickey had gone limp on me. Da went in further, and he had his handkerchief to his face, and Setanta was panting, with his purple tongue hanging out. 'God Almighty.'

Da could barely keep himself standing. 'Jasus Fuck and all that's good, get me out of this cesspool of juvenile sexuality!' There was the housewife from the Fairy Liquid and this girl in a bath of Radox, and thousands of other poor souls lost in the purgatorial den of my iniquity. In that blackness floated the disembodied dreams of every wank I'd ever had, and Da was blessing himself and staggering like a drunk.

I was in the reformatory bed, and Da was watching me through the small curtained cubicle. It smelt of spunk in there, a claustrophobia of sexual anxiety, forty lads going at themselves, a river of spunk staining socks. That's what we used, old socks on our hands, like puppets, that smell of feet and spunk, the hard crust of sweat cutting into our mickeys. If you were caught at inspection with your sheets stained, you got the fuck beaten out of you. You got duty picking the cigarette butts out of the urinals with your bare hands as punishment.

Setanta shouts, 'Holy Jasus, that's not Brother Seamus Riordan, the hurling coach, is it?' I screamed, 'That's a lie!' but Da plugged his ears and tripped and slid on the ground, and he was covered in this sticky spunk. He roared, 'Jasus, tell me no more!' Off he dashed. Setanta said, 'Come on now, let's not have another sexual exposé on the priesthood. We're better than that,' and then he burst out laughing and headed off after Da.

I dragged myself out of the stall, and I was limp, humiliated and shaking. My balls were in the hammock of my underwear, and I could feel them moving by themselves. I looked at Bill Hayes' trailer, him, his wife and children all asleep. I went by the window, and Bill Hayes was sucking his wife's toes. He was leaning into her with that mountain of back hair glistening with sweat, devotee at a temple. I moved away silently. I got back into the car. Sandy was awake.

'So we've got that out of our system, have we?' Sandy laughed so hard the car jiggled.

I said, 'Go shoot yourself up, you drug addict!'

He stopped laughing and said, 'We all got our demons, my friend. We all got our demons.'

The whine of saws high up in the mountains was coming to its seasonal end. The quarry pit was letting men go each day. Bill Hayes got me a week under the table loading cut lumber onto trucks. It was good to earn money and get it in cash at the end of each day. It ended up being only seventy-two dollars, but when we'd been down in the town getting our supplies at the beginning of the stay at the campsite, I'd seen fifty-nine-dollar Greyhound Bus tickets that could take you across America, or at least back up to New York. I got a sense of security in just having the money, and Sandy seemed to know that he didn't own me any more. I measured everything now against the rawness of those first months of sickness and depression. Bill Hayes said that down near Texas there was honest money to be made for any man that was willing, and I thought about that some nights, because now I could think of leaving. I had the seventy-two dollars hidden in a plastic bag down by the river, and I went down to check on it from time to time, and it was there when the time was ready.

I rescued a grasshopper down there from this rock, marooned. It stood there, miserable, and it didn't seem like it could bring itself to jump for land. I touched it with my finger, thinking it would jump, but it had outlived the season. I took it into my hand and took it back down to the campsite, and it still clung to my finger. Bill Hayes said grasshoppers brought good luck, and he gave me a jar, and I put the hopper inside and got some leaves and tall bits of grass. Bill stabbed the lid with a few air holes. I gave it to Angel as a present.

I spent hours in the car listening to the radio with her. Sometimes she'd have me rub her ankles. She asked me about back home, and I told her the kind of shite that I knew she'd like about the greenness of the fields and the crash of the ocean, the great storms that came rolling in. She asked me if I'd ever seen a leprechaun. I said I hadn't, but that I'd seen their little forts, the small ringed stones that lead to their secret world underground. She just smiled and said things like, 'They're real good at makin shoes, isn't that right?' I said, 'Yeah, that's right. They are great lads for makin the shoes.' It was nice in there in the car when the cold came on us, real cosy just under the blankets and drinking coffee. I told her the story of Leda and the swans, the lovely children turned into swans by their evil stepmother and the long roaming of their Da over the world to find them, when they were there in Ireland all along. I told her how they screeched in their swan voices when he passed them late in life, and just his tears on them made them human again. I didn't even know the real story or nothing, just made it up for her.

The running awaited me each day, morning and evening, a stubborn animal that needed to be taken out onto the roads. Addiction had taken over, that automatic urgency to run took me out whether I liked it or not, and that was the trick, to get the mind hooked, because the body can do a lot more than it ever lets on. I centred my eating and sleeping around the morning and evening runs. After the first month at the campsite, I'd felt the drag of endurance, felt that my body had switched over to a new mechanism for burning calories, knew that I was eating into the fat reserves. My trousers were like a sack on me, and I was swimming in the reformatory jumper. I was pretty much a mobile scarecrow, but that's what I needed, to be lean.

I paged through my log in the front of the car and saw the rise in mileage from that first week of forty-five up to a hundred now. I had put myself into a trance of endurance, that's how I liked to think of it. I had that capacity of mindless endurance where I could make my brain a dormant mass of grey matter, devoid of longing or anger, compelled towards only a drawn-out battle against my own body. I lay there and switched back and forth between the two parts of my brain, part animal and part human. I sat there and added up the total mileage since I'd arrived at the campsite. It came out around five hundred miles. Usually a summer base of distance running was around twelve hundred before a runner had honed down the body weight and could really consider going near the speed work. I wasn't going to be able to challenge any of the decent runners until the new year.

I put the log down and stayed still for a long time. Bill Hayes' wife had come outside. I wiped away the frost on the window, and I could see her looking over at our car. She washed in the barrel of rainwater like she always did and then stood there and combed her hair. I couldn't make out her face, but I felt inside me this yearning to kiss her just once. She went inside again. The sky was still grey outside, morning coming later each day now. I had the horsehair blanket over me and my reformatory jumper and two pairs of socks on. I got out of the car and pissed off by the trees. I came back and set the fire and waited before getting the coffee ready. I was thinking of the run by the Thompson farm, about four miles up near this sulphur pond.

I wasn't going to get my breakthrough into Central Tennessee this side of Christmas. It was a sullen fact as I worked in the rising light of a cold morning, my breath fogging. I had been in America since June, five months at this stage, and I was halfway towards fitness. If it was just a season back home, I could have started into racing now and let the speed work come through racing, but there were no races. The main thing now was not to lose focus, to stay injury free and maintain the distance work. I thought only of the running. It was what was going to save me in the end. The coffee came slowly to the boil, a seething tar which I poured for myself and Angel. She kissed me good morning in the grey of the car. It was damp and smelled of sweat in there, and I felt sorry for her, but she never complained. She sat up and drank slowly.

I left with the pull of endurance at me, that runner's fix needing to be released in miles of exercise. It must have been the same way for Sandy back at the motel, that insomnia of a drug addict always roaming for that next hit, feeling the sensation of life impinging again. I needed nearly fifteen miles a day to stun my brain, to make it a hostage of physical endurance, to keep my mind from thinking about Da and Bill Hayes' wife.

A cop came by our site and wedged himself out of his car about a month after Bill Hayes had beaten the man. The cop was holding a styrofoam coffee cup in one hand. He asked us if we'd seen anything unusual at the campsite when the man was beaten into a coma. Bill Hayes took off his woollen cap and wiped his massive forehead and said, 'When you got three children, you sleep like a log,' and then he put his cap back on his head and chopped wood with a grunting effort.

The cop shuffled over and asked us, and we said we'd heard nothing, but Sandy said that there had been a card game, but with the dark we saw nothing. The cop said, 'That man is a vegetable is what he is. Ain't no figurin if he is ever goin to come round.' The cop looked at me and said, 'You that kid that's been seen running all over these parts, isn't you?'

I nearly died, but I said, 'Yeah.'

Sandy looked at the cop and said, 'He's training for the Olympics is what he's doin.'

The cop drank from his cup and said, 'That is something all right. You his coach then?'

Sandy said, 'Shit, I guess I am his coach and all.'

A tow truck came and broke up the stalemate in the conversation. The tow truck man said, 'You heard they found that kid,' and the cop said, 'Naw!'

'Oh yeah, it's all over the radio this morning. Up by them old mine shafts they found her, tied up and hungry, but safe.'

Sandy flinched and looked at me and then at Bill Hayes. Sandy said, 'That kid local or something?'

The cop turned and cocked his head sideways for a moment, like he was suspicious, but all he said was, 'Shit no. It was a kid from that Camp Yogi back up the way, one of them city kids. Someone just went in there and kidnapped the poor kid, just like that, bout a week ago.'

Sandy shook his head and said, 'Go figure. That is goddamn low. A kid and all. Jesus Christ, what is this world comin to? I suppose they was lookin for a ransom.'

'Twenty thousand in small bills is what I heard,' the tow truck driver said. 'I mean, shit, any goddamn fool is goin to know the government is goin to pass funny money when push comes to shove, mark them goddamn bills.'

'Twenty thousand,' Sandy said. He shook his head and looked at me.

I held my breath, and Bill Hayes swung his hatchet with a particular vengeance. The cop looked around and saw the cars. He looked at the tow truck man, and they both saw Angel. The cop said, 'She sick or something?'

'Pregnant, if you call that a sickness,' Sandy said, and his laugh was pathetic. He stopped too abruptly and just made this stupid face.

The cop put the coffee to his lips and drank and swirled it around before swallowing it. Bill Hayes' wife came out with a child on her hip, and the tow truck man said, 'Morning,' while the cop settled on Sandy's arm. Any eejit could see the track marks. 'You all related or something?' the cop said.

Sandy said, 'We just neighbours is all. That there is Bill Hayes and his wife, and he got hisself three children.'

The cop and the tow truck man went over by the other site where the man had been beaten. The cop surveyed the area and moved his foot around like he was looking at something, but it was nothing. They came back again. The cop was shaking his head. The tow truck driver was saying something in a low voice. He spat on the ground, and when they were back in front of us he said, 'Well, that's the story all right. Kid is safe, and thank God for it. You know it was someone in the vicinity that done it, cause that's what this expert from Atlanta was sayin.'

'They got any leads?' the cop said.

The tow truck driver shook his head and smiled, 'Shit, Ernie, you is the goddamn law round here! Have they got any leads, shit!'

The cop held the coffee over his big belly and settled his gun belt with the other hand. 'Kidnapping is a federal matter, Chester. FBI was handling all that. They don't tell me shit. They just came in here and swore us all to secrecy is what they done.'

'Ain't that some shit,' the tow truck driver said. 'You inspire no confidence in the general public, Ernie.'

The cop said, 'I take each day as it comes. Ain't no point bein a hero. They got the FBI and them college-educated assholes for real crimes.'

'Guess you is obsolete. I mean, they got the experts and all, crime lab and forensic experts to beat the band, and hell if they didn't just find that kid and all.'

The cop had a jaded face of hanging jowls. 'You about finished insultin me?'

The tow truck driver spat on the ground and said, 'I guess I am,' and then the cop said, 'We better get this show on the road.'

I stood there and tried to look relaxed.

The tow truck driver's radio hissed. 'That'll be the shop.' He went and hitched up the fuckup's truck and headed out of the campsite. The cop followed with his lights flashing, but the siren was mute. He stopped and rolled down his window. 'You think of anything at all, you come on down and let me know.'

Sandy said, 'All right then,' and he waved after the cop.

Bill Hayes kept chopping wood.

Sandy shook his head and touched his chin, and he said, 'I just don't goddamn believe that.'

Bill Hayes stopped. He was steaming. 'That kid local or something?' mimicking the way Sandy had asked the question. Bill Hayes just held the hatchet tight in his hand and said, 'Sometimes it's best to keep your mouth shut, Sandy.'

I turned my head back and forth between them, using my good ear to catch what they were saying.

Sandy had that stunned look. 'Hey, you is preaching to the converted, Bill.' His eyes were just blinking away with the truth blinding him. He looked at me. 'I didn't say nothin bout up in that motel to that Lyle Carter or nothin, did I?'

'Who can keep track of what the fuck you say, Sandy? I mean, hell, that cop saw your arm as plain as day.'

Bill Hayes said, 'You run Camp Yogi by anybody else?'

Sandy bit his lip and said, 'Shit, I wasn't meaning nothin by it. I was wastin time is what I was doin is all.'

I just couldn't believe it. Who knows what the situation was really, Bill Hayes by himself, Bill Hayes and Lyle Carter, Lyle Carter by himself . . . Bill Hayes' wife was off in the trailer. Angel was in the back of the car, but she had the window lowered. She heard all the shite that had taken place, but she wasn't going to say anything at all at this stage.

I was stunned, a total ignoramus in the middle of shite that was over my head. I just stood there, and Bill Hayes said, 'I got you a goddamn job. I put my neck on the goddamn line for you, Sandy!'

'Bill, you ain't thinkin I did shit with no kid? Jesus H. Christ Almighty, what you take me for?' Sandy looked at me and grabbed at my arm, 'Shit, I ain't been out of your sight in all the time we been here. I don't even know where this goddamn mine shaft is or nothing.' Sandy had that look of desperation.

Bill Hayes was obstinate and looked at Sandy. 'I can only go by what I hear you say out of your own mouth is all. For all I know you could have twenty thousand ransom stashed somewhere.' Bill Hayes went back to chopping wood.

Sandy half laughed, but he was scared. 'You think I wouldn't have got my ass off this goddamn mountain if I had twenty thousand?'

I went off for a run, like a dumb animal retreating to its burrow. I went way up by the cold pools of still black water and felt scared that, by some chance, I was running straight for the mine shaft in some conceit of the devil's to really fuck me. And I said to myself, 'What's the point?' I looked into the dark pools. The sun was high and cold. I stayed there for half the day and considered my options. There was fuck-all really for me, if you considered that I had no money, just enough for a bus ticket. I had burned my bridges in New York. I stayed still for a long time.

Reason settled eventually, and I said to myself that things had passed. The cop hadn't seen anything other than a group of poor fuckers trying to survive. Maybe that's all that cop had been thinking. I looked up into the heavens, 'Was that you, Auntie Bridie?' because I always felt that maybe my Auntie Bridie was watching over me. I'd read up at the altar, the prayers for the faithfully departed, and I mentioned her name and asked for her to be commended into Heaven, and I thought that should count for something, if she had any influence up there in Heaven. And then I thought to myself that she had five boys of her own that needed helping, and how would she have even known I was in America? She was dead before there was ever any mention of scholarships to America.

Then I said to myself, maybe it was my Ma that was dead, that it was her that had saved us, and I felt this burn of humiliation that I hadn't ever called her or nothing. I remembered the look of her at the airport and that dead cement of her poor face, and she could do nothing as I fucked off into eternity and left her behind without a decent word of thanks or remorse or nothing. And when you looked at it that way, she could just as easily be getting her revenge on me for what I done to Da, and the money, and how I disgraced the whole family and left my brothers without any hope of ever getting anything in the town because of what I'd done. That was probably the real truth, haunted by the unsettled ghost of my dead mother.

I went down the mountain like a shot. I got the money from the river, and down I went into the town. I got twenty dollars in change, and my eyes were filled with tears when I phoned the local sweet shop. I was half-crying, and Mr Daly was sharp on the phone. He said, 'Your mother is up dyin in the hospital, so she is.' He called me 'a dirty bollocks' and 'an ignorant cunt' for the game I'd played on my Da, but I didn't listen to him. I roared, 'Tell me the number of the hospital, Mr Daly?' He kept at me, and then his wife came on all soft and still, and she paged through the directory and gave me the number. I could hear Mr Daly in the background, cursing me to some customer who said, 'He's a bastard of the highest order,' and this other woman shouted, 'you devil incarnate,' like she had gone up to the phone itself and roared. I just hung up the phone and repeated the hospital number to myself as I ran across to this store and got a pen to write the number down. Then I just walked around like a zombie and stopped myself from cryin, but just barely.

I worked on the courage to call the hospital, but I could hardly open my mouth to speak. When I did, it was to vomit in this alleyway. I retched up fear and loathing and despair, and I felt that my Ma was dead all right and that she was lost in Purgatory. St Peter said there was no way she was coming through the pearly gates, because she was the mother of me, and so she burned away in a pit of screaming penitents, howling her head off and despising me because I was holding her hostage in Purgatory.

But my Ma wasn't dead. I got through on the phone. It was late over there, past visiting hours. This old nun's voice was cranky as fuck, but when I said I was calling from America she softened up. She told me to call back in ten minutes, and they'd have a phone in my mother's room. When I called, my mother answered, and she was talking very low. She asked me what was wrong.

I said, 'I'm sorry for everything.' There was an echo in the phone, the cable stretching between two continents. I closed my eyes and tried to imagine her before the sickness, tried to think of her in her wedding dress in that photograph in the living room, but all I saw was that image of my Auntie Bridie in the hospital bed when she was withered up and nearly dead. My Ma laboured and breathed into the phone.

I said, 'Ma, do you remember when I was about three and you had me in for the Irish Dancing, and I was in there, and it wasn't going well at all, so I just packed it in, and out the door I went, and the police found me ten miles out the Dublin road, still running . . . Do you remember that, Ma? Wasn't that the way it was?'

I heard her breathing into the phone. She said, 'That's how it was all right, Liam.' Then the hard breathing again. I tried to stop myself from crying. She said I'd done a terrible thing to my Da about the ten thousand dollars. I could say nothing. I heard her voice break and come back again, like she was speaking to me from the grave.

'I'm tryin my best, Ma, I am.'

She said she loved me, but she said, 'Don't you come back here for nothin, do you hear me? Your future is over there . . . No matter what happens to me, I want you free of this place . . .'

'You're going to make it, Ma. I know you are.'

A nun's voice broke in on the conversation, and said, 'Will

you say a prayer with her now?' We said a Hail Mary slowly, the three of us, and the nun said, 'Are you saying the rosary?'

'I'm not,' I conceded.

'You should pray to our intercessor, Mary.'

My mother's breath was wheezing, but she managed, 'Sister, he took our Lady's name at his confirmation.'

The nun said simply, 'There is always guidance for those who honour the Blessed Mother.' She ended the phone call with a 'Father, Son, Holy Ghost,' and the line went dead. I wept until it was dark.

The wind sucked around me up at the campsite. I turned my good ear towards the rush of wind, heard the cry of animals and birds in the dark night. Then I put my palm to my good ear, and there was only the sound of my heart racing inside me. It was a strange lonely sound, the whole universe of stars up there in that cosmic coldness. It made me shiver and close my eyes. Then I took my hand away from the good ear and let the world fill my head again. I was damaged from everything, lost out here in the middle of nowhere. I was afraid to even try and go home. There was nothing but death waiting over there for me. I got into the car in a daze of nausea, stunned and silent. My mother was dying. I would never see her again. The realisation burned inside me. I caught deep sobs inside me and held them. Angel was curled up, but not sleeping, just there in her own purgatory of pregnancy. It may have been fate, but nothing came of the kidnapping or the man in the coma. Nothing was to bring this to an end, no tragedy, just a sullen deadness. We went on living, and the running took its course, but there was a sense of futility about everything now that it got cold. I felt a rawness at life, at its impartiality and how some men went unpunished for crimes and others suffered, and that was the way it was to be.

I got out of the car and was there near the fire, asking myself, 'Why the fuck does cancer run in families? Why are those born innocent going to die because of something in their blood? No matter if they live the life of a saint, they are going to suffer pain and shit blood in a hospital until they waste away to nothing, because it has all been pre-ordained. I mean, where the hell is the justice in hereditary illness?' Speaking to my mother only made me more bitter, more a head case. I'd been spending time thinking on what had fucked me really.

I got back into the car and turned and looked at Angel. 'Can I tell you something?' I said.

She was there, obscured like some tuber buried underground, a strange and humiliating pregnancy. She said, 'Sure.'

'You know them dreams I have?'

She nodded.

I didn't know where to begin, how to start. I said abruptly, 'I'm just trying to figure out what the fuck I did to deserve this.' I felt self-conscious, and I had no right to start into upsetting Angel, but I couldn't help myself. I said, 'Did I ever tell you about my cat? I know it sounds stupid, but that's where it all started, this downward spiral.'

She said, 'Your cat?'

'Yes, my cat. Well, here goes nothin, as they say. All right then. When I was a young fella, I had this grey cat. Now, at the time, I was into the choir and bein an altar boy and all that. I was under the sway of the good priests back home. I read about the lives of saints and all that, especially the miracles Jesus used to do for his friends. You know, the miracle of the loaves and fishes, turning water into wine, healing the lepers.'

Angel looked at me and smiled softly. Her hands were interlaced over her stomach.

'Anyway, things were going all right, and then one day my cat died of some illness. I was out with the dead cat in the shed. I was nearly ten years old, and I said, "Come on God, make the cat live." I mean, who cares if a cat rises from the dead? It's not going to change history or nothing. I gave God a few chances. I even went to school and said some prayers, and the class said a prayer for my cat. I didn't say anything about wanting a miracle to the teacher or anything. When I got home, the cat was still not of this world. So I spread my hands out over this box that I'd made as a coffin, and I said, "Arise, poor pussycat! Arise!" The cat was stiff as a starched shirt, and it didn't flinch or nothing. There was something coming out of its arse and its mouth. But I closed my eyes real hard, and I said the words again, spread my arms out, but no go on any resurrection. So, I must have gone a bit insane or something, and I got up and said, "Hey you, up there. Yes, you, Wanker God. I'm not arsing around down here! How about one of them miracles that come by so easy in the Bible?" No luck. I said, "Hey bollocks, how about the sweets money I saved and sent off to the Africans that you let starve? Yeah, you bollocks, how about my sweets money?" But no go, no sign, just silence. So I went inside, and my Ma had a tablecloth set, and there was my favourite tea for me, fish fingers, chips and beans and ice cream with wafers for dessert, and I ate the stuff in silence because my Ma had done something decent for me. I didn't taste any of it, though. Da gave me a sup of his Guinness, because I was always after him for a drink, but it tasted like ditch water. My Da said he'd bury the cat for me, but I wouldn't hear of it. I was still expecting the miracle. I knew the story of Job, who God put through these trials, and he passed them in the end and got into heaven.'

Angel unlaced her hands and looked into my eyes. I flinched and lost what I was saying. I had this lightheaded feeling of embarrassment. 'Go on,' she whispered.

'Well, I bargained down with God that all I wanted was a few minutes to say goodbye to the cat, but the cat was stone cold. Then, I only wanted her to lick my hand the way she did when she was alive, but she was hard. My Da came out and said rats might come around if we didn't bury her. I said to my Da I would be happy with a sign on the shed or somethin, some hint that she was up there in heaven. I covered her and left her in the shed overnight, and I thought about the way she was when she was alive, and I bawled my eyes out. It was the first thing that had ever died on me. The next morning, there was this scrawl on the wall above the box. It said, 'You'll never walk alone,' but I knew it was my Da's writing, because the cat wouldn't have said that.

'I buried the cat, went out after three days and dug her up, but there was no resurrection or nothing. She was flattened by the weight of the earth, and maggots were getting into her. I knew she was gone for good then. I was sad to see her dead.'

Angel leaned against me. I felt her warmth.

'I was off servin Mass a few days later and didn't give a fuck about religion. I was an atheist altar boy. I was in union with Satan. I went down the aisle and blew out the candles people had lit for the dyin and the sick. I saw Jesus on the Cross, and I said, "Morning, bollocks! How're those nails in your hands and feet?" I said, "Hail the King of all Cat Killers!" and then I went and saw St Therese and a few other saints, and I laid into them and called them every name in the book. And then I went into the sacristy and got ready for some fun with Mass. I wanted to really fuck up Mass. I didn't ring the bell when the host was raised, and the priest looked at me. But I didn't give a shite. When the priest gave out the communion, I held the gold plate under each granny's wattle throat and caught the crumbs of Christ's body, but when we turned to go back up to the tabernacle, I flicked the plate and let the body of Christ fall onto the carpet, and then I walked his flesh and blood into the red carpet, and I fully expected Hell to open up and swallow me, but it didn't. I did that for about a year, desecrating the body of Christ, blowing out the candles and snotting anywhere I could in the church. And then, one day, Father Keogh sees me wiping the crumbs off the plate, and he loses it. He took me aside after Mass, and he got to the bottom of the cat's death and my atheism. But instead of it turnin into a parable of forgiveness and reconciliation, Father Keogh beat the livin fuck out of me, and I never served a Mass again. He told me to forget about confession, because a sin like that was eternal damnation, no question about it. He called me "The Devil Incarnate"!'

Angel had her hand to her face. 'You was only a kid then. God knows that. Kids don't know what they're doin.'

'You don't think he's out to get me?'

'Are you sorry now?'

I shook my head. 'I don't know what I think any more. My mother's dying of cancer back home. I'm never going to see her again. You know what it's like to be banished from your own country?'

'Why can't you go back?'

''Cause it's not so simple, Angel. I snuck into America. If I go out, there's no coming back.'

'Maybe you could tell em about your mother?'

'There's no speakin to the American government. I'm an illegal, plain and straight.'

'How you ever going to get legal?'

'Get that scholarship. Or marry someone, and that's not likely.'

Sandy came back and said, 'What's goin on here?'

'Just speakin about the Resurrection and miracles is all,' Angel said.

Sandy said, 'You want to hear about miracles?' Angel said, 'Not really,' but Sandy said, 'Why don't you shut your face, Angel. That ain't funny.' Sandy touched me on the shoulder. 'Let me tell you this one. I read this about a year ago. This killer buys a pizza, and he takes it home, and he opens it, and he starts screamin, cause the face of Jesus is lookin up at him from the cheese. I mean, this guy just starts screamin he is sorry, and Jesus is just starin up at him, and he knows there ain't no escaping justice, and when the cops come he tells them he did this killin. He tells them Jesus is in his pizza. They had this picture in the paper of the pizza, and you could see Jesus in the pizza all right.'

Angel said, 'I don't believe that.'

'I saw the goddamn picture Angel. It was the face of Jesus all right, no mistake.'

I got out of the car and stretched and got into my gear. Angel lowered the window and said, 'You ain't a bad person.'

Sandy said, 'What the hell is that all about?'

I found it hard to maintain my body temperature with the running and with the shite clothes I had. I was already compromised with the heavy training, feeling the drain of constant exercise, and now the dampness sank into me and wrapped itself around my neck. I needed better food. Eggs and coffee weren't enough. I hated the starch of potatoes, but there was nothing else. I sat there peeling the skin and gouging the eyes out of potatoes and cooking them like some primitive man. I slept after the morning runs, which I didn't get done until nearly noon these days. Then I only came back to climb in the back with Angel and curl up and face the door and await the evening run. We went nowhere, did nothing. It was stark when you had no money, when immobility settled like a plague. Central Tennessee seemed to get further away with each day. Sometimes Angel leaned into me and put my hand on her stomach. I could feel the baby inside her. I wanted to tell her to forget what I'd said about God and all that stuff. I wanted to help her escape in the end.

I ran with a resolve of animal stubbornness, sheer exhaustion where I saw nothing except the blackness of some nihilism, and then I stopped and knew I was losing it, and I beat my chest and made grunting noises and wallowed in the kind of insanity that you might find at a mental home, but it was conscious. Maybe that is what the nutters say as well. Come to think of it, didn't the insane have voices speaking to them in their heads?

One day, we parked the car down at the doughnut shop for relief out of the rain. We went in to see Darlene and drink bottomless cups of coffee. Darlene had a bruise under her left eye, a glistening slit like she'd been cut. She didn't look at Sandy, and that's when I knew he'd hit her.

Sandy drummed his hands on the counter and made coughing sounds. 'Can we get a little service round here?'

Darlene ignored him.

Sandy said out loud, 'They call this the change of life.'

Darlene was taking an order at a table. She said nothing.

We were trapped, with the glass fogged and weary patrons getting edgy on caffeine. Angel brought in the hopper with her and left the jar on the table and watched it. People stared at it, and Sandy said, 'Don't make me want to kill that thing, you hear me, Angel? Jesus Christ, I hate those things.' Angel didn't say anything, and he just sighed and got up, said something in a whisper to Darlene and left for a while.

Darlene looked at Angel. 'What you see in him?'

Angel looked at me and then at the table.

Darlene turned away.

I waited for something like the sound of police sirens or gunfire to erupt, and I had a statement in my head about what I would say when the police came and took me away.

I spent the idle time looking at the hopper in the jar. I moved a blade of grass to its head. There was nothing as mysterious as its face, this minute alien contrived of such detail, with its huge black compound eyes and its eerie hideous tiny face of writhing feelers servicing the mouth, holding grass as it ingested it bit by bit. You had to ask yourself what order of universe could come up with such a creature. It represented a universal cold arbitrariness. It proved the non-existence of a God with any human sense of compassion. Fuck churches and altars and sacrifices and the rosary we used to pray back home for a good career and a happy death. Fuck it all, is all I had to say there in that doughnut shop with the soap operas playing in the background. It was better to believe in nothing and at least understand that I was alone. It wasn't even a melancholy realisation, just a fact of life.

Angel was watching the soap operas.

I said, 'You mind if I set him free?' I went over to the door and tapped on the jar. It was raining in sheets. The grasshopper remained in the jar, and I slapped on the glass with the heel of my palm until it fell and then caught itself in midair. Wings grew out of its back, and it disappeared into the greyness of the small town.

I went across to the bank and got more change. I didn't know what I was going to say. I just phoned up the hospital and asked if my Ma was a patient and they said she was.

'So she's still alive?'

The voice said, 'Excuse me, but we only have living patients here,' and then the voice said, 'That's not you, is it?' Oh Christ, it was Maura Connelly, who I'd gone to the pictures with a few times, from down the lane. 'So how it is over there in America?' she said to me.

I didn't know what to say, but the defences were down, and I said, 'I'm living like a tinker, to be honest with you, Maura. I'm living in this campsite with hillbillies. There's a chance I might be up for aggravated murder and an accessory to kidnapping. I'm trying to decide between the gas chamber or lethal injection.'

Maura laughed and didn't believe me. I was glad she didn't believe me. 'Go on with that. I always knew, despite everything, that you were going to make it. Your Da was in the other day, and I was telling him about how I used to ride my bike home from school some days, and how you'd come out of nowhere and start racing me and the other girls, and how you could run faster than we could cycle. You remember those times, don't you?' Thank fuck the phone started asking for money, because I didn't know how to end that conversation. The phone just went dead.

Good ol Maura Connelly, down at the hospital. Christ, what I wouldn't have given to be back home and have a decent start all over again, no more messing with Frankie Cooper and Eamon Bolger and getting mixed up with the robbing and the granny bashing. You could be sure that Maura was getting herself a decent wage at the hospital, living well and still going to the pictures with the lads. She was all right, not great looking, but on the level, sane and a great sense of humour, and fuck, let it be said, 'She could make a good cup of tae.' Jasus, I was becoming more like my ol man every day.

I was standing in the phone booth and just thinking, and then it came to me. I'd seen *Airplane* with her, and Jasus that was a hilarious film. It was the kind of film that made you fall out of the seat laughing. That was something I missed all right, having a watch of the ol films down at the Savoy, now that I thought about it. That, and getting a bag of chips and a fish and a big bottle of cider. I used to pool my money with the lads for cigarettes and a few bottles of cider, and we went down the lanes and got the girls drunk and played spin the bottle in the winter weekends, all huddled together and scared out of our minds, but in control, and just having a laugh, and closing my eyes, and feeling the secret lives of girls. It was those memories that hurt the most, the simple things, nothing big, just a normal life was all.

There was an eeriness to the transatlantic call, because you'd be speaking to them, and yet you couldn't go back home. It was like a seance with the past.

I met Sandy coming across the road. We went back into the doughnut shop, and he ordered a slice of cherry pie and split it with Angel.

Darlene poured more coffee. She said, 'You lay a hand on me again, I'll kill you, I swear it.' Then she just walked away.

Sandy just waited and stayed silent. Then he said real loud, 'You know, she shaves her pussy.' The other patrons turned and looked at Sandy and then at Darlene.

I just stared at the grapefruit halves with the red cherries behind a glass showcase, along with meringue pies and apple turnovers and miniature boxes of Corn Flakes and Shredded Wheat.

Sandy dug into the cherry pie.

And then Darlene drew a gun on Sandy in the booth. She pointed it at the back of his head. 'You asshole, take it back, what you said. Take it back!'

Sandy's mouth was red with cherry pie like he'd already been shot.

A man in an unbuttoned denim shirt said, 'Darlene. You got a boy to think about.'

Someone else said, 'Shoot him!'

'Take it back!' Darlene screamed.

Sandy kept his head still. 'Prove me a liar then. Let's see your pussy.'

Darlene's mascara ran down her face in two tearing streaks. She cocked the hammer. Sandy smiled and closed his eyes.

The man with the unbuttoned denim shirt got up and took the gun out of Darlene's hand, directed the barrel towards the ground and uncocked the hammer. Darlene ran into the back of the shop.

Sandy opened his eyes again with a look of shock, a kind of regret that he was still alive.

We left in the aftermath of silence. Sandy spent the rest of the day putting his index finger in the back of his head where there should have been a hole, going 'Pow! Pow! Pow!'

Salvation

The weather broke in an early afternoon of brilliant yellow, a
sharpness that gave me a headache. It was the kind of weather
that stung the life out of your body if you went out in it. 'How
bout that run then?' Sandy blew smoke off to the side in a thin
blue jet.

I didn't feel much like doing anything, thinking of my Ma
dying over there at home, and what was the point of going on
at all? Death would come in the end, and it was all obscurity,
and that was that. Central Tennessee, scholarship, no
scholarship, what the fuck did it matter? I was thinking
maybe they were more sane over in England or Australia. The
running had landed me in shite. I had to face the fact of the
matter now.

'Let's go!' Sandy said into my face, and I forced myself up
out of the seat. I was exhausted. We set off in the car for a
long stretch of unpaved country road. Sandy wanted a time
trial, something to give me some sense of pace. I could see
Sandy was assailed with sullen boredom. I warmed up and
came back and got into my shorts and put on my manky old
reformatory school shirt with the pale blue, well faded crest,
and laced up my shoes. I was thinking of Maura Connelly
again and chasing her home after school. I liked that life of
schoolboy ease. I was more like my Da than I let on. I just
wanted security and a little house and a bit of cash in the
pocket. That was all, really. I was pathetic, but that was it. I
knew my limits.

I got going on the run but felt like shite and wanted to end it
and sleep, but Sandy was smoking and staying pace with me,

the car burning oil again. Soon it would be dead, and where would we be then? Disaster skulked us. Sandy looked at me but said nothing, flicking ash out the window. The long vapid silence added to the gloom. I saw the apparition of Angel in the back looking at me. She lowered her window and said quietly, 'Remember, one day you'll look back on this, and it will make the future all the more special.'

I wanted to say, 'What future?'

Sandy turned his head and said, 'Angel, two open windows is one sure as hellfire way to get a goddamn cold.'

I was out on the last stretch of road, at about mile nine, when I came up on a pack of runners from the local high school labouring up the same hill. Sandy crawled by in the car, this hearse, with him, and Angel in the back, and the smoke making everything invisible. I ran beside the car, forced to keep pace so as to stay out of the smoke. We passed the pack without so much as a word said between us. The runners stood off to the side of the road and coughed as they were consumed by the smoke.

It was a long three-quarter-mile ascent into an obscurity of low clouds. Sandy flung an empty bottle of whiskey out the window. His eyes caught mine. 'You is good,' is all he said. The poor saps were down there, invisible in the smoke, bewildered.

At the top of the hill was the coach of the high school team, in his tracksuit and his stopwatch around his neck. Sandy pulled over and got out and started talking to the coach. The smoke from the oil dissipated, and up came the pack from down below, rising slow. Sandy read out my split and shouted, 'Let's hit the shower, Champ!' Then he burst out laughing. 'If there's one thing I hate, it's goddamn sports!'

The coach said, 'We got practice in session, if you don't mind,' and put some distance between himself and Sandy. He called down to his runners, 'Let's hustle!'

The runners were ragged and exhausted. The coach called out splits and tried to separate himself from Sandy, but Sandy started shouting loudly, 'Come on you worthless pieces of shit!'

The coach turned and pushed Sandy and said, 'You goddamn drunk!'

Sandy scoffed. 'I may be a goddamn drunk, but I got an athlete here that can kick your guys' asses any day of the week. I ain't training goddamn pussies. I'm willin to bet you a thousand bucks that my guy could kick the shit outta your so-called athletes!'

We were on the side of a mountain, obscured from the real world, a band of primitive creatures drawn back to a time of physical endurance. I looked at the runners and they stared at me, a snarling unease of physical antagonism. A fog filtered through the trees, and it was cold and rain unfolded in a soft mist. We were in this stalemate.

Angel shouted, 'You're bein stupid, Sandy. You come on now.' She put her head out the window of the car. 'We don't got that kind of money.'

Sandy turned and said, 'Shut it, Angel. The coaches is in conference.' He smiled at me and winked at the runners.

'What kind of race are you talking about?' A conspiracy of nods emerged. The coach was a heavyset balding fucker with a whistle and four watches hanging from his neck.

'How about a relay. That's right, a goddamn relay race. I'll bet you a thousand that my guy can beat your best three guys over three miles.'

I hesitated, 'Let's hang on a second here, Sandy.'

Sandy turned and looked at me. 'You ain't goin to tell me, after all the shit you put me through, that you want out?'

'You sayin they run a mile each, and he runs the whole three miles?' the coach said. He scratched his head and looked at his own runners. 'What do you guys think?'

'Make it your best five guys, and they each run a mile each,' I shouted. Sandy hesitated and looked at me, but I held up my hand with my fingers spread open and said, 'Five of them!'

'Okay then. So what do you say, you chicken shits?' Sandy really laid into the runners, but they said nothing. They were looking at me with this disdain, like I was a caveman or something. I was in the shite gear from the reformatory school, looking like a vagrant, with my hair long and wild. I had faint blotches from the burns in the summer. They showed in the mottle of red from the cold. I felt like a mutant, but it only hardened me against them. I was the outsider, the immigrant scraping to enter America, a cockroach from the motel back in New Jersey, something that survives. I was the personification of hard-fought longing, fear and loathing and determination, fed on rabbit and potato, bedded in a car, wanking into cold toilets, dreaming of a past long gone. I was a hard sight. I could see in the way they looked at me, with fear and disgust.

The rain began again, as it had earlier. The runners got into a small bus, like I had, back before all the shite with the granny and all that.

'You take care you chicken shits!' Sandy shouted and made a chicken noise and put his thumbs under his armpits and flapped his wings. 'You goddamn disgrace to bipeds!'

The coach stood there in the rain and wiped his face to a sheen of moisture. His face was pocked with acne scars. 'You got a goddamn loud mouth.' He looked like he was going to hit Sandy, but he didn't. The rain was really hammering, the sky invisible. 'I'm goin to take your goddamn money, asshole. You got yourself a goddamn race.'

Sandy extended his hand across the scratch of falling rain. He was soaked to the skin.

The coach didn't accept the hand. He said, 'So how am I going to get in touch with you?'

Sandy's face was red in the cold rain. 'You don't. I know where you are. I was thinking of something like Homecoming weekend. You got one of them, ain't you? This here fella is a goddamn international runner from Ireland, I'll have you know right now. I want a goddamn spectacle, you hear me?'

The rain was going like the hammers of hell down on them, and I got into the car.

The coach shook his head slowly and said, 'There ain't nothing I like better than taking a fool's money. If he's so goddamn great, how come he ain't on scholarship?'

This took the wind out of Sandy's sails. The coach left. The bus took off down the hill. Sandy got into the car. He was shivering, and the car reeked of menthol rub I'd used. He rubbed his hands together and said, 'You ain't going to prove me wrong, are you? You're on the level with me about this running, right?' He seemed anxious for a moment, the raindrops beading on his greasy face. His breath fogged, and he wiped the window. 'Maybe we got a way of making it after all.' Angel looked at Sandy. He said, 'Don't even start. If I didn't have your fat ass along, I wouldn't need to be involved in shit like this.' That settled her down into a slump.

Sandy looked at me and said, 'How bout you run back to camp. I'll get us dinner ready.'

He basically threw me out of the car. I ran an extra eight miles, long and slow, back to our camp, nearly twenty for the day. I was sick at this stage, laid out with the cold and no real food, the pang of hunger and exhaustion stalking me. The coffee had gone cold inside me. I went into the woods and squirted out this runny shite and began running again. It was already getting towards dark, the sun obscured in clouds. I felt that solitary existence of killing and eating and silence out in the mountains, the bewildering rains that drove the animals to the higher ground in a humiliation of cold. I thought of my ma dying and my da drinking and cursing my name, and I thought of that granny that I'd beaten up, and the cook back in New Jersey, and of that fuckup in the coma and the child that had been kidnapped, and I thought of my wanking and grinding the body of Christ into the carpet, and of the nights of slaughter down in New York, with the faces of immigrants dazed in the glare of brilliant fluorescent light, and the whine of blades cutting into bone, and the pink worms of meat coiling into cold fat sausage.

I was running through a nightmare. I stopped and called out Da's name. I stood there shaking, screaming his name. I could feel him in there inside my head. I saw him in the train station hut, waiting for the kettle to boil, hacking away with the coughing as usual. I stood there and watched him move slowly, lumber in a hunch with his fist at his chest and his tongue coming out of his mouth when the heavy coughing passed. I was looking at Da sitting there with the towel over his head, and it was a sorry sight. I said, 'Da, I'm on the comeback,' but he wasn't listening.

A few days passed of easy running. Sandy cooked me potatoes in their jackets, and I ate like a savage and tried to keep warm. A grim atavism overcame me. Survival was all that I thought about, hibernating against the cold. I could feel my heart inside me, pounding, and I listened to the static of dormancy, the crouching stillness of an animal waiting to strike.

Things were ending, a season of change that left only us and Bill and a few stragglers at the site. Even Bill Hayes conceded that his children needed better. He was sending them to live with his mother in South Carolina for the winter. It was pretty gloomy back at the trailer all right. Bill Hayes took his children to pick berries. They spent the day crushing berries, and his children were filling the jars, and Bill was sealing each jar with a rubber ring and a glass top.

Me and Sandy were walking around, and Sandy was happy as Larry because of the upcoming race. He told Bill Hayes about the race, and Bill shook my hand and said, 'See, shit pays off in the end, don't it?' And Sandy said, 'But don't it just. We got a thousand riding on this race, and that ain't figuring side wagers. I figure three thousand or more is what we're looking at, and that gets us clear down to Texas for a warm winter and all.'

'I didn't think you had that kind money?'

'Ain't sayin I have it now. I got that Darlene down at the doughnut shop. She takes the money to the drop safe at night. The way I figure it, we borrow the proceeds and make us a return on an investment.'

'You run that by her?'

'I got her round my finger, Bill.'

'You made up since she pulled the gun on you?' I said.

'Shit, that's old news. A woman like that can't afford to shoot no man. Change of life women is hard up for action.'

Bill Hayes said, 'Shit, that could be trouble, Sandy. Not

telling her you want to borrow that money.' He looked at me and shook his head.

'Jesus, Bill. I got her shaving her pussy for me. She's goin to give me that money, don't you worry none.'

We were all just standing around, and the ground was hard with frost. Bill was drinking whiskey. He had his gun in his other hand, and it was stained from the berries. It looked like dried blood. He tried to smile, but he had other things on his mind. I could see he hadn't reconciled giving up his children like that. It looked like one of them grim American situations where a father blows the heads off his wife and children and then himself and leaves the world wondering what the fuck went wrong.

Bill Hayes said, 'I want you to share a meal with us,' and it had a weird spirituality to it.

'It would be our pleasure,' Sandy smiled. Bill drank his whiskey, and they went off to kill something to eat. Sandy turned and said to me, 'You stay warm, you hear? You is my salvation.'

It was a decent evening, and Bill Hayes' kids were beautiful. They looked like their mother. They were quiet and soft spoken. They didn't cry or nothing. I watched Bill Hayes' wife, and someone like Maura Connelly was nothing compared to Bill Hayes' wife, because American women had a different kind of beauty, a sexual ravishment or abandonment where they gave themselves up to be fucked in hard embraces, or at least that was the way I was seeing them, that is, the ones I'd seen in America anyway. Bill Hayes' wife smiled at me, and I smiled back. Fuck, I was starved for her attention. I needed an anchor of human touch and not to be wanking myself off like a degenerate out in the shed.

Bill Hayes was helping his children with the preserves. They were spreading them over bread and smiling and eating. Bill Hayes and Sandy were fairly drunk, and, though you could still feel the mistrust, things had cooled off between them. Nothing had come of anything. Bill Hayes had been shitting bricks over the past weeks since the cop had come round, but he never let on to anyone, just remained stoic and waited. Looking at him there before me, I thought he was amazed that he had gotten away with beating that fuckup into a coma. There was this ease in him that I hadn't seen in ages. He proposed a toast to my race, which was fairly decent, and Sandy clinked his glass and knocked down a shot and said, 'Barkeep, pour me another!'

And then all hell broke loose. Bill Hayes' wife said, out of the blue, 'Bill thinks our kids is unnaturally small because I didn't have breasts big enough to feed em, ain't that right, Bill? Isn't that what you said? These kids is too small because I didn't let them drink my milk?'

The trailer seemed to clamp around us.

'I think what I said, if I remember correctly, is that I thought you took the kids off mother's milk too soon. That's how I remember it said.'

Bill Hayes' wife said, 'Okay, yeah, maybe it was like you said. But I don't like women with big breasts, and you know how you get big breasts, don't you?' She was looking at Angel, who lowered her head.

I felt sorry for Angel, because she was alone with her pregnancy and didn't know anything, and her breasts had become bigger than Bill Hayes' wife's. I could see poor Angel looking down at herself.

'Having kids suckin on your breasts is what makes them big and flabby. Maybe some men like women with flabby ol tits, but I want no part of flabby ol tits. Bill went with a woman with flabby tits, and he thinks there ain't nothing like em, cause Bill's mother is one fat ass with big ol tits, I might as well tell you, cause you're goin to be seeing her soon.'

'Now I don't remember sayin that at all. You got that wrong. And how bout leaving my mother out of this?' Bill Hayes showed his teeth in an irritated smile, but he didn't want any trouble. It was like with the fuckup, and now I knew what Bill Hayes was capable of, and so I waited. Bill Hayes went on about his business and helped his children spread more preserves. He wiped the jars clean and touched their heads and said, 'You're doing a fine job there. You give them other jars two weeks or so and you got yourself real preserves.' Bill used a pen and wrote the names of his children on each of the jars.

Bill Hayes' wife just wouldn't shut up. She said, 'I always say, if you're going to have flabby tits, you might as well go whole hog and get yourself a flabby ass. I mean, you gotta see Bill's first wife, Marsha. A goddamn fat ass that could black out the sun. And you know the funny thing? She kicked his ass out. Kept his kids, and that was that!'

Bill Hayes only hit his wife once, but it was enough to put a dent in the trailer door. A jar broke and poured its mush on the trailer floor like a wound opening up. Bill Hayes' kids caught their breaths and held them like they were going under for air. Bill Hayes led us all out of the trailer, all except his wife, out to the fire, which was going nicely. He poured coffee and hot cider, which he had gotten special for his children, because he knew they were going to do a good job with the preserves even before they had started.

Bill Hayes' wife threw Bill's clothes out onto the ground, and he clenched his fists until his knuckles turned white.

We were all sitting in the car the next morning, in the aftermath of a foul breakfast ruined by too much rain. We were watching for Bill Hayes' mother, and she came. She was a house all right, the kind of shed that could have housed the infant Bill Hayes. We didn't get out of the car or nothing, just watched things transpire through the window.

Bill Hayes' wife didn't weep as she sent her children off, because she didn't have any tears left. She was in shock. She ran after the car, putting her hand to the window, and the children did the same with their hands. Bill Hayes' wife was a fast runner. She had the body for running. She had long thin legs. I watched her follow the car. It was a sad parting. It reminded me of emigration.

Bill Hayes came over, and Sandy lowered the window, and Bill Hayes said, 'All things hole up for the winter, I figure, why not children?'

Sandy waited until things settled. He went out and spoke with Bill Hayes, who was staring into a spit cup like he was trying to read the leaves of tobacco. 'You want to get out of here for a while?' Sandy said.

Bill Hayes' wife came back from the road. She had this mark under her eye. She just went straight to the barrel and washed her face in defiance and then submerged her head for a long time. Bill Hayes just looked at her when she came up, but he said nothing, and she went into the trailer.

Sandy and Bill took Bill's car down out of the mountains. I knew they were going to get drunk. Sandy said, 'I might just go visit that coach and get things started. You get that run in, you hear?'

Bill Hayes' wife came and sat in the front of our car and blew her nose into a handkerchief and said she was leaving Bill. Her left eye was half closed. I felt a pang of longing just to hold her. She said the first two children weren't even his children, that they'd only met two years ago, when she was a waitress in Charleston. She said, 'Don't you see the way he favours his own boy? Ain't it as obvious as day?' To be honest, Bill Hayes was the same kind man to all of the children, and I said that to her.

Bill Hayes' wife had been drinking a lot, but she said, 'I appreciate honesty. Thank you. Maybe it's all in my head.' Bill Hayes' wife wore a tee-shirt and no bra. Her nipples showed. She leaned toward me, and I felt them against me, that small pressure of hardness. She kissed me on the side of the face and smiled. She said to Angel, 'Where'd you find this diamond in the rough anyway?' Her eyes and nose were red from crying, but she was really a beautiful woman, lean and long like a swan. She was the kind of girl I always wanted back home, the prettiness that doesn't need make-up or anything.

I got out of the car and walked around for a while. The day had dried up, and it wasn't a bad day at all. A wintry light filtered into the car. The clouds were flying through the sky, and the wind was strong. I went back to the car to get my running stuff, and to get away from trouble.

I was dazed, and the days had become a blur. I felt defeated. My mother was dying on another continent. I ran off, and Bill Hayes' wife came into my head, into that grey landscape of ghosts, among the roamings of my Da and his dog, in there where my mother lay dying. I felt myself unhinging, unable to keep things straight, lost in a world of past memories, abandoned among refugees. Bill Hayes' wife emerged, and I was thinking of her in one of them Catholic uniforms, the tartan skirt and the socks rolled down to her ankles and black shoes, the curve of her calves giving you a hint at the rest of her legs. I would have liked her to have been like that, to live at the end of my street back home with her Ma and Da and brothers and sisters. I'd have come around and kicked a ball near her house and done a few headers and juggled the ball to show her I was good at the sports.

Maybe I'd have kicked the ball through her window and gone on in to own up and say I'd pay for the window. I'd run by her coming home from school, wait for her to get out of school and lash by her, I mean really piss up the road, passing bikes and the milk van, and show that I was a flyer. If she took the bus into town, I'd race the bus, pretend I didn't see her or nothing, just race after the bus from stop to stop, gaining distance when the bus stopped, and then have it catch me, go even with it on the long hills into town, because that was the kind of shite I'd done back home with girls I was in love with. Fuck, where had time gone at all, the good old days back home. Even at the reformatory I got out and ran over by the housing estates and got myself a girl now and then, copping a feel down by the canal, getting into their knickers with my fingers was all, nothing else, but it was enough for the kind of life we stole from the reformatory, enough to get you through the shite dinner at night, enough for the night at the study halls where you stared into the books and saw the words and the numbers scramble themselves, enough for the late evening prayer where I prayed for my family and for my running.

It was a disquieting beauty Bill Hayes' wife and Angel shared, a smell of tired sadness that wanted to lie down and be held. It was making my head dizzy, the languid ease with which these women gave of themselves, the way they spread themselves apart for men. It wasn't disgusting or anything like perversion. It was simple life, the sort of thing that went on out at the Island Field by our housing estate, where the real gorgeous looking girls who went to the comprehensive school took their drink with Teddy Boys who came back from England for the holidays to drink and take the girls out to dances and dinners and then fuck them off out by the airport hotels or in the burnt-out old houses. Then the Teddy Boys fucked off back to England, and the gorgeous girls were pregnant and got the shite beaten out of them at home, but even when they were pregnant and we used to laugh and shout at them and call them fuckbags, they still had this way about them that you knew if you were the last man on earth they wouldn't do it with you.

When I got back, I heard Bill Hayes' wife saying, 'I swear I won't leave my babies.' Angel sat up and touched Bill Hayes' wife's hair. Then they saw me and wanted something to eat.

When we were eating, Angel said, 'He's gettin hisself a scholarship to college, ain't that right?' and I said, 'I am,' and felt self-conscious with the three of us all loaded into the car.

Bill Hayes' wife pushed her long hair behind her ear and tried to smile weakly and said, 'He hit me, that son of a bitch!' I just wanted to hold her. She smelt of tears, and her legs trembled. I saw a mark on her leg where he hit her. She saw me looking and let her eyes meet mine. I nearly died just being there with her like that. She said, 'It must be somethin to have a future,' and I felt special, and my head was dizzy.

Angel wiped the misty window. She spoke sedately. 'I got a past is all for now.'

I looked at her.

Angel said, 'Ain't anything ever come to any good with me and men. I been looked at since I was eleven, when I didn't even have no period or nothin. Men, they got that way of lookin at me.'

Bill Hayes' wife said, 'Amen to that.'

Angel said, 'He seen me back there. Right? I've known the bitterness of men these past years. I've tasted everything inside men when they come, felt men go small in my mouth, go small inside me down there. I swear to you, that's what's inside me. It ain't just his baby. It ain't one man's baby. It's all that stuff from them men growing in me . . .'

Bill Hayes' wife just looked at me. 'I been with a lot of men, too.'

I wanted to tell Bill Hayes' wife to shut her face.

Angel had her head down, speaking into her stomach like she was talking to her baby. 'The things I done for him . . . He said to me, "There is women who ain't women at all, but angels put on earth to ease men's pain." He gimme my name, "Angel. It ain't like sex really," is what he said. He'd say anything for a fix, sell me anywhere. While I sucked, he injected. His veins collapsed, and my insides opened up until I was as cut and raw as his arms.'

Bill Hayes' wife looked between Angel and me. She said, 'Jesus Christ. You plannin on leavin Sandy?'

Angel looked at me. 'I got a plan. You can't tell Sandy this, but I got my own money with me.'

I remembered the twenty she had given the salesman down at the supply store. Wind whistled outside in the coldness. It made the car rock slightly.

Angel said again, 'I'm trying to survive is all.' She looked at me. 'I want you to promise me something.'

I looked at her and nodded. She looked at Bill Hayes' wife and said, 'Is this a normal dream for a pregnant woman? I got this dream that I'm going to give birth here, in this car. You see, Sandy don't know it, but in his head he wants me and this baby to die.'

Bill Hayes' wife said, 'I dreamed I had a dog inside me when I was pregnant.'

Angel whispered, 'You told me that, Alice.'

I took hold of Angel's hand. 'You're not going to have that baby in the car, Angel.'

Angel shook her head. 'It just might happen, if you don't help me. See, I got this plan. When it's time, I'm going to get him away from me somehow, get him out of this car, and I want you to take me down into that town, where I can have my baby like I'm civilised and not some animal.'

I stayed still, felt her warmth close to me.

'Why don't you leave now?' Bill Hayes' wife whispered.

Angel said softly, 'What you waitin for, Alice? Your children is gone from you.' Then she took hold of Bill Hayes' wife's hand and said, 'I ain't tryin to be cruel. I'm sorry. I don't got the money for livin and havin this baby all at once. I got to wait until it's time.' Angel looked at me, 'You didn't answer my question. Will you take me down there when the time comes?'

'I will,' I said.

'I'll name him after you, if you want,' Angel said softly.

'You don't have to.' I looked away for a moment and then said, 'If it's a girl, my Ma's name is Kathleen?'

Bill Hayes' wife said, 'Why couldn't I have a man like him?' I felt a flush invade my face. It was the nicest thing anyone had said to me in literally years, but this wasn't about me and her, it was about Angel. I looked at Angel. 'There must be something better than this for you, Angel.'

'There is, but I got to get this baby born first. I got to get it out of me, and then men won't be afraid of me no more.'

Bill Hayes' wife looked out the window and whispered, 'It ain't that simple, Angel. It just ain't.'

'Maybe you could make us coffee or something?' Angel said, and I got out of the car. I made the coffee, and I was wondering just how long Sandy and Bill were going to be. I was breathing shallow breaths and looking at the road off out of the campsite. It was a strange feeling of longing I had for both of them. Each one had their own softness. Each one was more than I'd ever have hoped for back home, and look at the state of them here, abandoned like me. You had to ask yourself how people like that survived, and then I remembered. I was one of them really, existing on the periphery, in motels and campsites, scrounging out an existence on day-old doughnuts and cheap coffee, eating cold cans of beans, sleeping in a car.

I came back, and Bill Hayes' wife was saying, 'He's got a big dick, but he don't know what to do with it. He just sticks it in there, like he's checkin the oil in his car.'

It was the kind of thing I didn't need to hear. It made me sick. I looked at Angel and felt sorry for her. She smiled at me.

I left them and went off in the cold and walked around for a very long time and thought about how much I missed having a girl to hold. Even the reformatory days had their joy. Even back then I used to get them Love Heart sweets, and during the night prayer I'd go through the pack, until I found one that said 'Be Mine' or 'I Love You,' and keep them in my grey uniform trousers and wait for the time to fuck off over the wall and give it to some girl. But Bill Hayes' wife and Angel were other men's women, long gone from the stage that I was at, soft women who longed for love, women who had opened themselves up to love and childbirth. Sex was bound up with all sorts of eejits for them, dependence and fighting and abuse and screaming and regret. I didn't even let myself think about it now, but Angel had fucked anything and everything up there in New Jersey, she had been with that cook and had driven him demented with love or something. I'd seen them in that room on our last night, and who knows what she really would have done in the end.

I wanted to be with Bill Hayes' wife, even though she was a stupid fucker. She wasn't much older than me, really, maybe twenty or something. Fuck! I stopped on the road and turned and came back to the site, dragged by some unconscious yearning. It was a joyless walk of tired exhaustion and longing, and this was all shite, because I should have been thinking of the race and not have been letting myself catch a cold. I went into Bill Hayes' trailer and slept on damp blankets in the place where she slept, and I cried and thought of home and thought of her as living down the road from me again, and she had no children or nothing, and I wasn't going away from home, and because I had her I wasn't going to suffer any indignity, unemployment and all, because I would have her, and we'd be together by the fire, and we'd manage somehow, and maybe the running would work out back home, and I'd get myself a job based on my being pretty good at the running, the way the hurlers and the footballers in the town got to be bank clerks and agents with the insurance agencies.

I was cold, that sort of coldness that only human love can warm. I was in a trailer, a tinker's despair that nobody would believe back home. I mean, I said it plain out to Maura Connelly, and she laughed, because who would have ever believed it could be like this over here at all? I lay still, and the cold wrapped itself around the day. I felt the loss in the trailer, the silence of Bill Hayes' ruined family.

I got up, and it was a stark day of brilliant coldness of fogged breath. I made soup over the fire. Bill Hayes' wife said, 'We got some smoke jerky you can have.' I fed them again.

Angel was trying to figure out when she got pregnant. Bill Hayes' wife was counting months on her fingers, and she kept saying, 'No, it couldn't have been then.'

I was in the car again. It was a day of longing, there with Bill Hayes' wife looking vulnerable as hell, and her small breasts inches away from me, and her eye half shut, and that mark on her leg. I felt sick that I could be attracted to this sort of pain, that I could abandon the image of my mother dying. Bill Hayes' wife was talking utter shite. She said to Angel, 'You know you can comb hickeys out of your neck?' Then she said, 'Angel, this ain't goin to help this time, but there ain't no better contraception that shakin up a can of Coke and just poppin that lid right down there.' She pointed to her crotch. 'Coke kills sperm. You know that, right?'

Angel just smiled.

Bill Hayes' wife shrugged her shoulders. 'Hey, I been around enough. I'm just tellin you what I know to be true is all.'

I nodded like an eejit.

Angel smiled again. 'It kicks. You can feel it.' Bill Hayes' wife felt the stomach, and then she took my hand and put it on Angel's stomach. I felt the pulse of Angel's stomach, and then something kicked inside her. I smiled.

I couldn't see Angel's face when she said softly, 'I got a miracle of life inside me, but you know, I don't think there is a God.'

I ran late in the afternoon, out of boredom, and thought I was going to die. I had logged over twenty miles between the two runs. I had a chill in my back, and my legs ached. Only creatures of migration could understand the deadness of fatigue that settled and lived inside me. I was doing the training all wrong at this stage, too much useless distance with no balance of speed, no tempo runs, no system of peaking and tapering, just pure slogging at the miles. I came back down and got undressed and shivered in the trailer and looked for something warm to put on, when Bill Hayes' wife opened the door and saw me and stared. My penis was the size of a radish from the freezing cold. She came into the trailer, and the door closed softly. I moved crabwise by the jars of preserves and other provisions and wanted to say something, but nothing came out. I was bewildered, ashamed of myself, and embarrassed. Bill Hayes' wife turned off the light. The cooker pilot light whispered in the dark. I could feel her tongue on my fingers, sucking. I lay down. I felt her warmth press against me, ease me back against the damp bed. She put the comforter over us and settled herself beneath me and held me like that until I stopped shivering. She took hold of my hips and settled me slowly. 'I want you to fuck me.' I tasted the damp warmth of her armpits, kissed her softly, breathed fitfully. Tremors ran up my back. I kissed her swollen eye, tasted the blackish bruise. She put one of her breasts into my mouth, made me kiss each nipple. Her tongue moved slowly to meet mine in the wet darkness of her mouth. She guided me towards her, put a finger gently to my lips, impressed a still silence of mutual longing. She arched her back, and I felt a swooning sense of falling through the universe.

I understood why men will do anything for women, why wars are fought. I felt the heat of longing, the dormant sweat of Bill Hayes rise from the covers, smelt her there beneath me. I closed my eyes, and everything throbbed in that centre of dark wetness. I had found a home for my longing. I dug into her back, holding her.

After a few minutes, she moved me gently out of her. I

hesitated and felt her legs come around my waist, felt the arch of her feet on my hips, felt the dampness of her against my stomach. I stared into her eyes, and she drew me inward again. She tensed and held me, and her hand guided me. It took me a moment to realise fully what was happening. I felt the pressure, the seam of her insides giving in a slow tear, a slow warm descent, and I stopped, but it was what she wanted. She set me in motion again. I had been relegated to her arse. Her tongue became a slug in my mouth. I wanted to pull back, but she wouldn't let me. She put her mouth to my bad ear and gritted her teeth and forced herself into me and locked herself against me. She was saying something to me, but I heard nothing, just her tongue against my ear. I felt every inch of her insides around me, eating me, a sludge of darkness like original sin.

I stayed inside her and grew small, slipped from her, and nothing mattered. I turned into the wall of the trailer. She leaned into me and touched my neck. 'I can't afford to get pregnant,' she whispered.

I said nothing and felt the dirt down there on me, and I wanted to say, 'What the fuck is so wrong with me?' She traced her finger down my back, and I felt a surrender towards exhaustion and eased into sleep, closed my eyes. 'You gotta save Angel,' she whispered.

I said, 'I will.'

'Maybe you don't see it, but she loves you. You know that?'

Her breath was on my back. 'I don't want to steal you from her. She knows we're here together.'

I kept my eyes closed. I didn't really give a fuck if Bill Hayes came back. I was dazed, but, Christ, I wasn't long under when, nightmare of nightmares, on the horizon of sleep were two shadows convened in conversation. I moved toward the inevitable, and there was Da, speaking in earnest to Setanta. Setanta looked up and burst his sides laughin, and he lifted his tail to show that pink asterix of arse and wink at me. Da looked and said, 'Ah stop, and don't be cruel, Setanta,' but then he nearly broke his sides laughing.

Setanta raised and lowered the tail and kept grinning and winking and showing his pink arsehole. Fuck if I wasn't demented. Fuck if the sun back there all them months ago hadn't made me a head case.

Da put his hand to his mouth to stop himself, but he couldn't. He burst out laughing in snorts, until he got control of himself a few minutes later when Setanta stopped with the tail. He gave a shiver and caught his breath and took a look at Bill Hayes' wife. Thank fuck she wasn't under the siege I was under. Da said, 'Do you get a smell there, Setanta?' The dog grinned and said, 'You mean like shite?' Da said, 'Exactly. Like shite. Only dogs and Protestants would be at that game.' Setanta looked at Da, and then Da said, 'Sorry there, Setanta, not all dogs, yourself excluded of course. Let's say only Protestants and queers do be up to that sort of game.' He gave the dog a wink, and the dog winked back and raised the tail again, but Da said, 'That's all we'll have of that now. Too much of a good thing spoils it.'

Da turned his attention to me again. 'First time in the saddle and all, God love you. You'll be a sexual spastic from now on, mark my words. Ah, God love you. That reminds me of this recurring nightmare I have about playing first division English football, where one minute I'm Kevin Keegan on the ball, racing at this goal, and I'm listening for the cheers from the crowd, and suddenly there is nothing at all around, and I realise I'm playing fourth division English football for Carlisle F.C., and there's about three skinheads in the stands, and they're only there for a fight, and they don't give a fuck about the football or nothing. Shocking revelation, son, the passing of our professional football dreams . . . But where were we anyways?' Da scratched his head and said, 'Ah yes, tell me, have you heard tell of the commandments by chance, the "Thou shalt not covet another man's wife" commandment and the "Thou shalt not steal" commandment? You know, we're talking major sin here, son, not to mention, "Thou shalt not kill", because who the hell knows how things ended back up at the motel, a man bleeding like that? We're not talking three Hail Marys and an Our Father here, now are we bollocks? God, but it must be grand to make a complete fuck of the commandments. How about "Honour thy father and mother?" And how about "Thou shalt not lead thy old man on a wild goose chase for ten thousand pounds"? What the fuck are you trying to do at all, put the icing on the commandments, not only coveting other men's wives but sticking it up arses into the bargain, if you don't mind. Sodom and Gomorrah is where you should have gone. You'd have gotten in, no bother at all, no visa required for anyone who is a major bollocks of your calibre.'

Da brought his fist to my face, and he dislodged his front tooth the way he did when he was royally pissed off, and the whole plate of spittle and tooth snapped at me. 'I can safely say now that you are, without a doubt, the biggest bollocks that ever walked the planet. Do you know that me and him walked the streets of the town, in and out of post offices and banks, day in and day out, until that poor dog's paws bled from the walking we did. We badgered the fuck out of bank managers and told them to check at the central bank and the international banks. I wanted my money, and I was prepared to tear the place apart if they didn't find it, because it was there, and somebody had the money. And not a sign of the alleged ten thousand pounds, as if I shouldn't have known all along, but I said to myself, "Could I have the biggest bollocks on planet Earth who would take it upon himself to actually call across the continents, across the Atlantic Ocean, where our ancestors drowned and died in an effort to save themselves from poverty, from famine and death. Would a bollocks be so hard as to scam his own Da, to feed a phone box to set his own Da astray like that?" I gave you the benefit of the doubt, because we are a nation of mourners. The dirge of emigrant songs haunt us at night. They are our collective unconscious, our guilt and reconciliation, and I said, "No way, no way," what with the stationmaster singing your praises and commending your return to the fold and the sincerity in your voice. Didn't I have to buy drink for anybody and everybody, because everybody was saying, "I've heard your boat has come in, so I have," and so it was, drinks on yours truly, while I was off at the post office and at the bank, roaring my head off, and the poor dog in no fit condition for walking, soldiering on beside me. Jesus! I think you are the greatest bastard that ever was born. There was no money in the end. The bill was sent up from the pub, and I went down there with a cashed-in Life Assurance Policy, a meagre pittance after early withdrawl. I set it down on the counter and paid up, and nobody was the wiser. Your infamy is secure with me and the good Lord, bollocks. You caught me out, you did, from a continent away. I concede to your evil genius.' With that, Da gave a bow and pitched over and roared.

Setanta licked the tears from Da's eyes and said, 'You evil genius.'

I don't know how I got out of that trailer at all, but I managed for my trousers and socks and the shoes and got out of there and walked around in the cold. Everywhere Da came out of the dark and swung at me, massively drunk. I went and sat beside the fire in the deck chair, shaking and knowing that there was something wrong with me. I could hardly move, shaking and looking back at the trailer. Fuck if I couldn't get her out of my mind either, and that soft burn of penetration, like a seal of mortal sin, and my mickey stained with her arse, no doubt the colour of a lifetime smoker's finger.

It was dead dark when Sandy and Bill came home, polluted. I watched Bill Hayes' wife go and hold Bill. Sandy staggered over and opened the car door, got in and slammed it closed. When everything settled, I opened my door slowly and leaned in. Angel was staring at me. The car was filled with an intoxication of alcohol. She took my hand to her face and smiled obliquely and said, 'You're too hard on yourself.' I took my hand away and went and got out of my clothes. I stood and shivered and washed the spunk all off me in the freezing shower by the toilets, and my Da just stood there and put his hand to his head and shook it and said, 'I never understood you. I never did, and I never will.' Then he turned and walked into the woods and disappeared into the dark. I shouted after him, 'Da, wait! I got this race that's going to save me!' but he was gone.

Surveillance

The following morning was one of those mornings of cruel finality, when you ask yourself, what is the point of living, and then you realise just how hard it is to come up with a way to die without the possibility of pain or botching things up.

I paged through my running log, trying to piece together my training, but mostly just trying to forget things. The coffee was a cold tar mixture, and the eggs never boiled at all. When I cracked one open, it poured out its sticky contents all over my trouser leg like sticky spunk. I wanted to scream, but it was restraint and fear that held me. Bill Hayes had been shouting through the night. He threw his wife's clothes out into the mud and slammed closed his trailer door. I could see her sobbing, and I thought that maybe she had told him about me. What comes out of the arse after you do it, stains or something, and Jasus he'd know what the hell was what. I watched her go and get into one of the old cars, and she didn't look at me. I braced for some attack. Soon afterwards, Bill came out in his long johns and boots, and, though he looked at me, it wasn't with anger, but with the jaded face of a man who feels lost. He said, 'Let me in, Alice. Honey, please.' It was like the wolf at the door of the three little pigs, 'Let me in by the hair on my chinny chin chin!' He looked hideous. I watched him get into the car. It began to rock and made a squeaking noise. He was screwing the shite out of her, suffocating her with his massive weight, that big incompetent mickey of his between her legs. Everywhere I looked I saw the colour of sperm in the melt of sleet.

Sandy and me went up to get the traps through a slosh of

muddy water and fresh snow, the sky rolling fast in an embankment of clouds. The river had become swollen. With each step, the ground sucked at our shoes, the dirt oozing over our ankles.

We were on our way down with one big rabbit when Sandy said, 'I ain't got but forty dollars left. That's about enough gas money to get us halfways to goddamn nowhere,' and he left it at that, saying, 'I'm looking to this race to save us. You been hitting the road these months, and now you got to come through for us and for yourself.'

'You don't have to worry,' I said, and we went down the hill.

Back at the campsite Sandy said, 'Why don't you do the honours with this rabbit.' He set down a big pot of water and started the fire, but the wood was wet and it died. He went over to the car where Bill Hayes and his wife were holed up. He said, 'We don't got no fire, Bill. If and when you get finished, I could use the help,' and then he set off to the toilet.

Bill Hayes came over with his acetylene torch to help us with the fire. He was in the long johns, and the buttons were undone to the waist. He took his beard and gathered it and put it into a rubber band he had around his wrist. He pointed the finger of blue flame into the wood and studied it intently, like he was doing invisible welding. He didn't look at me, but he said, 'You give me one good reason why I shouldn't beat you till you piss blood?' I looked up at him and said, 'I'm only one half of your problem, Bill,' and just kept staring at him. 'I hope you aren't planning on beating me into a coma like you did to that fella.' He never made eye contact and stayed still until the wood reddened and ignited into flame. His teeth emerged from his beard as he rose and straightened himself. He smelt of sweat and whiskey.

Sandy broke the stalemate when he came from the toilet. 'Bill, I think I owe you a beer or two.' He went to the car and took out a six pack, and the two of them went off to the trailer.

There were so many things to be done, all useless things that occupied the day. Angel watched me from the back of the car, wiping away the moisture, and it was like she was waving to me. There was no heat in the day, but it was a brilliant cold light that hurt my eyes. My eyes were watering from onions. I had a fork between my teeth. It was supposed to stop the tearing, but it didn't. I set the fork down and sniffled and spat and used the back of my hands to dry my eyes. I could hear Sandy and Bill laughing in the background. It was only ten o'clock in the morning, and it seemed we'd been awake for days. Sandy was fast on getting drunk again. I looked at the shadow figures of him and Bill sitting by a window in the trailer with their heads only feet apart, leaning into discussion. I knew we didn't need the complicity of anybody else right then, especially with what Sandy was planning.

Bill Hayes' wife got out of her car. She went off to the toilet, and then she washed in the rainwater and got back in the car and tried to start the engine, but it wouldn't catch. It hacked like someone coughing. Bill Hayes looked out the window and came to the door, and he shouted, 'Don't make me beat you!' I was afraid to look at him. I understood the quietness of his children. Bill Hayes was a big man.

I just got into the back of the car, into the makeshift bed, and slept. I awoke and Bill Hayes was working on starting the trailer, without success. I got out of the car and skulked around the place, keeping away from him.

Bill Hayes' wife was folding the blankets from the broken down cars. She had on make-up, and her hair was tied up in a bun. She said to Angel, 'We're going to get our babies.' She went over to Angel and took her hand and said, 'You can have that rainwater, Angel. I want you to have it.'

I lingered for a few moments. I had cut the gore out of the rabbit, the compact jelly mess shining in the mud. A bird stood in officious doom. I watched the bird paint its black face in the sanguine gore. It withdrew its head in sticky strands of mucus, cawed in alertness and excitement, hopping tentatively around the guts, watching my advance.

I didn't say anything at all. I just left on the road and ran slow and long, the kind of running I didn't need before a race, but I had to get away from them. Time was going like that slow cancer inside my Ma, a sullen grey creeping toward death. I was frozen and exhausted. When I got back, Bill Hayes and his wife were gone. Sandy was cooking something on the stove inside Bill Hayes' trailer. He handed me a tin of condensed milk, and I drank its sweet heaviness.

'Okay then. I need help with Angel. We might as well move her over here.'

Moving Angel was like repotting a plant, but we got her moved into Bill Hayes' bed. Lifting her, I saw that her ankles had become really swollen. They looked like they needed draining, the way my Da used to apply a bread poultice to draw out infection. They had that bloated sweatiness of infection. Sandy saw it, too, and just made a face that said I was to say nothing.

Sandy brought soup to the boil and poured it into three bowls. I sat at the small table in the trailer and ate. Angel said, 'I don't feel hungry right now,' but Sandy said, 'Shit, you ain't eating just for yourself. You eat this now. Come on Angel.'

Sandy opened a tin of peaches he found in the cupboard and showed them to Angel and said, 'How bout dessert?'

Angel just looked glumly into her bowl of soup.

'We're out of the woods, Angel. Don't you understand? We're in the clear with him running. This is the break we've been waiting for. I been eyeing this here trailer all this time, and it just falls into our lap, just like that, not that I didn't put a word in to make Bill feel guilty and all. Shit, he just about broke down crying down in the town. I got him good is all.'

Angel had black cavities for eyes, ghastly looking, now that she was out of the confines of the car, now that you could get a sense of perspective. 'You ain't ever to bet with money you can't afford to lose. You ever hear that said, Sandy?'

'Hogwash!' Sandy said and touched Angel on the forehead. 'Maybe crankiness just comes with the territory.' He winked at me, trying to draw me into the discussion, but I said nothing.

With that, Angel turned into the thin wall of the trailer.

The trailer seemed huge compared to the car. Sandy took the bowl of soup away. The propane heater glowed in a crown of blue flame. I smelt its sweetness. We sat looking at one another. Sandy said, 'You want to read what that says?'

It was a note Bill Hayes had left. I looked at it and read it slowly: 'There ain't no point telling you not to break in here, because I know you will. That ain't a judgment. It's a fact. I've always abided by common decency. I don't begrudge no man from taking what he needs. Take what you need, and leave the rest as you found it. I don't want to have to go and kill you, Sandy! Bill Hayes and family.'

Sandy laughed. 'I got a good mind to burn the goddamn trailer to the ground. Where the hell does he get off riding his high horse, "That ain't a judgment. It's a fact." He wants a fact? I'll give him a fact. Fact is, I might just burn this trailer to the goddamn ground.'

We shared the canned peaches. Sandy set some aside for Angel. He was still pissed at Bill Hayes and the note, and there was no getting him off that point. He looked at me and said, 'Sandy Bridges is a malignancy, and if I serve one purpose it this world, it may only be to say, "Keep your goddamn doors locked, cause I am out there, waiting for opportunity." Bill Hayes deserves to have his place turned inside out, and I'd be doing him a favour if I decide when I'm through here not to burn this goddamn place.'

I looked at him. 'Sandy, you broke in.'

'Just shut it, you hear?! We got other things to discuss, like surviving. Now listen up. We got two weeks before Homecoming. I asked this man that just come for the weekend over there, and he knows when they have their Homecoming, and it's big here in this town.'

I slurped the thick peach juice and listened and felt the tremor of exercise in my hamstrings. I was on for a strange race, against a pack of Americans. I looked up at Sandy and said, 'What's Homecoming?'

Sandy stopped with his spoon in mid-air and dropped it. 'You're shitting me, right?' Then he burst out laughing. 'Oh my sweet Jesus. Ain't you in for a goddamn treat.' I put my spoon down on the table and just stared at him blankly. He laughed until his eyes were wet. He got up and said to Angel,

'Honey, what's Homecoming? Jesus, if that don't beat all to hell.' He was screaming laughing. He mimicked my voice and said, 'What's Homecoming, Sandy?' He went out of the trailer and off in the direction of the man who had told him about the Homecoming. He was cooking something over a fire. Sandy said, 'Have you ever heard of such ignorance in all your born days? He wants to know what Homecoming is. Jesus H. Christ. Homecoming. I ask you, sweet Jesus . . .'

'Who wants to know?' the man said.

'My runner, that Irish guy I been telling you about.'

Angel lay out on the bed, quiet, but she said, 'You don't really think I'm going to let him do this?'

'Why not?' I said.

She looked at me and whispered, 'Vanity of vanities, you're going to ruin us. I can feel it. Maybe we should take that money now and just get out of here before it's too late.'

And so began our surveillance of the cross-country team for the next two weeks. Sandy became a commando, stalking the hills above the high school track, putting a watch on the different runners. He conceded that I knew what was what, since the fourth and fifth runners were useless, and that was where we were going to win the money, the loose links in the chain.

It was a glorious afternoon of sunshine, and the weather had warmed up. We were wedged in on the side of this hill on this escarpment of rock, looking down on creation, as the song says. It was the only way to get an accurate sense of what the fuck I was up against. Sandy was dead keen on getting all sorts of times down on the runners. We were awaiting the cross-country team's illustrious appearance on the track, so we could catch their speed on the quarter mile around the track. 'Where the fuck are they,' is all I had to say. Sandy assured me he had found out that Tuesday was track workout day.

In the meantime, we hung around, and Sandy was at the drinking and smoking pot he'd got from up in Bill Hayes' trailer. He had this little pipe he kept putting to his mouth. I stood there rubbing my hands together, because it was on the cold side if you didn't stay in the sun, but at least it was dry, and now we had Bill Hayes' trailer and a bit of decent living space.

I was there sitting on a rock, watching the proceedings below, this expanse of playing fields and armies of sports teams doing this and that. It was a bit of a laugh all right, the spying part. To tell the truth, I'd never seen such a collection of palsied stupid fucks in all my born days. America succeeded by sheer numbers, by its size, because on a one-on-one basis, there they were, total eejits that couldn't catch balls thrown into their chests, quarterbacks that couldn't throw with any accuracy, underthrowing, overthrowing until it just made me want to go on down there and tell them to go the fuck home. They looked like spacemen down there in their helmets, doing push-ups and sit-ups and running backwards and then forwards, and still, for the most part, they looked like absolute shite. Now, I might not have been the man to comment on the American football, because who knows what goes on in that game, but Jasus Christ almighty, I had to laugh at the state of the kicking game. I'm talking about poor fucks that couldn't kick a ball twenty yards with any accuracy, and, if one kick managed to get itself over the bar, the hoots and the hand slapping and hugging was pathetic. I could have got a couple of lads from the Limerick Regional Rehab Centre out in wheelchairs, and they'd have done a better job. I said to Sandy, 'Hey Sandy, why don't we fuck the running, and let's see who can kick a ball down there?'

Sandy came over red-eyed and smiling. He looked at me, and then at some poor fuck attempting a field goal. He seemed like he had to focus, because his head seemed to tilt like it was going to fall off. 'Maybe you don't get it, but this country was built by hands.' His eyebrows arched, 'That's right my friend. Hands!'

I interrupted him and said, 'Wait till you see this shite, Sandy. Down there. That fat eejit about to go for a field goal.'

This stupid fucker in a helmet ran and sent a wobbly

banana kick that went way left and didn't come near going over the bar, and then the kicker came and conferred with the stupid bolloxes spotting the ball about wind direction or some shite like that.

'Proves my point exactly, don't it?' Sandy said and inhaled more smoke and held it and then exploded in a rush of air ages later, like a man come up from the depths of the sea. His voice had a raspiness from all this breath-holding business. He leaned into me and said, 'We got football, basketball, baseball, all-American sports played with eye-hand co-ordination, cause that's what built this nation, not running your goddamn ass off around no field, not kickin goddamn balls from here to there. I don't even think of running as a sport in any real sense, or goddamn soccer for that matter, cause the legs ain't got nothin to do with the advancement of the human species.'

'What are you talkin about? Didn't we have to outrun what was chasing us back down there in Africa?'

Sandy put his hand on my shoulder, and then he put his hand in front of my face and wiggled his thumb. 'I would like to introduce you to the opposable thumb. Opposable thumb, meet the biggest dumbshit in the world. Biggest dumbshit in the world, meet the opposable thumb. Oh, I see you don't know about the opposable thumb, then. Well, let me explain this, dumbshit. The opposable thumb is what got us out of the goddamn trees. It's what let us make tools and build shelter and get out of the goddamn cold. It wasn't our legs that did it, cause we ain't shit when it comes to speed. We didn't outrun no goddamn tigers down there in Africa. No sir, we trapped those motherfuckers and ate them with our hands.'

I really hated the bollocks. I had a good mind to say, 'Fuck off then, and that's me out of here, fuckface. Go fuck yourself and your girlfriend, because you are nothin but total shite, a drug addict loser who is going to end up getting his arse ripped to shreds in some American prison,' but all I said was, 'I never thought of the eye-hand thing before. Interesting point, Sandy. Point well taken, Sandy,' and, fuck, did I taste the bile of profound hatred. It reminded me of the kind of hatred I had for Da through the years when he laid the law down at home and hit the head off us if we said shite.

But you know what, Sandy was right about the running thing. The fucker wouldn't let it go. He saw through me all right, because I was pretty red in the face, and I stubbed my toe in the ground the way I did when I was on for a fight. 'Let me tell you something, shit for brains. You don't know shit about this country. If it wasn't for me, you'd be back in that goddamn motel, gettin used by that guy that come calling for you every night and taking you off to work. If and seeing you're so goddamn smart, why the hell ain't you in some fancy college with your scholarship, like that coach said? Don't give me shit about something going wrong where you come from. I ain't buyin that shit here. I know what I'm dealing with. I'm dealing with a goddamn piece of goddamn human wreckage, that's what I'm lookin at. I ain't stupid, you hear! And don't think we came upon them runners by chance, because it was no chance but Sandy Bridges himself who thought of tracking their asses down for this race.' He had shouted everything. His face was a flame of red. He roared again into my face, 'Shit, I just don't know any more!'

A whistle blew down on the grounds of the high school. People were looking up into the mountains, unable to pick out where the yelling had come from, and then they resumed their games. I looked between the break in the bushes and watched the players look away from the mountain and gather in a huddle and then break and fan out across the field. Four fat coaches conferred on the sidelines.

Sandy went up out of the bushes and onto the road, and I thought he was going to leave, and that would have been that. Maybe I'd just walk on down there among the players and just stand in the field like a gombeen man and wait for the law to come along, and who knows how the hell they really threw you out of the country. I should have found out, I suppose, back home if they had the right to fuck you in jail and then deport you, or if they could only deport you, and, if they did, who had to shell out the money? Maybe they kept you in jail until the money was sent over, and then they kicked you out, because I couldn't really see how the fuck they'd see you off on Aer Lingus and let you have a nice flight, courtesy of the American government. Maybe the Irish government got stuck with the bill. Either way, if that was going to be the case, I'd my mind made up. I was going to drink myself into a coma on duty-free whiskey and become a national disgrace and poster-boy for emigrant rights or something. Maybe I'd wake up out of the coma and be totally fucked with loss of the right side of my body or something, and I'd be jerking and squinting and talking out of the corner of my mouth and snorting and telling my story on *The Late Late Show*, and Gay Byrne would be looking at me and sayin, 'And now let's hear from the Mammy.' And I'd say, 'Gay, the Mammy is no longer of this earth,' and Gay would make a cathedral of prayer with his two hands to his face and make some face of absolute piety, and then they would put up the relief fund number where proceeds were being held by the Bank of Ireland on my behalf. I'd let this snot hang out of my nose and make that rocking motion of a poor ol spastic until there was enough money for a colour telly and a record player. At least there'd be some security in the job as Ireland's leading prodigal emigrant fuck-up. I'd be up for all sorts of government schemes for free medicine, a house, no doubt, and free on the buses and the trains.

Sandy wasn't gone at all. He was only up refilling the weed in his pipe. The fucker was unflappable when he was on the weed. Down he came with that glazed look of drug inducement. He said, 'Maybe it's time we had us a talk about American sports, what they mean. I think it my civic duty to speak to you on behalf of the sporting conscience of this nation and tell you, a prospective college athlete, what the hell it's all about.' He had that congenial smile and kept up with the voice of a sporting announcer. 'Ladies and gentle-men, if you will direct your attention please . . .' and then he burst out laughing and said, 'Come on . . . Shit, if that ain't funny, come on . . .'

It was a laugh all right. Fuck, if you couldn't have a laugh, you were fucked, so I said, 'I suppose I don't know shite about anything.'

Sandy took the joint to his mouth and inhaled deep so his incisors showed, and he held the smoke until he looked like he was going to burst, and then he let it all out in a rush of air. I became a docile pawn again, and we went down the mountainside, followed along an animal trail until we were still high up, but close enough that we could actually see the expression on the athletes' faces. Some eejit got ready to kick a ball, and Sandy was shaking his head. 'Watch this now, cause I know you're going to go wild.' Sandy licked his finger and pretended he was checking the wind and said, 'Left of centre, going wide and short,' and this might have been the world's worst kick, because the stupid bollocks kicked a rut, and the ball went nowhere, and the stupid fuck hopped around holding his foot.

' "A disgrace," go on and say it,' Sandy said, 'cause in part you're goddamn right. That asshole don't know what the hell he's doin. But you see, that ain't the point here at all.' Sandy inhaled again and waited while the next fuckup misfired a kick and made Sandy snort and cough in a fit and hold my arm and splutter, 'Don't even say nothin. Jesus, this is even getting to me.' His eyes were filled with tears from laughing and the drugs.

We were just standing there behind the bushes, looking like two field marshals surveying their handiwork.

'Okay then.' Sandy spat and cleared his throat. 'You gotta have losers in any society. Ain't everybody going to play first string, ain't everyone going to catch the winning touchdown. No sir. That's a fact of life, and it ain't no secret, so why does some asshole come out here then, if he don't got a chance?' He looked at me and smiled and said, 'I ain't asking for an answer. I'll tell you why. We got us what we call "Participation Awards" like they was comin out of our asses. If you want to go to college, you better have played some goddamn sports, you better have got your ass out there, even if it was only to get it kicked up and down the goddamn field every day, cause when it comes to where the hell you go to college, you'd better have put in your time on the field. You'd better have taken the hits, cause an admissions counsellor is going to be looking over all the shit you've done, and he don't give a damn if you were all-league, or all-county, cause they got places for niggers who can actually throw balls and kick balls and bounce balls and run like goddamn hares. What they is look for is how you let yourself be humiliated. They like that. They get a good feeling that they ain't going to have no riot on their campus, because they already know you're the kind of herd pussy who lets the coach drill him, the kind of kid that drops and gives a coach twenty without saying a word, the kind of kid that goes home and learns play action fakes and options from the coach's playbook, the kind of kid that ain't going to make a deal with the next town over and sell the goddamn playbook. You see where I'm goin with this? You ain't done shit for the team all year, right, but when it comes to giving out awards, they're going to have to say, in a matter of words, "Okay, so we had three niggers here that deserve awards. They done caught the balls and put them in the end zone, they stuffed the balls into the hoops. So here are your goddamn trophies niggers. Now fuck off. But now, ladies and gentlemen, if I may direct your attention to what we are really honouring here this evening, let us, without further adieu, give you what you have all been waiting for this evening. Yes, let's get down to what really counts." And out comes this table of trophies as big as goddamn houses for "Most Improved," "Best Attitude," "Best Team Spirit." And the coach, he just about weeps, and he hugs his guys and says, "I asked for one hundred per cent, and they came and gave me one hundred and ten," and the guys pump their fists in the air and say, "We are number one," or some shit like that, even if they got their candy asses whooped all season, and it goes on down the line all night at the awards banquet. Varsity, first string, second string, Junior Varsity, right down the goddamn line until the towel boy shuffles up and says he's just glad he had the opportunity to pick up the goddamn jock straps.'

There was really nothing you could say to that, except to say that Sandy was an exquisite racist.

There was no sign of the cross-country team. 'I don't think those fuckers are coming, Sandy.'

Sandy was gone back up by the car. He began coughing in a fit and leaned on the car.

Sandy's voice was still ringing in my good ear. It was like when you get a slap, and there's this sting and stunned sensation, and you don't know what the fuck to do. I felt lonely and sad and stupid for what I'd done in the past. I wanted to get away, and still I stayed, because I didn't have anywhere to go. It was as simple as that, and maybe more. Who knows? I saw Sandy as some freakish version of myself, a know-it-all who was right most of the time, but what was the point of knowing the truth? What was the point of saying the obvious, because it didn't do shite for you. All it did was make you a nutter, and you got a chip on your shoulder and began mouthing your philosophy on life, like anyone gave a fuck, because all the people I've ever known who actually made it never had shite to say about anything at all. They just got down to the business of living and living well.

I sat on a rock and thought of poor Angel, left for most of the day now that we had some place to stow her up at the trailer. I felt something bad was going to happen. I could feel it, and what about my promise to her to get her to a hospital in time? Anything could happen up there to her. It was criminal to leave a girl like that up where she was alone with no hope of escape if something happened.

Sound travelled a great distance in the cold, and I could hear the hit of helmets, hear the voices speaking. Sandy came down and looked at me. 'Maybe you just want to run up home. I got some business I gotta take care of, all right?'

I looked up at him and said, 'How are you going to get a thousand dollars to put up for your side of the bargain?'

Sandy looked down at me from the road. 'If anybody asks you somethin, you and me was here all afternoon, you hear?'

I nodded, and he started the car and drove away slowly.

My hands were cold, and my feet had a dull sensation of pins and needles from being in one position too long. I got up and jogged on the spot, and then something caught my eye. A swarm of girls came pouring out on the track from the gym. Jesus Christ, it was a pack of cheerleaders outfitted like I'd seen once about the Dallas Cowboys on the telly. They were in black and red outfits with short skirts, and they were wearing leggings and these fuzzy things on their shoes. It was getting towards evening, and the football players were standing around with the coaches, and you could tell the day was coming to an end. I went down further towards the field. I might as well have died and gone to heaven. If there was ever a time I wanted the lads from the reformatory here, it was for a look at this shite. Christ almighty, to think of the pandemonium that would have erupted back at the reformatory if, on our inter-city rival hurling day, the girls from the convent schools hiked up their knickers and proceeded to spread their legs and climb on each other's backs into pyramids, and mount and dismount in a flurry of acrobatic moves, and form the letters of our school, and then do a few cartwheels across the pitch, and throw the small girls into the air, and jump and spread their legs out so you could see their knickers as clear as day. There'd have been a total sexual frenzy. Lives would have been lost. The priests would have gone haywire and hurling sticks would have split heads open. I might as well have dreamt of aliens taking over the planet.

I was close enough to hear them talking, the footballers and the cheerleaders. I supposed they'd be talking about riding each other. This one girl with long legs and black hair sat on the track and put her legs in a 'V' and this footballer came with his helmet in one hand. He looked like an astronaut that had come back from the Moon. He slowly eased her upper body forward until her chin touched the ground, and her hair spilled on the track. He said to her, 'Crystal. You want to go get something to eat after this?'

She rose and took his arm and said, 'Sure.'

'How bout pizza?' the footballer said.

'That's my favorite, Brad,' the cheerleader answered. Her torso flowered, and she leaned backward until her hands touched the track. 'You do that calculus yet?' the footballer said.

The cheerleader said, 'I got stuck halfway through.'

They weren't talking riding at all, nothing like that, only about eating, like any normal people would be talking about, and not riding. I was looking at them, and they couldn't see me. I was afraid to move. I had come down too close. I waited until the track cleared, until the coaches went off talking among themselves.

I went out onto the track and jogged in the settling evening light, warming up for a few two-hundred-yard sprints. The track was old and lain bare, a light sprinkle of cinder rutted into a groove in each lane. I ran slow along the inside lane, breathing in the silence of what had been an uproar only half an hour ago. The grounds were hemmed in by the surrounding trees. I saw car lights off in the parking lot heading off onto the road. It was strange to think of driving back and forth to school. I stopped and watched the flicker of lights up at the school. I was like a space alien, watching, invisible. It was nothing like the reformatory, the grim silence of feeding time on the winter days, the lines of lads forming and marching across the yard to the awaiting tables of steaming food.

I went by the bulletin board of school records and stopped. The two-mile relay record was fifteen seconds slower than I'd run myself. But a runner called Marshall Haines had a 1:53 half mile and a 4:24 mile record, set last Spring. I stood there and stared at that mile record. Jasus, that wasn't a bad time, and try knocking out a sub-4:30 after running four miles beforehand. Fuck! I just stood there, and my heart raced inside me. It wasn't going to be a cakewalk after all. I looked back at the two-mile relay record and did some maths in my head. Two of the runners had to be worthless as shite for the school to have a crap two-mile relay record like that. That's where I'd have to work like fuck, hack into the two shite runners, gain distance on them. Still, if they put Haines on the end of the relay, I'd be fucked. I didn't have raw speed. Two hundred yards out, and I was fodder for half-arsed eejits if it came to a sprint. If all the stuff at the reformatory hadn't gone on, I would have worked on my speed, because speed is something that has to be developed when you're young. Endurance comes with age. But I never got around to the speed, because things had turned against me.

I went off and ran along the dark rut of the inside lane. I felt the sweat forming under my clothes, that same stink of heat I'd come to live with, that biscuity smell of the sick who piss on themselves because they can't help it. When you can smell yourself, you know things are bad.

I stowed my trousers and shirt on the first step of the grandstands. It was dark now. I ran by the light filtered from the school, a backdrop of gunmetal grey. I did a few sprints and went off to the two-hundred-yard mark. It was all there, beyond the reformatories, the motels and campsites that I had haunted, the schools and the normal girls and fellas, the long hallways of learning where people spoke decently and had futures, not the margin of sickness and disease I'd occupied. I ran fast in a fit of fury, because I knew the running was the only way into that world.

I was going to do eight times two hundred yards with thirty-second rests. I got going good, leaned into the turn and got the arms pumping well, hit the straight and hammered home. It was a different feeling altogether to get the arms swinging, completely unlike the long distance, a nauseating sickness of oxygen debt, a burn in the lungs. By the third repeat I was shagged. The pain in the veins was excruciating, like it must have been for Sandy and his drugs. I could feel the pressure of blood behind my legs and where my arms bent. The throb of pain at the temples told me I was on for a horrible migraine headache. I always got them headaches at the beginning of the hard speed workouts. I ran slow between the repeats, trying to take deep breaths, rubbing my temples. I had to take a minute rest on the last set of four repeats. I vomited up bile at the end of the sixth repeat. The threads were hanging from my mouth, spools of yesterday's dinner. Jasus, the track was a different beast, the clinical measurement of distance, the grim knowledge of where you are at all times. There was no subterfuge with the track, no mindless games of the cross-country or the road where you could lose yourself in the hemmed-in wetness of a hedge, the twists and turns, the ups and downs that let you slip in and out of cadence, catch on to different terrain. I always ran with people and places in my heart, the fields of animals, dogs barking, old houses and farms, the dead places where people never went anymore.

I was on the second-last two hundred yards when I heard Da call from out of the dark. 'Keep the head down, lean forward.' When I finished, I looked up at the stands, but there was nobody there. Still, I felt him looking at me, burning through the dark inside my head. I felt a severe loneliness, running there by myself. But there was no Da, no nothing, just myself and his shadow receding. It had come to that. I hadn't the mental endurance to resurrect him for any reason now. He just skulked there as a distant memory.

I did the last repeat and just buckled there at the end of the track. I had my eyes closed, everything pulsing inside me. I had my hands up to my temples to stop the pain, squeezing the veins against my skull. Christ! I recovered slowly. I was totally knackered, the muscles twitching on me, the calves sore from being up on my toes. I got back into my clothes and hobbled back up into the mountain. I stopped at the gap in the trees and stared down at the track, its perimeter outlined in the darkness of cinder. The school was squat in the background. It had come to this, an absurdity of battle in the heart of nowhere, for my survival. I turned and headed off, holding my head like it was wounded. The headache roamed from the back of my head forward, crouched at the top of my skull before fingering down over my eyes in that usual agony of half-blindness. I ran for the campsite, knowing the pain was going to get worse. Movement at this stage was the worst thing for the head.

It was dark in the mountains. I ran slow. I had no choice. I felt the loneliest I had ever felt in all my life, wishing for the comfort of my old bed, the days of youth where I shrank from the world with this pain I'd inherited from my Ma's side of the family. God almighty, those old days at school when the migraine reared, rushed home by headmasters with my head in my hands, those days where I was delivered into my Ma's arms, taken up to the back room where she'd draw the curtain and make everything dark, even at midday, place Da's cough bowl in bed with me for the vomiting that always came with the pain . . . The smell of menthol made me think of poor Da.

I leaned over and hacked until my eyes watered, nothing but a dribble of bile. I lay down, off to the side of the road, in among the trees. The pain got that bad that I didn't want to live, a total submission to death. The whole brain must have swelled inside my skull. I curled up into the foetal position. If I'd had a hammer, I'd have cracked my head open.

It must have been the anxiety of the race or something that did me in. The fear of the past rose up inside my head, because out of the dark came this horse, a horse I'd raced back home at the reformatory. Our town was one of those places where they'd put a number on the backs of two flies and bet on them walking up a pane of glass. When they saw me out in the fields, banished from real running because of what I'd done to the granny, the horse and me were up for grabs. It didn't take them long to come up with the idea of the race. Christ, I just wanted to erase the whole thing from my head, that infamous race when things went haywire for me.

I tried to turn away, but I couldn't move. The horse's nostrils smoked in the cold of my dream. It came toward me. 'Jockser,' I said. 'It wasn't me that done it to you.'

The horse's eyes stared at me, then they turned towards this wintry yellow light and the reformatory opened up before us, the dark receding into a reel of film, a projector light filling the dark aound us. I went and stood beside Jockser. His head touched against me.

On this pulldown projection screen was the static sepia of my past. There was Jockser being dragged out of a shed in a harness of heavy rope, his big bloodshot eyes turning back into his head as he protested the pull of rough rope.

I was out along the canal among the dog men warming the dogs down. Off on the field, crows descended to peck away the bloody rabbit corpses turned in the churn of mud from the dogs.

I was watching myself do all this, along with the horse there beside me. The projector wheel turned slowly, a clicking sound of time passing. I turned around, bewildered. I shouted, 'Are you there, Da? Is this you doing this?' But there was no answer.

A cap gun smoked against the sky, and a shower of dogs dashed at Jockser's legs, sending him into a frenzy and off onto the narrow winding road up towards the Danaher Pass. A tractor followed in a farting splutter of blue smoke. The lads in their studded football boots ran along side me and the horse, spitting and cursing, 'Go on, Granny Basher!'

I watched myself go for the steep rise off by the quarry of salt mines, going down first into a field of bewildered cows, out along the embankment of the canal where the ground made a squishing sound. The camera work was jittery, sporadic images of me against the mountains. I emerged in a narrow break in a hedge, and struggled against the give of shale and broken stone on a long incline.

Jockser was off on the long narrow road, the long way up the mountain. When he saw himself up there on the screen, he made a breathing sound through his nostrils. He was in a shocking state, hobbling amidst a sea of dogs, knackered but still ahead of me. I was off at the edge of the screen, coming out onto the road. I watched myself tuck in behind the monstrosity of his dark flanks.

The camera followed past the dark grottoes of choked purple thistle, our silhouettes slipping in and out of the embrace of Our Lady's outstretched arms. Her face had been eaten by rain and wind.

I put my hand against the horse, both of us staring at the projection screen. The horse's eyes glistened in the light. I said, 'I'm sorry.' I looked around for Da or Setanta, for any sign of life in the dark behind me. Nothing.

I braced against the inevitable turnaround, an abrupt barricade of men in a car on the screen. The drunken bolloxes hooted and slapped their hands and got out of the car, waving their hands in the air. Jockser made a neighing sound of pain and didn't have the power to rise on his hind legs. But there was no sound with the reel, just the static silence of the projector.

Jockser scraped the floor when he saw himself buckle in a fit of exhaustion and collapse into the gorse. A man sent a boot into Jockser's side. I watched Jockser turn and make a rocking motion and make himself upright. I was out of breath, standing in the silver mist of the frames of brown memory. It was like staring at life through an onion skin. My lungs burned. Jockser swung his head in a weary swagger and hit against me with his monstrous head.

On the long descent the legs went out from under Jockser on a turn. His huge frame rolled and collapsed in silence. The dogs circled in a scrum of fury. I was there kicking at them, driving them away. I saw that much of myself on the reel, my face twisted up with screams.

The left leg was broken above the fetlock, a splintering bone sticking out in a jagged-toothed cut. The camera went in there with a level of uneasy intimacy, the wound bleeding a grey pool. Every time Jockser moved, the bone cut the skin.

You could see me roaring. I was saying, 'Fuckin bastards!' I was screaming at the sky and then screaming at the camera.

I couldn't help crying there before the projector. Jockser put his head down. I smelt his animal warmness. My eyes were filled with tears.

Jockser's hoof dangled from a flap of useless flesh, the bone showing with each step. You could tell he was finished. We made it down together side by side. The camera pulled back and there was the school field and the throng of people rushing at us.

'You fuckin bastards!' I roared inside me.

You could see the frost gleaming on the stiff grass. Winter shadows stretched across the land. A bonfire crackled. Stunned men parted crabwise into a semi-circle as me and Jockser came towards the finish. I didn't cross the line. It was painted in whitewash. Men were pointing at it. Someone had to come across first. I brought Jockser to the edge of the line and then turned aside in defiance. You could see the men going wild. Jockser hung his head, and blood poured from his mouth. The greyhounds whined with instinct on the reel, straining for the bleeding leg.

In the silence of the film, a crisis brewed almost immediately over bets, an angry fight over how things would be settled, since neither me nor the horse ever crossed the line.

The film ended for a few moments of darkness, then a scratch of film appeared again. Jockser was abandoned to the obscurity of a shed. There was a man with a long-barreled fowling gun at his side. I was there beside Jockser in the old running clothes, covered in mud. The man pushed me aside. I saw myself crying and wiping my nose with my sleeve.

Then the gun smoked, and all you saw was blood against the grey wall of the shed. The film ran out again. I turned and the horse was gone. It was all darkness. I felt this coldness around me, this shuddering sensation.

A car went by on the road. How long I was out, I don't know. It woke me. I was soaked to the skin, numbed by the cold, shivering, but the headache was gone. I coughed, and the head had that vast clarity of painful silence, like walking in a cathedral. I got up and just started walking. I looked around for the horse. I said his name, 'Jockser,' but he wasn't there. It was that defiance, the not crossing the line that had done me in back home. After the nightmare of the race back home, a longer study hall was instituted without reason or justification, a complete jail lockdown of impending doom. I was blamed for it all and sat there anticipating having my head stuffed down the toilet at the breaks. It was what did the ear in on me. The remainder of my days at the school were a nightmare of solitude and derision. I was banned from the running and sent down to the old nuns to peel a mountain of potatoes when the other lads went off with their football and hurling. That's what had killed the running for me back home.

I got out of the ditch slowly, the legs locked in stiffness from the run. I was in shock, I suppose. Rising from a ditch and just going on like nothing happened. But that's what I did with a will to survive that even I didn't understand. If someone had said to me, 'Can a man sleep in a ditch and live through the night and then just continue on his way?' I'd have said, 'What sort of life is that? No, if it came to that, I don't think a man would live.' But live I did, and up I got in that grim resurrection, and off I went like an ol tinker. It was part of the evolutionary process of survival, the mould on cheese and bread growing in the cold of the cupboard back home, the microbes that live in the arse of animals, the cancer cells that fed inside my mother. Ask them the meaning of life. Survival.

My left calf was a knot of pain. My jaw hurt from the strain of the sprints, and my shoulders felt like they had been pulled from the sockets. I was hemmed in by physical frailty, reduced to walking slowly. The heat came back into my body, a slow invigoration as I got moving. These headaches were my punishment for original sin, a priest told me once at a confession before my confirmation. He spoke to me through the mesh of that small confessional about pain and suffering, about Jesus and the nails hammered into his hands and feet. I told the priest about my Da, about the coughing, and about my Aunt Bridie and her stomach cancer. I could see the head moving in the dead light of the confessional, that half-dark of subconscious guilt, me wanting to know answers to questions that nobody could answer. 'We suffer our earthly crosses, for the flesh is finite. Its pain is temporary,' was the kind of shite I got. 'Deliverance lies on the other side of the flesh.' He said to me, 'Think of hell as a hundred thousand times the pain of that migraine in your head, and it never ends, not in a year, or a thousand years, or a hundred thousand years, but goes on for infinity.'

I got up to the campsite somehow. I got into the car. I found two tin cans, canned hash and glazed sweet potatoes. I ate them in the dark, and then I slept and thought of absolutely nothing.

I recovered from the night in the ditch after a few easy days. It's amazing what the body can take, let alone the mind. I was almost giddy, with a certain longing to run headlong into battle. The time had come, an unconscious need to have things go one way or the other. It was probably the feeling of men who go to battle fronts after waiting and fearing. I scrapped the long distance that last week, tapered back to a series of sprints and slow running for the warm-up and cool-down. I ate like a wolf, stuffing myself with all them cans of food, shoving platefuls of beans into me. Sandy watched in amazement. He liked what he saw, grinned and opened up cans for me and heated them on the stove inside the trailer. He liked that ravenous look of hunger in me. I was a transformed man. You don't crawl out of a ditch without asking yourself what the fuck is your destiny.

Angel saw the look in my face, too. She was watching me crouching in anticipation of escape, feeling me edging away from her, slinking from what I'd promised her. I could feel that break, not wanting to catch her look. She was nearing giving birth. Her stomach had grown huge, a big egg under Bill Hayes' sheets. She just lay there in the trailer, propped up by a few pillows. At any time the bleeding could start, the descent through the birth canal. How the fuck did she cope with that nightmare? The silent fixity of fear was hidden behind her thin wasted face.

Eve of Destruction

The evening before the game was a Friday. I could see the bonfire burning off in the distance. Sandy had allotted us a few hours to hang around town while he got the money from Darlene to put up for his share of the bet. I felt those pre-race jitters that make you yawn and fart and wish you'd never thought about running in the first place. Self-doubt is a nightmare, even for the most resolute. I sat still and listened, stiff with anxiousness, breathing hard, wishing I could just go unconscious and wake up on the starting line.

Sandy was smoking pot and leaning into the wheel. I could see he was thinking, going through things in his head. He'd kill Darlene if it came to it. I could tell he hated her, that frankness of disgust was there on his face as he drove. He'd fucked her a few times, that grim ordeal of taking off her nurse's shoes. 'This little piggy went to market . . .' He had told me in detail the whole deal, how he peeled away her polyester tights, spread her sweating sausage legs, tore off her knickers for a go at that hairy bush. He went on about the fat of each arse cheek, the grizzle of hair from her arsehole down the sides of her legs, and her huge stinking cunt. 'And you know the worst part of it all? She thinks she's lettin me have some, like she's in control, like she's doing me a favour.'

I could see how you might want to kill someone after something like that. I granted him that in the trailer one evening, after he'd done the dirty deed and gone through the ordeal in detail again. 'Fat Cunt' was her official name now at the campsite. 'Fat Cunt better not back out on me. Fat Cunt better live up to her end of the bargain. Fat Cunt deserves to die. Fat Cunt deserves to be set on fire.' Me and Angel just let him have his way. 'Hopefully, Fat Cunt isn't going to get us put away for life,' is all I was thinking.

It was a cold night, a clear sky overhead. The moonlight poured through the trees. I yawned again, and Sandy said, 'What the fuck does that mean? That yawning?'

'Nothin,' I answered.

'Don't get tired on me now. You got a job.'

I said, 'I know.' The tension was brutal.

We came out of the mountain, rolling in neutral to save petrol, the way we had when we killed the dog. We moved with this inertia of gravity in all the things we did at this stage, pulled by exterior forces. The tragedy of life was that there was no free will after a certain stage.

We drove along the small main street through this blaze of colour. The town was a carnival of banners painted in garnet and black. Everything was a flicker of light and sparklers. 'Go Warriors!' was painted in windowfronts, images of bonfires and Indians in headdresses. Even the doughnut shop was offering doughnuts in the shape of an Indian's head. We passed Darlene, alias Fat Cunt, dressed up as an Indian Squaw, and Sandy lowered the window and whistled.

Darlene came out into the street, and Sandy said, 'How!' and raised his hand.

'Maybe you want to give me an hour, Sandy?' Darlene said. I could see that look of apprehension in her face, now that Sandy had come for the money.

'Jesus, you ain't gettin cold feet on me, Darlene?'

'You sure he's goin to win, Sandy?' Then Darlene looked at me and said, 'You goin to win this thing? Cause I can get into a hell of a lot of trouble if you don't.' Darlene shook her feathered head, a scavenger bird with that pucker of red lipstick smeared on her face like she'd been eating something dead.

Sandy said, 'Jesus, Darlene. Worse come to worst, you say some guy threatened to kill your kid. That's all you gotta say. We live in a dangerous world. I'll write you a goddamn note, Darlene. Shit, men are always threatening women these days.

And anyways, ain't we been through this? Shit, he's going to win. Ain't that right?'

I said, 'Yes.'

'I'll be around,' Sandy said and rolled up the window. He took a long drag on the pot, held it in his lungs and then let it out slowly. 'A fat cunt like that needs to be beaten senseless. That's all there is to it.' The sentiment lingered in the confines of the car.

'Don't do nothin stupid,' Angel said softly.

'I already done somethin stupid. I hooked up with your ass. Now shut it, Angel.'

The town was thronged like I'd never seen before. Small armies of squash and pumpkins stood guard along the sidewalk, cut into ghoulish faces with small candles burning inside them. Shops had put tables out onto the path for big close-out sales. Old cars had been turned into parade floats which blared music. Fellas in their letterman jackets leaned out of the windows, pumping their fists. One car had a huge bullhorn mounted, and a voice kept blaring, 'Go Warriors! Go Warriors!'

I looked back at Angel, and she looked at me through the glow of light.

We pulled into the back of the pharmacy and parked among literally hundreds of other cars. The whole mountain-side of people had descended into this parochial maelstrom of paint and noise, the blare of horns and drink consumed in public, grills cooking hot dogs and burgers, men sitting in the backs of pickup trucks playing cards, old vans from out of state selling Grateful Dead tee-shirts and POW shirts and flags and incense, the same transient peddlers I'd seen up in New Jersey. People milled around the vans with cash.

I took Angel by the arm. She walked slowly. Sandy went on ahead, looking back and pointing at different things. The pharmacy was selling candy floss and toffee apples for fifty cents. Ace Hardware would paint your face up like an Indian for seventy-five cents. It was done by cheerleaders. The money went to buy new uniforms. The girls were long and slender with those pleated skirts and tasselled shoes. They reminded me of Bill Hayes' wife. Sandy got his face painted red with white war lines along his cheek. When they leaned over Sandy, I stared at the beginnings of their pale arses, but I wasn't fooled by any of it.

Me and Angel sat at this table beside the window in a pizza place and had a slice of pizza. The store owner had sponsored three football players. Their pictures were posted along with their stats for the year on the window. Carl Rogers, the star quarterback, had a crewcut and a thick neck in his photo. A quote attributed to him read, 'You gotta believe!' There was a picture of the coach there as well. It said under his picture, 'Luck is 99% hard work!'

'I feel old,' is all Angel said, nothing else, while we ate in the glare of the pizza joint at a rickety table. I felt self-conscious. She was staring at me and then at them outside. I could see blotches in her face. She could see the haggard tiredness in me, the ragged haircut I'd given myself, the old mottled skin from the sunburn must have looked like shite. We were fine for each other, as long as our suffering was contained in the darkness of cars, as long as we saw only each other in the sad proximity of desire up at the campsite. It was disquieting to be on the outside, to look like shite in the real world. I looked like some young IRA hunger striker, the long black hair and white face of absolute resolve and defiance. I didn't know if I'd ever recover at this stage of the game. I was a day away from destiny, but it didn't feel like salvation any more, just survival.

Angel ate her crust. I could see her looking at the prices. She wanted another slice. We might as well spend now. This was the end of things. I got up and didn't say anything to her, just got another two slices and sat down again. She ate slowly and methodically, almost dazed. 'You ain't scared bout tomorrow?' she said, between bites, holding the crust away from her mouth.

'I've a good chance,' I said. I leaned toward her, speaking almost in a whisper. 'This is my last chance in America. I'm going to hammer into them.'

Angel looked at me. 'You think you're going to go on down

to that college after all this? They going to take you, you think?'

'Depends on the time. Fast time and I'm in, I suppose.'

Angel smiled at me. She whispered, 'I think you're going to win.' I felt a flush invade my face. Her hand reached across the table and lay on mine. 'I know you're going to win. I can see it in your eyes.'

I had this shuddering sensation of feeling in my stomach. It was the nicest thing someone had said to me in years. I took a long drink of ice water. My head was on fire. It was hot from the giant baking ovens. Sitting there seemed to make it like things were normal for us, just two people sitting in America eating pizza in the small warmth of a mountain town. I looked at Angel, and she knew what I was thinking. I didn't say anything.

Angel kept her hand on mine. 'You remember, you promised me you'd take me down to the hospital when it's time?'

I nodded, 'I will. I'm going to wait and see things through.'

Angel shook her head. Her face came close to mine, her long hair falling in tangles of dampness. 'You don't have to.' She squeezed my hand. 'I don't want you to.'

I got this tunnel vision, everything falling onto her small gaunt face. Her eyes had sunken into dark rings, but they had that beautiful blue still, that colour I'd seen back at the motel before things got so fucked up. She had survived, like me, the months of captivity with that psycho Sandy. Angel had never once complained, abandoned to the back of the car, just waiting all those long days, when I had at least the release of the run and my fixation on Bill Hayes' wife. I'd seen her sleep through the storms, through the terrible rains with the car rocking against the wind, just huddled up in those stale sweaty blankets, saying nothing, waiting with that baby inside her. How many times had Sandy slipped inside her with me up front, the sickening moans in the darkness. Maybe I'd never let myself believe it before, but I was in love with her. We had an ease together, a quiet peace I'd seen between normal people back home who weren't on about sex all the time, the kind of people who went walking hand in hand out the Shannon Banks.

Angel began eating again, slowly. I watched her small hands, the old scars healed but a few marks remaining from veins she hit. We were there, with all these people around us, but nobody knew what we'd been through. It was our secret, stowed away with that time of hopelessness. 'We've made it.' I squeezed her hand gently. 'We made it, Angel.'

Angel looked at me. The table rocked slightly. 'You don't got to make promises you ain't going to be able to keep.' She looked into my eyes. 'You don't owe me anything, you hear me?' I could see the tears making her eyes shine. 'You got a place to go. You're going to go on to that college.'

The heat of the ovens was roasting the place. I had to lean my head forward and take a breath of air. 'Listen to me. I'm not like him. I'm not going to abandon you, Angel.'

She looked away and half opened her mouth, holding back tears, her face obscured by her hair.

'Jesus. What the hell do you think I am? Christ, listen to me.' I should have been up resting at this stage. Still, hunger stalked me. 'You want more?'

Angel nodded.

I got up and got in line.

Some guy ahead of me turned and said, 'What the hell's that smell?' and I stared straight into his face.

'You that Irish guy?' the guy shouted. 'You that hotshot runner?'

I said, 'What's it to you, bollocks?'

'You smell like shit! You know that?'

The group laughed, and someone made a snorting pig noise. 'Smell like a goddamn pig!' the guy shouted. 'How about washin with some Irish Spring?'

Some other overweight bollocks with a neck like my thigh said, 'That your skanky-ass girl?'

The blood just rushed to my head. I lashed out with the boot, right into his balls, grabbed his hair and kicked the fuck out of his face before anybody could stop me. The place was in an uproar. Hands grabbed at me, restrained me and buried my face in the ground. 'That ain't fightin fair, you goddamn asshole,' someone shouted.

I eased, and out came the pizza man, and he said, 'Get this asshole outta here.' I was literally tossed into the street.

The crowd of high schoolers jeered from inside the pizza joint. I got up in a rage and banged on the glass. 'Fuck all of ye. Go fuck yourselves! Just you wait until tomorrow. I'm goin to kick the arse out of your Warriors!' I got a spit up from deep inside me and let it fly at the painted window, then I walked off towards the car. I was shaking. First real time out with anyone my own age, and this shit blows up in my face. That's what it was going to be like all right. I was a freak, the skin rash and the recovery and the smell and the hair, all of it.

Angel came out, and I waited by the pharmacy. 'I wasn't hungry anyways,' she said.

'You're not a skank!' I shouted, and then, for some stupid reason, I was crying. I put my arms around her, like an eejit. 'You're not.' There was an awkward retreat after that, when I got my senses back. I took my hand away and went into silent mode.

We waited in the back of the car, hearing the sounds of roaring and drinking outside. I had that urge to start the car up and get away into the night. I wanted to say to her, 'Let's go up there to the site, get the money and make a break for it!' What was stopping us? Fuck all. I turned to say that and stopped myself. I was only thinking like that because I was afraid of the race. I wanted an out. That fight was going to get the whole town against me tomorrow. I stayed silent, burning with humiliation to have been showed up like that in the pizza place. It was my fault though. I mean, what the fuck was the point in going down into the town looking like shite, not even washed or nothing, hair chopped like it had been done with a knife and fork? That was what they were going to see tomorrow, some savage immigrant in his stinking shorts and faded reformatory jersey, standing there trying to take them on. I was an aboriginal, some pathetic sight. Jasus Fuck! Why had we come down to this dump? I should have stayed put up at the trailer, that's what I should have done, and not got involved in what that stupid fuck Sandy was doing. It was none of my business.

When Angel was asleep, I went out and poured money into a phone at the far end of the town, out of the glare of lights and voices. I shouted, 'Fuck Homecoming!'

I heard the voice at the other end, the static background of noise. 'It's you, isn't it?' said Maura Connelly on the phone, working the graveyard shift, two in the morning over there.

'It is,' I said. 'Cut the small talk Maura. Is my Ma goin to make it, Maura? Tell me the truth?' I was on the edge of crying. 'Fuck! Is she alive, Maura?'

She was still alive. I blessed myself. 'Thank Jasus,' I muttered. 'I'm coming home to be with her. I'll not be kept away! I have a right to see my own Ma!'

Maura calmed me down. God love her, honest girl like that helping me. I told her how I was hiding in America, told her where I was, the state of me. I'd gambled and lost out, totally ruined myself. I said, 'Maura, you wouldn't recognise me. I'm like one of them IRA lads, one of them hunger strikers. Well, that's me, Maura. I look like one of them lads. I swear to fuck I do!' She was silent on the other end. 'You go up there, Maura, and tell her not to die, that I'm comin home to be there. You hear that, Maura? Go on up and tell her I'm not abandoning her. I'll be fucked if they'll try and keep me away from her! She's my Ma!' I trailed off slowly, 'Tell her . . .' I felt my throat tighten. 'Tell her I love her.'

I was stunned into silence when the phone went dead. The cool evening wrapped around me. This lad and his girl went walking by me. They saw me buckled there by the phone. I was crying. I heard the lad say, 'He's probably drunk is all.'

I crouched down there by the phone and put my hands to my face and cried. I cried for all sorts of reasons, but mostly out of fear. Tomorrow was looming now. Fuck! Jasus, there was one lad who could ruin it all for me, that bollocks and his 4:24 mile. Christ! I didn't know if I had it in me. I shrank from that time, curled away and wished that bollocks would die or something. Why the fuck was I racing horses and running against teams of runners? Why the fuck wasn't I normal?

I got up and straightened myself out. I said, 'Get your wits about you, you stupid fuck!' People saw me and moved out of the way. 'You're scared. Isn't that it? Well, isn't it?' That's what I was running from, the humiliation of what might happen tomorrow, the fear, yes, that was it, the fear. I was scared that I'd lost everything from them days in the reformatory, that the gift I'd been given had been taken back from me. God had said, 'This bollocks had his chance!'

I roamed the streets and went out on the edge of the town, and my legs were heavy as lead, and my shoulders were cold and my neck stiff. I tried to run to ease the anxiety, but my insides were in bits. I went off back up into the mountains by myself, running slowly. I was crying inside, heaving sighs of breath turning to fog. The sky was clear overhead. It was cold back in the mountains, and dark, a limbo world of stillness, my haunt. I went up the long ascent to the campsite, the long slur of life filling my head. I saw my Ma at the airport in her hat and coat with her handbag on her knees. Good ol Ma, always there with the dinner, feeding us and making our beds, the leanness of my Da's money, her burden to make it last, rummaging through bins of turnips and heads of cabbage, unconsciously weighing differences in ounces in the fat mottle of her arm, making the butcher trim the fat off meat, stubborn and insistent, but smiling and always discussing the weather as she fought her ground at the markets, adding flour to everything, to the meat, and giving us the pancakes with lemon and sugar to stuff us up. You imagine things like that never ending, that they go on forever. It's something you've always lived with, her presence, the smell of food fryin, the way she scalded the teapot, the same old song again, them breakfasts in bed and all that.

I'd gone from a child to a man in the blink of an eye. Maybe it wasn't the emigration, just that time of life when everything goes mad inside your head. I had fuck for an education, beaten around, down in the shite classes with the dossers and hard men. What the fuck would I have done in any country? Wasn't that the point? I was a waster. I'd done it all to myself, laughed at the priests back from the missions, laughed at the collection boxes they gave us for the hungry, roared my arse off laughing at the swots up in their rooms burning the midnight oil while I scuffed around outside with the Corner Boys and the Boot Boys, and no wonder I ended up knocking that granny's head in, because that's what boredom and no future drives you to do in the end, the inevitable self-destruction, the internal mindbomb when you know it's too late.

The tears were streaming down my face. I was shaking. I tried to start Bill Hayes' old car. The key was in it, but it was dead, not even a turn of the engine, lights dead, battery dead, and I didn't know fuck about cars or nothing. I just sat there and put my head on the wheel and cried like I'd never cried before. I said, 'I'm sorry for what I've done! Are you listening to me up there? Help me, God. Help me!'

Da knocked on the window and said, 'Are you going my way?' He opened the back door and let Setanta in and then got in beside me in the front. 'There now. Would you cut off the waterworks,' he said, taking his hat off his head and wiping his forehead. 'Self-destruction yet again, is it? Ah, don't I know your game all too well. The feigned headaches when you'd not done the homework, rolling around the bed, and then up by ten, when it was too late to go off for the school. Don't think your productions fooled me. And the injuries with running. That time Dennis Higgins from Dublin was to meet you up in Galway, and you saw the time he had coming into the race, and, next thing you know, your knee is banjaxed on you. Limping here and there, making them ol faces all day and night when somebody looked your way, you passed on the race. Scared out of your arse, weren't you? You'd come to like racing against the older lads, humiliating them at the finish. Now the shoe was on the other foot. You were scared out of your head, you soft ol bollocks, running away from a race like that. Ah God, nobody knew, but I did, and stood by you all the same.'

I shouted, 'That's a lie!' but it was no good. Da was staring through me.

'So things is come to this now,' he said. 'The Big Day, and you're off up here by yourself. Great day to start a fight down there. Great day to think about cutting out and making a run for it. Different place, same ol story. Hiding and slinking off. Listen to me. You take the bad with the good, that's the way of life. Get stuck, and, Jasus, it won't always work out, but you have to dig in there, stay your ground. Do you hear me?' He turned so he was facing me. 'I know you want out of this. I can see it in your eyes.' He pointed at the dark outside. 'Well, let me tell you something fierce about life. There's worse things in this world than what you've been through. I know you have dibs on suffering, but you're in the ha'penny place by all accounts. You've basked when the going was good, and then headed for the hills when things didn't go your way. Well, let me tell you now, you've come to a dead end.'

Da lit a cigarette, and Setanta's face showed in the back of the car, but the bollocks stayed quiet, listening.

'It's humiliating for me to have to speak to my own flesh and blood like this. We were never a family of quitters, do you hear me?' He waited again and reset his hat on his lap. 'Did I ever tell you about Patsy Flynn, the old train driver?'

I said, 'Leave me alone. Please, Da.'

Da rolled his eyes and said, 'You know what your whole problem is, what's been the problem all along? It's your story or no story. Well, maybe you might want to just shut your trap for a bit and listen.'

I felt the plague of tiredness. It wasn't Da at all is what I was saying to myself. I shouted, 'Stop doin this to yourself!' I hit my face, tried to sting life into me, get myself normal, but the image remained beside me, Da pulling on his cigarette. He said, 'If you're finished with that outburst, I'll proceed.' Da leaned around and put his hand on Setanta's head and gave it a scratch. 'There's a boy for you, no mental derangement or nothin. Sound of body and spirit.'

'He's a dog! Make him emigrate. Stick his arse off on a plane, and we'll see how he manages!'

Setanta growled, and Da said, 'Jasus, leave the defenceless poor fella alone, for God's sake.'

I just put my hands to my head and made a humming sound until Da gave me a clatter on the bad ear, and it was like waves breaking on a shore.

'Now listen up, for the love of Jesus. Now, where was I? Oh right, Patsy Flynn . . . Well, Patsy Flynn has the greatest untold story of misery I've ever heard in all my days. You see, for going on thirty years, Patsy Flynn drove out and back between Limerick Junction, three times a day. And on each journey, he passed under bridges with young lads with their shite in plastic bags the way you'd bring home a goldfish from a fair. They'd wait there for the train to come, and then they'd let go with a smattering of shite and piss, right at the window of the train. For years, poor ol Patsy Flynn thought it was disgusting, but he'd laugh it off, the game of eejits, the passage of boyhood. But he got older, and the anticipation grew more unnerving. He got himself a wife late in life and had four children, and maybe it was the knowledge that he had to get up now and make a living with this kind of carry-on that gave him a tic under his left eye, just a wink every twenty seconds or so, but it got worse. Jasus, you should have smelt that train engine! We washed it down, repainted the thing, but nothing would stop the onslaught of shite. We had police out on bicycles to scare off the lads, but they just roamed from bridge to bridge or just went down the steep embankments to launch their shite. And I say shite in the general sense, but, my God, there's shades of shite, consistencies of shite, states of insides that have all orders of disease and stuff wrong with them that neither you nor I'll ever know, green runny shite, hard brown balls of shite like pellets, a slur of beige shite, black shite laced with blood, shite filled with roughage. He tried to explain it to me once when I was washing down the train. It all came flying at him, the stuff of breakfast, dinner and tea, an army of young bolloxes lashing the stuff, a nightmare of human waste. And the worst of it was that it didn't happen every day, so it was the anticipation of the whole thing that got to him. And this wasn't to mention the cats tied down to the tracks, like maidens in distress in a cowboy western, tied there and waiting for the train to come and cut their heads off. And there were three suicides in his time on the train, all dirty deranged bolloxes who put their deaths on the conscience of a train driver. They just materialised out of nowhere to make his life hell. He slammed into them, staring into that nightmare of track running out ahead of him into the heart of the country. I saw Patsy between the goes out to the junction, me in the shed, and he'd be talking to himself, then off drinking down at the Whistle, eating a feed of dinner and the eye winking away and the hands trembling. He said shag all to anybody about what was going on out there. I knew only because I worked with him. It never left my lips either. I just let him alone with the problem. He barely got out with his sanity, got off the drink and survived. He has a son a doctor, and the girls married well, one to an accountant and another to a solicitor.

'You see that now, a man who bore a cross of personal affront for thirty-odd years, and he survived to see his family settled well. He pulled through everything. He was on the brink, mind you, time enough, and then he'd drop a comment about his son, have a schoolboy's essay or something in his pocket with top honours. I went for a drink with him one day when he came by after he was retired, and he said to me, "Did you ever have to read Dante's *Inferno* in your day?" and I said I did, and he said, "It was like a day in Disneyland, that Dante's *Inferno*. I think I served my time in hell on earth." And Jasus, it was true enough for him, but he was smiling when he said it. He was taking medication for the twitch. There's few that would have survived it, I said. He asked about your running. He knew your story in the early days. Sure, it's all we had to talk about. He told me about his son, the doctor mind you, top of the class. The son had "a big house and a lovely car and a gorgeous wife and four beautiful children," is how he put it. The son didn't visit much. He never brought the children or the wife. The son was more in with the other side of the family, who had a longstanding family medical practice that stretched back two generations in this town up North. Patsy Flynn said, "But Jasus almighty, don't they go by the name of Flynn now. The whole practice has the name Flynn attached to it. The name Flynn is respectable in that town. If your head is at you, you go up and see Dr Patrick Flynn. If your child is sick, you go up and see Dr Patrick Flynn. If someone is dying, they call out the name of Flynn." Patsy rubbed his hands together and smiled at me. Patsy died the next year, and that was that. There's no history attached to him, no memorial to him, to what he saw out on the tracks. His son came in his Mercedes Benz, with no wife or children, down from the North, and he said a few perfunctory remarks, and you couldn't detect the Limerick accent at all. A train whistle blew out on the tracks, going off into the distance, along by the graveyard wall. I saw the puff of smoke, that train heading off to the bolloxes with their bags of shite in hand and the cats tied to the track. I looked at your man, Dr Patrick Flynn, and God almighty, not even a flinch of memory at the sound of that whistle. It all went into the grave with Patsy.' Da stopped abruptly and shook his head. 'Patsy Flynn, may you rest in peace.' He made the sign of the cross. Then he breathed deep and long, and Setanta licked his hand.

Da looked up again. 'Survival is the name of the game. Surviving any way you can. The name lived on. You see, that's what was important to Patsy. The name got important in that town his son went to live in. A train driver was resurrected a doctor. That's how Patsy Flynn saw it.' Da turned his head on his neck and yawned and took another pull on the cigarette. His face showed in a shift of shadow. 'Maybe it was no story at all, if you didn't know the man the way I knew him, or the generation we came from, where we looked to our sons to fulfil the dreams we had.' Da waved his hand in a benediction of smoke. His face grew dark. He set his hat on his head again. 'I'm talking shite is all. Maybe when you have a son of your own, you'll understand what I'm on about. When you set something of yourself out there into the world, it's a part of you forever.' Da leaned toward me and whispered, 'You were our legacy, your mother and me. It was as simple as that. You were our future. We wanted for nothing but your own happiness. Do you know what it's like for your mother up there at that hospital staring into the dark, and you out roaming the world, lost?!'

Da struggled with the door. I tried to stop him. He shrugged me off, that butt of a cigarette in his lips and that grimace of defeat in his face. 'Let me go. I've said enough.'

There was nothing for it in the end, the struggling and the shouting. Da and Setanta went off into the dark.

I was asleep when Sandy drove into the campsite. 'I thought you fucked me over!' he shouted, grabbing at me. 'Fuck! Why the hell didn't you tell me you were goin on up? Jesus! Fuck! What the hell are you trying to pull?' He had a thousand dollars in a paper bag. He held it up before me, and I didn't answer. I got out of the car and went over to the trailer.

'Assholes ain't even going to count this till Monday, and still that fat cunt frets like she's going to get caught. I had to fuck her in the back of that goddamn shop to get the money out of her. You hear me, asshole? She played me good back there, getting what she wanted. You hear what I'm sayin? It ain't all about you. Running is the easy part!' Sandy pulled out that big mickey of his and just held it, pointed down with his chin at it. 'You go on down and fuck her! Go on! You stick your dick into her fat cunt! Yeah, that's what it takes sometimes. It takes someone to go down there and talk sweet for goddamn weeks, and it takes putting your tongue into her throat and then your face in between her legs, and then you gotta put your dick into her fat cunt, and you gotta say, "You is the best, baby!" You hear what I'm sayin? It ain't all about getting to the starting line!'

It was a good thing there was nobody left at the site was all I kept thinking. Sandy just held his mickey there like it was a weapon.

'If he don't get some sleep, there ain't going to be no race,' Angel said.

'Shut your goddamn face, Angel. This is all your fault. You bitch, get yourself pregnant and think I'm going to carry your sorry ass for the rest of my life. I ain't never asked for you to come with me. You dragged your sorry ass after me. Yeah, don't even look at me like that, you bitch. Why didn't you hitch up with that useless piece of shit back in Jersey? Huh? I'll tell you why, cause you knew he saw right through your whorin ass. He saw what you were in it for, tryin to hook onto any goddamn man that'll take your ass!' Sandy turned and glared at me, still with his mickey showing. He came towards me. 'Don't think I don't know what that bitch is up to. She wants your ass to take her. I ain't blind. I ain't deaf. I ain't stupid!'

Angel began sobbing. 'You lying asshole!' She tried to go at Sandy, and he went to hit her. I lunged and knocked him to the floor. I got up, trembling and breathing hard. I was ready to kick the fuck out of his face again, but he didn't move.

'Get out to the car, Angel! Go on, now!' Sandy shouted.

She went out the door. The wind pulled it wide open.

'You fuck off, you hear me? You dirty bollocks! You don't own me or her or anybody. Get it through your head, you bollocks!' I went out and got into Bill Hayes' car. It was nearly three in the morning. I sat there in the front of the car.

Sandy came out and went to his car and then came over and showed me the distributor cap from his car. 'Don't think about going no place, asshole. I think maybe you're too chicken shit to even run this goddamn race. That's what I think! You been talking shit to us all this time. There ain't no scholarship. You listening in there, Angel? You choose! That's right, you whore, you choose, and you understand this! That asshole don't got shit going for him. I'm too goddamn good-looking to be hooked up with a fuckup like you anyway. You hear me in there?' Sandy beat on the car. 'You heard what the coach said, that if he was as good as he says, he'd be on a scholarship! He's lying his ass off, Angel.' Then Sandy kicked at the door until it was totally fucked. He left and just blared the fuck out of music in the trailer. I watched his shadow from the car.

Pep Rally

I was down in the high school locker room, stretched out on a wooden bench, dressed in a heavy jumper and trousers and a blanket over me, getting up a sweat inside me. I stayed still, off in the back of the locker room, between the rows of grey mesh lockers. I hadn't slept well with Sandy acting the bollocks all through the night. I was trying to relax and think of nothing, like I did back home before the races, trying to fall asleep for a bit, but there were trainers wrapping up legs and arms, taping cleats around ankles. Footballers were stretching and rubbing globs of menthol into their arms and legs. The smell was suffocating, showers going full blast sending hot steam out into the locker room, coating everything with a hot fog. I felt the mist settle in a slickness on my face. Players hit mesh lockers. Others roamed down near where I was lying. They didn't notice me, stretched flat and motionless on the far end of the bench. Some went down on one knee and prayed. I could hear fitful breaths. The game meant that much in this town.

The coach called a meeting. I listened to him begin a long pep talk. He was shouting and then getting soft. I could hear the slap of skin on shoulder pads, the brief intimacy of words exchanged between coach and player. Then the coach would speak in general again, and the voice rose. At ten and two, the team was on the verge of going to the state elimination rounds. The Pioneers, the other team, were at nine and three and in a must win situation. It had never been so close in years, two teams with legitimate State prospects. The coach was going mad, banging things. He was shouting. They needed this win real bad, for the school, for their families, for the town, but mostly for themselves. They'd never forget this game, the last home game ever for the seniors. These were the guys who had grown up together, all through grade school and junior high and high school, all the same bunch. 'You've been working for this day your entire lives. You ain't going to know that till you look back when you go to college. That's when it hits you, when you don't see the same faces you've been growing up with all your life, and you ain't ever going to capture what it was like back home ever again. You hear what I'm sayin? I've seen guys come back here years later, and they want to talk about third down and goal to go in the fourth quarter, when they dropped a pass, someone intercepted the ball. I just gotta sit there in my office and look at them, cause there ain't nothing I can do about those demons in their head. I just say to myself, "Maybe you should have caught that ball." I ain't being tough, but what you do out there lives with you for ever. For ever. This is your contribution now. This is your time to shine. You've been growing up all your lives for this moment. You hear me? Community don't come with scholarships and it don't come with NFL contracts. No! There ain't anything more true than high school ball, cause it's community. It's family. It's what we represent as a town. You ain't playing for yourself. You know what I'm talking about! How many times have you come here, year in and year out, and you were sitting up there in the stands, wishing you could change the score, shouting and hollering and crying, yes crying, cause who wants to see their town humiliated? You are at home days later, and you go through it in your head, how you could have caught that pass or run that option, kicked that field goal. Well, this here is the day to make it all happen, your day of reckoning. It's your turn to show what this town is made of, you hear me?'

There was a huge roar.

'I can't hear you!' the coach shouted. 'You look back on games like this your whole life. Believe me. Who the hell wants to live a goddamn nightmare? Who the hell wants to be the class that let the big one get away from them? Ten and two ain't nothing without this win. We got a chance to go to State. Ain't no team here in twenty years was as close as you are today. It ain't yours to lose, you hear me? It's yours to win!' The coach was breaking at the throat by the end of things. I could hear the players making snorting sounds, holding things back. The showers were burning up the air.

I sat up in the hot fog. The coach had me going as well. I was sort of panting there, my legs twitching with nerves. I wanted to run out there and get into the race, but that was an hour or more off. Sandy had figured on an hour for the first half before I had to show on the track.

When the place cleared, I headed out into the long corridors of the school, and Jasus it was like arriving from another galaxy. Clean and polished, and the cold daylight filtering in long yellow fingers, bathing everything in stillness . . . What a humbling sight of cleanliness and community spirit, student art and organisations listed everywhere, bright colours slapped on walls, pictures of former teams lining the main corridor, football, basketball, wrestling, baseball, volleyball, gymnastics, track. There were the cheerleaders as well, the girls in front doing the splits and the big pom poms between their legs. All them smiling faces stared out from the past, the legacy of the school going way back with each class photograph. There was this memorial to former students who'd died in Korea and Vietnam, a bronze plaque embedded into the wall beside a huge trophy case with cups and medals and shields, everything shined up, this arsenal of pride. Outside, a giant flag with the impression of a warrior fluttered in the wind along with the American flag. I just gawked at the thing and got this lump in my throat. To be an American. Jasus, it was something all right.

I went slowly through the huge corridors, the lockers on either side, some of them done up in wrapping paper for birthdays. Each football player had his picture taped to the locker, and the position he played, just like down at the pizza joint. Jasus, you wouldn't think it was only a game against the next town over. The Americans had a way of fooling themselves. Jasus, maybe fooling themselves wasn't even the way to put it. They believed they were 'number one', a parochial mindset where they entrenched themselves in their own community. You could feel the stubborn pride. If you tell someone they're great all the time, it has to rub off. It has to mean something in the end. You become a self-fulfilling prophecy is what it's all about. Fuck's sake. Where I came from, we were always looking to the outside, to see what was better, on the telly, *Dallas* and J.R. and all that oil money, and *Charlie's Angels*, birds tearing around in the fast sports cars, the halter tops and tanned tits and white teeth and big American hairdos, and the lads in leisure suits, Steve Austin running around at eighty miles an hour stopping world terrorism. That's all we ever saw, the outside world beyond our fields, where life was really happening.

I passed a nurse's office, the shine of medical equipment, the glint of steel, along by the principal's quarters, the heavy studded leather backing of his chair, a string of diplomas on the wall. I stopped and looked at a door offering counselling on personal and career goals, these pamphlets on college choices, community colleges, vocational institutes, agricultural certificates offered by the state. Every Friday was Career Day. There was orange juice and cookies going. Jasus, it was something, all right, just to be slinking around the school and seeing all this. It really got me going in the head. If I had this kind of support, Jasus, wouldn't it have been a cakewalk? Love fest is what the American high school was.

What a laugh back home was, that dumping ground of humanity, where Father Francis took down a map every few Fridays when we had fuck-all for art supplies. That was our Career Day. We had a world map with pins and lines emanating out of Limerick to all the places former students had immigrated. Father Francis would ask us where we thought we'd be this time next year, and with each response, he laboured with the continental maps at the head of the class until he got the right map showing. Then he'd point to the place on the map and have one of us read from the encyclopedia about whatever country and city someone had mentioned.

Tony Gallagher was going down to South Africa, because his uncle Freddy was getting filthy rich on mining diamonds. He had all these wogs working for him. He shoved their arses down into the mines, and he just got rich. He had a big mansion and servants to wait on him hand and foot. For a while, everybody wanted to go down to South Africa, until five missionary nuns ended up in a shallow grave, because apparently the wogs were getting sick and tired of taking orders from the Freddys of the world. That put the skids on South Africa.

Kevin Nolan was going to Chile, down there in South America. He had a brother, Larry, thick as a plank, who went to our school and got the boot in fifth class. He went off to work in the merchant navy out of Southampton. He landed down in Chile and got himself married to this gorgeous dark-skinned girl. He ran a pub there in Santiago, right on a beach. Nolan wasn't lying either, because he brought in pictures of his sister-in-law in a bikini with these coconut sized tits, and she was there beside Larry Nolan, who was holding her in one hand and holding up a pint in the other. He was wearing these pastel-coloured shorts and sandals. We roared our heads off at the state of him. But Jasus, he had the woman and the pub and the money and the sunshine, and he was by far the thickest eejit our school had ever witnessed. The only problem was, who the fuck knew how to speak the Spanish?

There was Noel Fitzgibbons, runner-up in the county milk board's annual essay on 'Why Milk is Good for You', who always had pretensions of grandeur, a real pain in the arse. He came back one year and showed up drunk, in a tweed jacket with leather patches, for one of our Friday emigration bashes. He told a story of how he told a pack of lies to some Australian Jesuits down in Perth the first week he got to Australia. He said he had a Master's degree from Trinity College Dublin and got himself a job teaching English Literature to toffee Australian lads. He said, 'My only advice is, make it up as you go along, lads! Make it up as you go along!' When the letter from Trinity came, saying they'd never heard of him, he had already been giving the receptionist the muscle, and he got the letter off of her and tore it to shreds. 'Make it up as you go along, lads!' Fitz shouted, and put his hands up like he'd scored a goal. Father Francis was flabbergasted, but he just sat up at the head of the class like an ol crow. 'Make it up as you go along.' That became our immigration motto.

Then we got down to the reality of life on some Fridays and picked out places like Liverpool and Manchester and New-castle, where there wasn't much hope any more, but at least you could make a living on the building sites, or get yourself a diploma in food management or industrial relations, or become a salesman. You might get a job as a waiter or a stock boy, or cutting up vegetables in the back of some hotel, or putting fish fingers into boxes on some assembly line. It wasn't better than back home, just different, harder in many ways, but you got a wage packet at the end of the week, and them cities had decent football matches. That was another good thing, when you thought about it. And of course you weren't an illegal, though the IRA could make life pretty uncomfortable when they started in on the bombings. Then you had to watch yourself and try and change the accent. You put up with life, buying the duty-free spirits and fags on the boat home from England and having a bash every few months.

I just looked up at the career board and counselling office, my head going a million miles an hour inside. Fuck, what were half the lads I'd known doing now? All emigrated and started into life in New York, up in Toronto, down in Australia, over in England, on the high seas. They were taking what they could get and getting on with living. How was it that I'd fucked it all up the most? Why didn't I just give in to New Jersey and New York City and adjust and just hunker down in that Emerald Underground and wait my time for the American government to grant amnesty to all of us? That's what was going to have to happen eventually, all of the Irish roaming around with fuck-all for medical insurance, fellas like Aidan Hennessey, poor bastard in his early thirties, been in the Bronx for ten years, took a tumble off some scaffolding and broke his leg. I mean, the bone was sticking out of the leg, and his head was fucked as well, a major concussion that had him going on the blink, in and out of consciousness. So what do the boys do but get him patched up as best they could, get him stable for a day or so. And then out to JFK, plastered drunk, and off he goes back home on crutches. Aer Lingus thought he was drunk on the other side, till they saw the leg on him bleeding through his trousers and his eyes rolled back in his head. He was in shock from loss of blood. He was taken off on a stretcher, like a casualty from a war, but it wasn't in the papers or nothing. Aidan Hennessey was lucky, because the leg healed. He came down to the school one Friday. He was a big lad who'd played scrum half for the school. His voice seemed to quake when he talked. He said, 'If any of yous have half a brain, use the thing.' He brought his fist down like a mallet. He was off to America again in eight months, sneaking in through Canada. He was a hard character.

I felt a sadness inside me, the old memories of home, all them lads who came back and told us their stories, all the postcards we got from lads off around the world. Sam Giblin, some lad who'd been around in the sixties, now worked in New Zealand, and he named a bottle of red wine after our school, Xavier Reform. He sent a case back to the school. That was pretty impressive. We got a card from Johnny Riordan, who'd stabbed his own brother in a fight. Johnny was out working the oil wells in Saudi Arabia. He sent home a picture of himself up on a camel's back out in the desert. He had on his reformatory scarf around his head, like an Arab, and he was giving the old thumbs up sign. It said, briefly, 'The bad side: no cigs, no booze, no women, no pubs. The good side: no Mass, £800 per week sterling.' And he wasn't lying either, because his Da got a new Mini, and his brother was flying around on a new Kawasaki motorbike.

Jasus, my head was at me. Total exhaustion day in and day out, running myself into oblivion, for what, I had to ask myself. I regretted the day I left New York City at this stage. I just shook my head. Nearly a year on, and I might have saved a bit of money, who knows? The illegals made it somehow. I'd have met some normal people down in the Bronx, or in Brooklyn, got myself a trade on the building sites, got a skill. The point was to start simple and work your way up, get in with the Americans slowly.

The entire inside of the high school was empty, a silent network of corridors all polished and decked out in blood-red crepe paper banners for the Homecoming. I ran slowly through this silence. It was like I was the last man alive on the planet in that hollow echo of steps. I wanted to get out of this race. I was running into a trap, into a fiasco like I'd done with Jockser. Jasus, I hated even to think about that scene. Christ, it put me off the running for ages really.

Down in the cafeteria was this huge window that looked out on the football field. The fields were jam packed, this tight spectacle hemmed in by the trees going off into the mountains. Women were barbecuing off to the side in the outer field, getting ready for half time. Flags waved in the cold air. I opened the window, and the rush of noise came through in a hushed roar. I suppose all people are the same in the end, just looking for a bit of entertainment, just occupying themselves with their own small lives. I sat there and watched for a few minutes, and, I'll tell you, I wouldn't have minded just being down there in the stands, just enjoying myself for a day, just a nobody down there getting lost in the game. It was a cold, bright day, carrying sound across the fields into the mountains. I looked on at that perfectly contained game between two rivals, all the inadequacies of two towns wrapped up in the annual spectacle of a game. It was no different than the Limerick Galway games, or our rivalry with the Christian Brothers. That was the great thing with most people, getting down to the small things in life, fighting the small battles. It was something I'd never learned, always looking beyond a win to what someone was doing up in Dublin or over in England on the running front, staring through the mags on sports, the statistical sheets on races over in Gateshead.

I just stood there, and for the first time it really hit me. I don't think I'd laughed in over a year, and all I could hear was laughing coming in through the window, the whole town wrapped up in the game, eating hot dogs and cheering, and the lovely smell of steaks and corn. It was the same back home really, the dog races and the stout and the fish-and-chip vans coming into the field. It was great being a nothing sometimes, just the spectator. I felt the distance between me and them at that moment. Christ, it had been a long time since I'd had a day to relax like I did some of them Sundays back at the reformatory, when we got the afternoon off after a big feed of boiled potatoes, cabbage and ribs. We'd head off to watch the *The Big Match* on the telly, and the priests would open up the tuck shop and let us buy a few bags of sweets and packs of biscuits and tins of Fanta and Coke. The ol nuns brought us up tea and cake or pears and ice cream, if there was no mess acting. And during the rugby matches and hurling matches, there was always a bit of a laugh with all the people roving around the school. Sometimes we'd be playing the toffee Christian Brothers, and we'd get hold of a poshy and stick his head down the toilet or drag him around and pretend to hang him with his tie off the handball alleys, or make some pansy keep smoking Carrolls Red cigs until he started vomiting. There was the time a few of the lads set fire to a rubber Wellington when we were getting slaughtered by the Brothers in a semi-final match. The lads hid the boot down in the chapel. The boot smouldered away and filled the school with black smoke. It was coming out windows up on the third floor where we had our dormitories. The match was abandoned, and all of us lashed for the school and tore up the stairs and started flinging mattresses and chairs and books and holy pictures out the window. The priests down below where screaming for us to get out before the place went up in smoke. Jasus, there was uproar over the fire when this fireman brought out the rubber boot and said that's all it was, and there in the schoolyard was beds and chairs and glass. What a great old Sunday, the best Sunday I ever had in all my life, even though we got the fuck beaten out of us and had study hall right after tea, with no break for a walk or nothing. I liked all that stuff, just being in on the laugh, no pressure or nothing.

There was more roaring outside. Up went the Red flags. The Warriors had scored. The place was in bedlam. Car horns blared. I got up and felt lightheaded. The cafeteria was a huge place, like out at Shannon Airport cafeteria, all clean and shiny, the long line of vending machines packed with stuff. I said to myself, 'I might as well get the fuck away from this place.' It had nothing to do with me, this Homecoming and high school. A runner from outside didn't mean fuck to them. It was the football they were there to watch. I was thinking about just heading off and forgetting this race. I wasn't responsible for Angel or Sandy or any of that. This was the same misguided shite that got me into the robbing back home, hanging around with losers and following them. I just looked out over that field, and the people were into their small lives, watching their team carry their hopes and fears. I didn't belong to any of it. This was a football game. That's what this day was all about, the local heroes and nothing else. I felt the exclusion again, messing in things that had nothing to do with me.

All my stuff was up at the trailer. It would be easy enough just to head back up now. I had a good notion where Angel kept her stash of money. I'd take enough for a bus fare back up to New York, my share of what I gave up originally. I couldn't do anything for her and that baby of hers. I couldn't take care of myself, for fuck's sake. It wouldn't be stealing, really, because I was thinking in the end she was going to stay with Sandy anyway, and he was going to get his hands on the money, and it'd be gone on drugs in a day or two. I'd been a decent enough friend for her up to this. Now it was up to her to save herself.

I slank back down the long corridor. There was a part of me that knew I was running away from a race, and then there was a part of me that was saying that this was just useless shite I'd always let myself get involved in. I didn't know why I was leaving. I was just running away. Part of growing up was knowing when to walk away, just like them cowboys in the films, except they always did end up in the gunfights. Funny thing, that. There was always a shoot-out.

'Don't say it, Da!' I shouted, because I could feel him in there, shaking that capped head of his. I went back up that long corridor of the high school, and it was great, but it wasn't anything to do with me. 'It's not as if this means anything! This race doesn't do me any good, Da!' Da stayed still and said nothin, but there was that burn of pain inside my head. Jasus, so long from racing, and now look at me, running scared or acting right, how the fuck did I know? I mean, what point was there in getting involved in some poxy relay race? I could just as well do a time trial on a track and get a good sense of where I was physically. The race was going to do shite for a scholarship. I'd have to go on down and have a real race at Central Tennessee State before they were going to let me sign on the dotted line. 'I don't even know the order of runners. How the hell am I to have any sort of plan? What the fuck do you want me to do? Run on principle, let myself get fucked over?'

A race like this was useless for me, an uneven race of different talents all rolled into one. And if it was about money, well, fuck that, because I didn't see how we were going to get anything out of anybody, even if I won. I'd read in one of them English running mags about these African lads who came over for some road races out in Texas and California. The lads won, but then got screwed over by the race directors. They got these checks for winning, but no bank would cash them unless the Africans had a banking account with them, which, of course, they didn't. Why the hell would Americans just hand over cash to a bunch of Africans just in to grab the money and run? And why would anybody feel obliged to give us fuck if I won? They wouldn't. That's the height of it. They'd be shagged off that I'd made a piss of them. They'd be saying, 'Why the hell isn't that asshole off on a running scholarship and not embarrassing our runners?' Why wouldn't the local cops want to have a look at my visa. Yeah, how was I going to get out of that one?

I walked through the jammed parking lot in the school. I

had that look of an escapee, hunched slightly, breathing hard. I wanted to sprint off. And then there was Angel, sitting in the car at the edge of the lot. She saw me looking at her, but she turned her head away, like she knew what I was thinking. I went the other way, just turned and headed through the rows of cars, and I felt like vomiting. I had that rawness inside me. My heart was racing, this sudden grip of shame, but I had nothing to do with her getting pregnant, and her business was hers. She'd told me that herself, and she was right. You have to look out for yourself in this world.

I saw the runners off on the outer field warming up, a tight cluster of lads all come together to take me on, dressed up in Red and Black. My stomach just knotted on me. They said nothing, just ran by me, but there was this look of fear in them. This chill went down my spine. It was like that déjà vu of the old days of running, the interminable waiting and warming up, seeing the other lads rubbing in the menthol creams, speaking it over with the coaches. But I was a long way from all that now. I'd lost my nerve. I understood, at that moment, that I hadn't the heart for things any more. I just wanted to get away.

I went out into the street and headed away to the mountain road. The roar of the crowd receded until I was off under the canopy of shadowy light, going for the campsite. I stopped sometimes to catch my breath, to stop the shaking. It's hard to actually transport yourself physically away from everything you knew in life, but that's what I did, slinking away from what I'd thought I wanted all my life. The last months were a total waste. I was thinking of New York again, trying to tell myself that it wasn't as bad as it had been. I'd knuckle down and get myself sorted out once I was back up there, get myself over to England if things didn't work out. So fuck about the running. I was still young. Da'd been right about things all along. I should have got down to living and not dreaming. That's what dreaming and a big ego got you, nothing. I looked back, and in the distance was this huge water tower, like something out of *The Day of the Triffids*, some fifties monstrous radioactive looking creature on stilted legs coming to destroy everything. America was a dream to me. I got running again.

I heard a car coming up behind me. Angel's voice stopped me dead. 'What the hell you aimin on doing?' Her voice was hard and sharp in the cold air.

I could see my own breath in small puffs. I didn't even look back at her, just stared at the ground.

'I just don't believe my eyes is all. You running away like this . . .' She waited, and I said nothing. 'What the hell was all that training for, anyway?'

'You don't understand,' is all I could manage to say.

'Maybe I don't, cause I was never anything special. You were something special. You hear me? I seen it in your eyes. You weren't like all them others.' Her voice was trembling. 'You were something special,' she whispered.

The car puttered in the stillness, the cold light falling in slashes over me. I turned slowly. 'I can't do it,' is all I said. 'I can't.'

I stood there for a time, just looking around at the trees, at the place I called home, the encroaching coldness wrapping itself around me. There was no escape, really. I was in the same position as back home, left to stare into myself. I'd been literally running for years, and for what?

I just got into the car, and I put my hands to my face.

Angel turned the car around slowly without saying a word to me and drove in the direction of the high school.

Homecoming

A marching band roamed around the football field. I came across with Angel holding my arm, walking slowly. 'Winning ain't everything,' is what she said when we got to the bench. 'Just lining up there is something.'

I said, 'Thanks for everything.'

She whispered, 'Maybe you ain't as bad as you think.'

I did a few sprints, and the first half of the game was down to the last few seconds. There was no sign of Sandy anywhere.

The noise level was insane. The entire stands were packed solid. I ran towards the start, still dressed in my trousers and heavy shirt. The coach emerged from a group down at the starting line and said, 'We got to get this started now. Come on!'

I togged off down to my shorts and reformatory jersey. I did a few more wind sprints. I had my socks down around my ankles, like Georgie Best, dishevelled as fuck. A voice blared out over the PA system. The coach pointed to the starting line. I heard the word relay and my name and that I was from Ireland. A cheer went up. The stands were crammed. I looked at Angel, and she looked like death, really, to tell the truth, battered by life, the dark marks under her eyes, a nose too sharp for the smallness of her face. But there are other things besides looking like a million dollars. Maybe that was the first time I ever believed anything I'd ever thought in all my days.

The relay teams were introduced. Out came Haines, last. He waved up into the stands. I looked at him without any fear or resentment. All I noted was that he was taller and bigger than me, more of a half-miler, big strong legs like a good soccer player.

I lined up, and off went the gun.

Out darted the first runner at a sprint. I tucked in and let him off. The roar the first time around was intense, this punch of sound. I was twenty yards back. I heard the split at the first quarter, and I was right on the edge of fucking things up, led out too quick. I backed off the pace. Now that I was in this, I was going to do right. There was no way that eejit was going to sustain the pace out in front of me, no way. I eased and his lead increased to forty yards. I looked up and saw the stands packed and the people roaring all around me on the infield. The band was still playing. The cheerleaders were doing cartwheels and slapping their hands together.

In that first mile, I caught the runner. I came up onto the straight-away for home, and your man was exhausted, wobbling like a train, the head going from side to side. I went wide and passed him, kept the momentum going but didn't sprint. I didn't want to go near oxygen debt. If there were people not interested, they got interested as I pressed on, opening up a lead. I saw the coach lean into the track, roaring. I made eye contact with his face. His small face was lost in the centre of his head, surrounded by folds of skin.

By the hand-off, I was out by forty yards. I looked back and felt this roar of excitement as the next runner dashed out after me. Steady going was the way I had to proceed. I kept telling myself, 'Relax, this is all nothing at this stage.' I was already thinking about Haines. Still, a rush of adrenaline poured through me as I felt the runner gaining on me. I edged forward, looking back more than I should have. I put on a spurt and kept the distance between us, trying to break his will. I succeeded and got myself out beyond two miles, into that grey area where I didn't know what to expect. I could tell now that the coach had put his worst two runners first. It was going to be a war of attrition, a comeback attack on me.

The assault came quickly, over the last quarter of the third mile, a long sustained kick, and the runner came by me. Jasus, I was in the midst of it now, what I'd struggled for this past year. I put on a spurt and stayed with him into the turn. I said to myself, 'The mileage is in the bank.' Christ, all them long twenty-milers up around the old Indian trails, away from the sight of anyone, the undulation of the hills, the hard ascents to the clear lakes at the top of the mountains. I had that conviction of endurance. Fuck, I hadn't lost it. There is nothing more simple than the mind of a distance runner when the drug of endurance runs through the veins, when the mind gives itself up to the struggle, when it calls upon an older order of survival, a basic animal perseverance where time recedes and all you feel is your heart thumping inside you. I had that perceptible dip of the head and glazed animal look, the predatory sneer of a half-open mouth.

Through the fourth mile, I set in behind the runner, moving in a weightlessness that doesn't last. It was the old sensation of pounding restraint that I'd not felt in years. It was that sphere of euphoria you wanted to live within, but the legs were getting tired, my hip joints feeling the pressure of the track. I stayed in it, though, dwelt in the shite of my early life, in that cold fuckin shed where we changed and the rain came in on us, out with the greyhounds on the pitches, slogging the miles, past the cows and horses. It was all there before me in this silent film of static grey and black. Christ, now I was on another continent, running for my life. I had come that far over the years. I was thinking of what the lads back home were doing. It was night time, study hall as usual, four long hours till ten at night, the rain rattling the windows, the ol nuns getting the tea and the bread ready on the trays for after night prayer. It was strange to live in that slipstream between two continents, aware of the ghost of a former life still being lived. Christ, my Da was down home, visiting time over, back down at the house just staring into the fire, poor ol Ma locked away down by the river in one of them small rooms, hanging on to life. The threads of our existence spread out across continents, all the lads back home and abroad, the emigrants of small towns all over Ireland. We live desperate, silent lives away from the sight of our ancestors.

The runner blasted on his last lap, opened up a lead, and I

could do nothing about it. I could hear the people screaming. They'd come down out of the stands, pressing around the track. The town rivals gave in to the moment. It was about something other than two towns for a brief time.

At the change, I was twenty yards off Haines. I put the hammer down and closed the gap over the next lap, forcing him on at a pace he didn't want to run. There was only one hope, and that was to kill the kick in him long before the last quarter. There was really nothing left in me, but I clipped at his heels, made him break stride, made him rush ahead in spurts. By this time, the players were coming back from the locker room with their helmets in their hands.

Down the straight-away, and the crowd was on its feet. I felt everything tighten on me. Lactic acid seared into my calves, and my arms were burning. I went around him at six hundred yards and went for home. 'Come on, for fuck's sake,' I shouted to myself, but it was no good. Haines was a good one all right, and he got into that half-miler stalking position behind me, and I could feel him waiting for the kick. I struggled to lose him, but there was no use. On the last bend, he came out beside me. I tried to keep him on lane two, held him off just barely. The track was in an uproar, people pressed into lane two, and I could see the faces roaring at us. Even the football players were screaming at Haines.

I felt this race slipping from me, just leading and knowing he was getting ready to fly past me. I couldn't shake him. He had the raw speed. He came up on me, and I saw that expression of exhaustion in his face. His mouth was open, and there was spit on his face. I put on a last burst at the end of the turn, but Haines was bigger and stronger. He pushed at my elbow and gained the inside lane, and I conceded it to him, because I could do nothing else, and he went ahead.

I was a circus act, a racer against horses and dogs and teams of men, a beater of grannies, a thug who spat at statues of the saints, a desecrater of the consecrated host, an atheist, fucker of other men's wives, assistant to botched attempted murders, confidant to vague and malignant schemes to kill large segments of the population. I was all that and more, but I was also a human being. I had been too hard on myself all these years. Forty yards from the line I lashed back at everything that had ever hurt me with a blinding fury.

The hand of God must have got me there first, because I have no memory of them last seconds, no recollection of how I fell over that line first. All I know is that I was on the ground, buckled in sobs and calling out for my Ma inside my head. They had to carry me off the track. I was in bits, just shaking, not about winning or anything, but because I hadn't stayed up in the hills. I curled away into myself and wanted to be left alone with that truth. It was nothing about any of the people around me or anything. I was thinking of all the great battles waged inside all of us, the struggle to survive, the personal history that dwells in our hearts.

When I got settled, I saw Haines was in the arms of his coach.

The whole place was in bedlam. Cheerleaders were jumping up and down. I stood there and felt this sudden humility at just being alive. I went onto the bench, and Angel emerged from the crowd, and she kissed me on the side of my face and said, 'That's all you can ask of yourself.' I saw the lads just staring at each other, that sudden shock of being in the middle of something big. It was a small legend unfolding, a strange twilight experience of youth. I had no right to come in and take away the years of training they'd done, but I had come into a town in a foreign country, and it was on them for ever, the memory of this race, a small insular story in the foothills of an Appalachian town. They saw the look of someone who had nothing struggling to survive, the ragged journey of an immigrant. Maybe they saw their ancestors in my desperation. I affirmed something in their own heads, something about their own country. And to be honest, it took America for me to understand the things inside myself.

I went over to shake their hands, and they were decent about it. The coach put his hand on my back. I wanted a picture to send back to the reformatory like we got on them Friday emigration bashes. The local newspaper man got me bunched together with the relay team, and, 'Snap!' and that was it, immortalised forever. Then I got with the best-looking cheerleader, and the camera went snap, and I was only thinking of what the lads would be saying when they saw this. I knew what the lads would be wanting. I was laughing and giving the thumbs-up sign to the camera. I had the cheerleader with her arms around me and the crowd behind us all dressed up and painted for the game and the Homecoming. That's what it was, 'My Homecoming.' That's what I'd put on the back of the photo.

When it was all over, and the game got going again, Angel came out and put her arms around me, and I kissed the top of her head. She was crying. There was no sign of Sandy. I figured as much, and we just began walking off towards the parking lot. There was no mention of money or anything. I said nothing about it.

'Hey!' this voice shouted.

I froze, but it was only the man who'd taken the Polaroids of me and the cheerleader. He handed them to me. There I was staring out at myself. I had to laugh.

We were walking away when I heard this other voice, this Irish voice.

When I turned, there was buck-toothed, cabbage-eared Tommy Flannigan, from back home, just standing there in his Central Tennessee tracksuit, and he gave me the ol wink. He said, 'How's it goin?' and I nearly buckled. I managed to say, 'What the hell are you doing here?'

But Tommy was just smiling. He pulled on one of his big ears. 'I hear everything.'

I was just stunned. 'You heard about the race?'

Tommy said, 'Yeah, you know you've got some friends left on your side.' Then Tommy said, 'So is this the girlfriend or what?'

'Yeah, I mean. No.' I stopped and started again. 'This a friend of mine. Angel.'

Tommy winked at her. 'I bet you never saw a race like that, did you?'

Angel shook her head.

'So what's the scene here, Tommy?'

'Scene is simple enough. I have a certain somebody who wants to meet with you incognito.' He nodded in the direction of this big pudgy-bellied man in sunglasses. 'That there is the infamous Coach Mitch Harper of Central Tennessee State.'

I just stared at the man.

Tommy said, 'Jasus, don't stare. He's shittin bricks about NCAA regulations as it is. We're not supposed to come near you since you're an illegal. He's all head up there's spies here or something. You know the way the Americans are fuckin mad for rules.'

I looked back at Tommy. 'So what now?'

'He wants to meet at a restaurant over in the next town. If you have a car just follow us, but stay back. Just tail us.' Tommy said the 'just tail us' with this American Private Eye voice.

We were out on the road, me driving at 20 miles an hour. The car was totally fucked. I could see Tommy looking back at us wondering what the hell was going on. I couldn't believe it was happening like this to me. So many things had always gone against me. I gripped the steering wheel, staving off this tremor of tears inside me. Christ, of all the plans I had in life, for this to work out, to have them arrive just like that. I pressed the accelerator, trying to make the car go faster, but the car just crept along. Tommy looked back again. Fuck! Maybe they'd get nervous and just take off on us. We passed the doughnut shop where Sandy hung out. No sign of him. The place was closed on account of the game. The whole town was deserted.

I kept thinking I was really up at the campsite asleep. I could see Angel looking at me. I didn't know what to say. I knew she was probably thinking I'd leave her.

'That Tommy sure is funny lookin,' Angel said. It was the only thing she said on the drive. Her belly was huge at this stage, the greasy hair pulled back from her face. She was wearing a dirty old patterned dress, bleached out and worn thin. I didn't know what to say to her, so I kept quiet. Already there was this growing estrangement. I tried to open my mouth a few times, but there was nothing there.

The coach didn't shake my hand or nothing. He didn't even say hello. He was still wearing the sunglasses. He was nervous as hell. He said something to Tommy, and then Tommy repeated it to me. It was sort of funny, since we were all sitting at the same booth in this restaurant. Tommy said to the waitress, 'Separate checks!' and the coach nodded. 'We got to keep this above board. Coach isn't really allowed to speak to you.'

I said, 'Tell the coach I understand completely.' I was trying to look grateful.

The coach held out a stopwatch to Tommy. Tommy said, '23:42. Jasus, that's fast, Liam. Christ almighty. I heard you were training, but not like this.'

'Who told you that, Tommy?'

'A little bird.'

'What little bird?'

Tommy winked at me. 'Ol Maura Connelly back home called me up and told me your troubles. I got through to the priests back home, and they called a certain somebody, who'll go unnamed.' He nodded to the coach. 'Coach had been wondering whatever became of you.'

I looked at the coach. 'It's a long story.' I remembered the letters from him before the trouble with the law, the Central Tennessee State Stationery and American airmail stickers, the letter stuffed with brochures of the school. I kept the letters in my schoolbag, took them out and read them during lessons, looking at the name, Coach Mitch Harper. Christ, to think the chance was here again after all the stuff I'd been through.

The coach raised his voice, 'We could have the South-eastern Conference wrapped up solid.' Tommy said, 'Oh yeah, right.' He repeated what the coach said. 'We'd have a lock on it.'

I ate a big slap-up steak dinner and drank Coke and had buttered pecan ice cream for dessert.

'Does he have a major?' the coach said, plastering warm butter over a dinner roll.

'A major what?' I said.

Tommy said, 'Twenty Major and a box of matches!' and we burst out laughing, and neither the coach nor Angel knew what we were on about. 'It's the name of cigarettes. Majors,' Tommy said, and the coach said, 'Tommy, you want to tell him we got a real good Physical Education Department. You want to tell him how you are working out real well in it.'

'Kick a ball against a wall, swim a few laps, and get a degree for it. You get extra credit for a header,' Tommy said to me. 'Jasus, it's a laugh.'

The coach moved his plate away from him and started eating a toothpick. He said, 'Tommy, you want to cut the crap out?'

Tommy said, 'Right, coach.'

'You know, Tommy, I thought your friend hesitated on that last bend, like he didn't really want to go through the hurt. You notice that?'

The remark took me off guard. I wanted to say, 'What are you fuckin on about?' but I kept my mouth shut. Now I was beginning to look for signs of Da and Setanta.

'Oh the hurt. Ah right.' Tommy looked serious at me. 'The hurt is a big thing with Coach. He's only interested in people who can go through the hurt. That's his training method. Facing the hurt, conquering the hurt.' I could see Tommy was laughing his way through the whole fuckin thing, but I wasn't laughing.

The coach had no sense of humour. This was his job, I suppose. He raised his voice into this American bark for more coffee. He drank it black, without sugar.

I said, 'Tommy, do you think that your coach would think my time was okay? I mean, if he knew I'd done no speed work or anything?'

The coach said, 'Tommy, how many times have I said, it ain't the goddamn time, it's how you face the hurt. You face the hurt, and the times take care of themselves.'

'You're right there, Coach. It's all about the hurt, Liam. You see Coach used to be Defence Co-ordinator for the football team.'

I was getting a pretty clear picture of things, but the point wasn't to make a laugh of things. It was about working with people, not going against them.

The coach went on talking, 'You know Tommy, you and that friend of yours can be the nucleus for what we want to accomplish at Central Tennessee State. I think he might be the calibre of student athlete Central Tennessee State is looking for.'

I loved the way the Americans talked like that, 'the calibre of student athletes.' I was thinking that the lads back home would have burst their sides laughing at that. I couldn't imagine any of them priests addressing us like that. The coach took out an official Cross-Country Running Schedule. It had a picture of Tommy on the back on this lovely manicured golf course. The coach was playing in this bad drama along with Tommy.

'Oh look at this Tommy. We got two races out in California next Fall.'

'We're going to fly, right, Coach?'

'We sure are.'

I interjected, 'That's not a bad picture of you there, Tommy.'

The coach sat back from the table, chewing on the toothpick. 'Of course, we can't really be having this conversation right now, what with your friend here in America illegally.' He had his hands folded in an easy manner. 'Before I can legally offer him a scholarship, he'd have to be back to Ireland.'

I just looked at him. I saw his eyebrows raise above the level of the glasses.

The coach said, 'Your friend don't have to worry. I have a contract here for him to sign. All he has to do is send it back from over there. We want him on this team.'

Angel looked at me, and I felt her hand touch my leg under the table. I looked between her and the coach.

I said, 'Tommy, what if I'm already married to an American?' My face flushed.

Angel just stared at me. 'We ain't married,' she said quietly.

227

The coach was abrupt. 'That's a whole can a worms I don't think I want to open.' He got up and dabbed his mouth and took a mint from his pocket and undid the wrapper, and Tommy did the same. 'When you commit to a scholarship, you're not like other students. You're representing the school.'

Tommy looked at me, 'Yeah, you're not like other students.'

The coach and Tommy got up and went outside and left us alone.

I tried to reach out for Angel's hand, but she pulled it away. 'Don't do nothing on account of me. You hear? I been around before you showed up, and I'm going to go on after you're gone.'

'Jesus, do you think I'm going to just walk out on you?'

Angel just sat there looking at me. She was shaking her head. 'Everybody gotta look out for themselves.'

I could see the coach and Tommy outside, looking down the street, their car parked in the road, gleaming and new. Tommy was looking back at me. He wasn't smiling now. The coach had his arms folded over his sagging belly. He looked like he was having second thoughts.

'Maybe I got it all wrong, Angel. All them times up there at the campsite, I stayed because of you, not the running. I would have given up on that a long time ago, but I stayed to be near you.' I got into the booth beside her and held her. 'I know what I'm doing, Angel.'

Angel shook her head. 'We were stranded together was all, nothing more. Shit, I didn't even like you first time I saw you.' But I could see her eyes glossing with tears. I held her against my shoulder. 'I'm sorry,' I whispered.

She said something into my dead ear. I felt her breath, but no words.

Things were moving fast inside my head. I kept looking at Tommy and the coach out there. It was almost anti-climactic. I kept thinking that, at any minute, the coach would pull off this mask to reveal Da's head, and then this laughing and humiliation would start, and Da would be there with Setanta in a running outfit or something, and Da would be saying, 'There's no fairy-tale endings in this world, bollocks! Race, my arse! You're up at the campsite, bollocks. You never did run that race at all! You slank off up to the trailer. Welcome to my nightmare!'

But the coach kept his head on him, and Da never materialised.

Before going up to the campsite, Tommy gave me the change to call the hospital. Maura Connelly answered. It was evening again over there. 'Did you win?'

'Maura, Jesus Christ. Thanks for everything.'

'Did you win?'

'I did.'

'Anybody who can beat the bus up home deserves a scholarship. The city's not the same without you.'

It was an awkward silence for a few seconds. Then Maura said my Ma was stable, sleeping. There were new techniques these days to fight cancer. My Ma might be getting a colostomy bag, where they take out miles of your intestines and all your digested food collects in this bag at the side of your stomach. It might have seemed an awful way to live, but not if you wanted to live.

I said, 'Maura, thanks for what you've done for me.' I told her I was coming home for a while. I asked her to go up and tell my Ma, and to let my Da know as well. She said she would.

Back up at the campsite, there was no sign of Sandy. The coach and Tommy surveyed the state of the place, the old car, broken down, and the trailer. I could tell the coach wanted to get out of there.

I said, 'This is where I lived.' We sat in the trailer, and I turned on the stove, and I explained things, how I got there. I said, 'I want to be honest with you,' and the coach said, 'You're having this conversation with him, not me.'

This whole fuckin game was beginning to piss me off. The coach didn't seem to give a shite about anything except getting me back home.

I took out the ball of skin from my rucksack and set it on

the table. It was a disconcerting sight, this ball of translucent skin, hardened and stiff. It didn't have the effect it once had. I started into the long story of how things had gone, but then I trailed off because the coach just yawned and took another fuckin toothpick from a little box.

Tommy was giving me that look.

Angel interrupted me and said, 'Coach, I want to tell you, this ain't his child. We ain't married neither, and we ain't going to get married.' She didn't look at me at all. 'You can talk to me cause I don't got nothing to do with him.'

The coach said, 'I guess I can talk to you,' and he shifted his attention to her.

I could tell there were tears in her eyes. She went on about Sandy and the thousand dollars and the betting. She said he might come up here. This was where he lived with us.

The coach got flustered and said, 'Geeze awmighty. Gambling! Ah Christ,' and he seemed off the idea of a scholarship. He was shaking his head. 'Maybe this is more trouble than it's worth. I cannot jeopardise the integrity of the programme with something like this.'

Maybe that's what scared me the most, just how quick things could go haywire again. I said, 'Coach, I got nothing to do with any of that. I never took any money. Jesus, I swear!' I was getting frantic.

The coach just shook his head. He got up and settled his trousers on his arse. He went out for air, and we just sat there. Tommy said, 'She shouldn't have said that. Your man is ape about regulations. Come on, you have to figure things out quick. This shite isn't on.'

The coach came in again and said to Angel, 'You must have some folks you know?' He kept his back to me.

I just sat there, and the coach said to Tommy, 'Why don't you take your friend for a walk. I think we might be able to work things out.'

Angel just sat there and said nothing.

I felt a stunned silence inside me. I had been with her all these months, but I got up and went out the door with Tommy. We went down by the river where I'd fished, and we talked about the old days mostly. Tommy said nothing of any consequence. He told me about his workouts was all, and I said, 'That's great, that one,' or 'Jasus, that's a tough workout.' But I kept staring back at the trailer. I was shaking inside, because it was getting towards evening. I was afraid Sandy might just come back up and wreck things on me. Tommy looked at me. 'You don't ever want to get on his bad side, because there's no coming back from that side.'

I said, 'What am I supposed to do? Dump her?'

He turned. 'How many chances do you think you get in this life?'

We left the trailer after dark, all of us in the coach's car. We drove well into the evening. I fell asleep before we arrived at a fancy hotel where they come out and take in your luggage for you. We got separate rooms.

The rooms faced a domed enclosure with a big swimming pool as the centre piece. It smelt clean, of chlorine. I didn't swim or nothing. I called Angel's room, and she answered, and I met her down by the vending machines. We just sort of looked at each other.

The coach was getting through to her people. I didn't even ask her why she'd never done that before. I was letting it all just leave me at this stage. He was working to get things settled for her. There were clinics and services she was entitled to. She told me all this. I could feel the slippage, the slow release. 'Maybe when you're famous, I'll look you up.'

I half smiled at her.

'It ain't like I'm not going to know where to look for you.'

Tommy Flannigan was outside doing cannon balls into the swimming pool. He was still a fuckin eejit.

'I'm still going to name this baby after you . . . or Kathleen, like your Ma,' she whispered, and I held her in my arms.

I slept in the same bed with Angel one last time, huddled up against her through the night. But maybe it was the bigness of her room, the emptiness of space that made it feel different. I listened to her piss in the dark, and then she moved to the other bed in the room. There were people screaming and running around and jumping in the pool. It was the beginning of the end. I turned and felt the stiff starch of good sheets around me. I didn't sleep until well into night. I had the telly on in the background. I looked at Angel's shape in the other bed. There were the usual ol American car salesmen like I'd seen up in New Jersey, when I was trapped. But it was different now. I wasn't scared of people outside drugging themselves. I wasn't waiting on the Bogman to come and feed me and take me into New York City by night.

When I awoke, Angel was gone. The phone was ringing. The voice said, 'Let her go,' and then the line went dead. I knew it was the coach. It was fuckin surreal. It was like I was in the international spy business. If it wasn't for the fact that everything hinged on this, I might have burst out laughing, but I didn't. I was sweating and shaking.

Tommy Flannigan came by my room and wanted to do a morning run. I went out with him. I saw Angel with the coach in the dining room. They were talking. The table had a vase with a yellow flower in it. I looked at Angel, and already there was a distance between us. I didn't go over or nothing. Out on the run Tommy said, 'Sure, he's a bollocks when we lose, but that's life. Jasus, but you're very particular for someone who was livin in a fuckin tinker's caravan.'

We came back from the run, and the coach's car was gone. We had a sauna and then some breakfast. My picture was in the morning paper, the one of me lying on the track with my face all twisted up in pain. It wasn't the picture I'd wanted, not the one of the cheerleader and me. It wasn't one for the lads back home.

Tommy told me the coach rented us a car to get me to the airport. The coach was taking care of things for Angel. It was the expediency of cash, of having alternatives, that made things different now, that made things happen quick. I could feel myself giving in to him and his money, into the institution of Central Tennessee State. But the funny thing was I didn't feel grateful or nothing. It was just this fufilment of a contract, the coach doing what was necessary to secure me for the team. There was nothing between us really, no friendship. I was a runner he needed. It was just a business deal.

The rental car was huge and had this killer stereo. Tommy had the music up loud. I heard it fill the good ear, the other dead with a hushed silence. It had that smell of a new car, the leather seats, top of the line. God, to be using other people's money. I looked at Tommy dressed in the team tracksuit, both of us stuffed from breakfast. He looked clean and well, smelling of aftershave. We were belting around America because we could put one foot in front of the other faster than most other humans. That was the absurdity of things, the two of us from Limerick, from shite backgrounds, in this fancy car. The lovely dinner yesterday, the hotel, the swimming pool, the breakfast, the car, all of it there for the taking.

The deal was, I would fly to Atlanta and then up to JFK and back home. Tommy had bought the ticket for me, but I knew where the money came from. At the airport, I found a hair salon, and Tommy said, 'Give him a short back and sides and a cream rinse.' He was laughing. I just sat there, and this young woman fingered my scalp and temples, and I just let it all swoon inside my head.

Tommy came back with some coffee and doughnuts for us. He had that ease of American living, that affable smile, and Jasus, I could have sworn he was losing the old accent, and why not?

'We'll see you in August then,' Tommy said to me. He gave me a Central Tennessee State bag with a new uniform, along with tee-shirts and pens and key rings and a pair of runners and eighty dollars cash in an envelope. 'I heard your Ma was sick. Get her somethin nice from all of us at Central Tennessee State.'

I said, 'I will, Tommy. Jasus, thanks for everything.'

I went into the toilet and changed into the gear. I left the waxy ball of skin there inside a stall, just abandoned that past life. I was transformed in that instant into another Tommy Flannigan, dressed up in the gear.

'Remember the hurt!' Tommy shouted.

I got onto that plane, and up I went into the sky, out over the mountains I'd lived in.

Sandy was down there somewhere, with Darlene's money from the doughnut shop. Things would be tense. There'd be a threatening letter written by Sandy or some shite like that. Darlene could be dead for all I knew, or maybe she finally ended the poor bastard's misery and killed him. Jasus, I couldn't have taken that shite again, those battles between him and life.

I could see this line of highway amid the trees. The coach and Angel were down there somewhere travelling. I could feel the plane rising higher. I put my lips to the glass, closed my eyes and kissed her memory. I realised then I had never known her real name. She was passing into obscurity, a girl who'd promised to name her child after me, or my mother.

I took out the picture of me lying on the track, that grainy black and white like an apparition. The one of me and the cheerleader was there too, that stupid face on me with the ol thumbs up. I just crumpled it into a ball. It wasn't like that at all. No it wasn't. I kept looking at that picture of myself, and I was crying to myself, because I'd survived it all in the end, just like all them who left Ireland through the years. In a hundred years, I wanted a descendant of mine to look on that picture. It was my legacy, my emigration.

The plane banked and rose further, high above the clouds into a brilliant sun. I blessed myself for the first time in years. I was on my way home to begin again, back to the tea and bread, back to Da and his train station, to my ol Ma and the colostomy bag, back to the rain and the cold for a few months. I was thinking of the runs out back of the Limerick mountains, among famine settlements long abandoned and forgotten.